A LEAP OF FAITH

IRINA SHAPIRO

Storm
PUBLISHING

Ebook ISBN: 978-1-80508-649-9
Paperback ISBN: 978-1-80508-650-5

Cover design: Debbie Clement
Cover images: Shutterstock

Published by Storm Publishing.
For further information, visit:
www.stormpublishing.co

ALSO BY IRINA SHAPIRO

A Tate and Bell Mystery

The Highgate Cemetery Murder

Murder at Traitors' Gate

Wonderland Series

The Passage

Wonderland

Sins of Omission

The Queen's Gambit

Comes the Dawn

The Hands of Time Series

The Hands of Time

A World Apart

A Game of Shadows

Shattered Moments

The Ties that Bind

PROLOGUE

THE PRESENT

Louisa sank to her knees in front of the newly erected gravestone, not caring about the mud left by last night's rain. The morning was misty and cool, with raindrops sliding like tears off the surrounding trees and onto the forest of wet gravestones below. There wasn't a person in sight; the cemetery eerily silent and sinister. Even the birds dared not sing.

She rested her head against the rough, cool granite and ran her fingers reverently over the names of her parents, etched into the monument. It'd been a year, a whole year of grief, guilt, and terrible loneliness. The date of death would have been the same for them both had her father not managed to hang on for a few more hours, surviving past midnight, therefore, dying a day later than her mother.

Thank God, Doug had been there to comfort her and lead her sobbing from the Emergency Room of Lennox Hill Hospital on that terrible day. He'd made all the arrangements for the funeral and contacted all the necessary people, leaving Louisa cocooned in her grief. But Doug was gone now too. He had accepted a transfer to the Shanghai office and had left New York three months ago.

In all fairness, he had asked her to come, but Louisa had refused. She had her own plans, and they would be much easier to carry out with Doug out of the way.

"Mom. Dad," Louisa whispered, "I've come to say goodbye. I would never have contemplated this had you still been alive, but there's no longer anything or anyone to hold me back. There's no one left to stay for."

Louisa had never told her parents the truth. She simply couldn't find the words. Valerie wasn't dead, as everyone believed her to be. Louisa had found her, quite by accident, in a painting that had come to the museum from some estate sale in Virginia. The painting was dated 1608, but it was of her sister—no doubt about it. There was another painting, as well, from several years later, of Valerie's children, Finlay and Louisa.

Valerie was alive and well, living in the seventeenth century. She had cleverly inserted a clue into both paintings, probably hoping against hope that her art-restorer sister might somehow come across her message from the past. The hideous cupid clock appeared in both paintings, set to the same time. 8:10 – 2010, the year Valerie had disappeared when she'd turned the hands of the clock in the antique shop while browsing for souvenirs. She couldn't stand it when something was out of place and had tried to set the clock to the right time. How could she have known that the Cupid clock was a time travel device, one that had already sent one young woman back into the past?

It had taken Louisa some time to figure out Valerie's message, but she had, and she'd traveled back to England to confront Mr. Taylor, an eccentric hermit posing as a shopkeeper in a small English village. He'd told her the truth then. Knowing that Valerie hadn't suffered some gruesome death had been a relief, if a minor one.

Louisa wiped the tears coursing down her face and continued her monologue. "I'm going to find Valerie. Don't worry about me. I'll be all right. I've been getting ready, and I will not go unprepared like Valerie did. When I find her, I will give her your love."

Louisa kissed the headstone and slowly raised herself up. Her flight to England was leaving in the late afternoon, and she still had to drive out to JFK and check in. She wouldn't have any luggage, just the few items she was bringing with her to the past. She wouldn't need the rest of her possessions any longer.

"Goodbye." Louisa turned away and briskly walked out of the cemetery. It was time to go.

ONE

The idea initially began to take root on Christmas Eve, but Louisa pushed it away. Who in their right mind would willingly go back to the early 1600s? It was portrayed as being exciting and romantic in the numerous books and movies devoted to the period, but the reality had nothing to do with Hollywood. The seventeenth century wasn't all about beautiful gowns and dashing men armed with swords and flintlock pistols. The reality had been ugly and harsh. The 1600s were a time of hunger, poverty, disease, and mind-blowing ignorance. And that was in civilized England.

Virginia had been a primitive outpost, populated by a small number of colonists, who'd spent more time fighting for survival than establishing a prosperous colony for the benefit of England. Countless people had died within the first few years, and those who'd survived had harbored no illusions. They were on their own, and it was up to them to forge a safe and thriving community for future generations.

But Valerie had survived, Louisa reminded herself stubbornly. She had looked serene and radiant in the portrait Louisa had come across so serendipitously. She'd had a family. And they were Louisa's family as well, the only family she had left in the world. The thought of seeing Valerie again filled her with such longing, it was almost a physical pain, a sickness for which there was no cure.

She was just feeling maudlin, since this was the first Christmas without her parents, she told herself. Doug had left the day before to visit his family in Montana and Louisa was all alone on Christmas Eve, curled up on the couch with a selection of sappy DVDs displayed on the coffee table. Doug had invited her to come spend Christmas with his family, but she'd refused. She couldn't bear to be surrounded by his warm, loving family when her own family had been decimated. Doug's sister reminded Louisa of Valerie. She had the same quirky sense of humor and the ability to see the good in everyone, and Doug's mom would only make Louisa think of her own mother, whom she missed every minute of every day.

Louisa made herself a turkey sandwich, popped *Love Actually* into the DVD player, and settled in for the night. She'd briefly entertained the idea of going to Midnight Mass, but it was sleeting heavily, so she decided to pass, opting for the warm comfort of her lonely apartment. She was in bed by ten, wishing she could just sleep through Christmas Day and wake up on December 26th after the holiday was over. Not that the pain would go away, but at least she could look forward to returning to work, the only place she could still find some semblance of peace.

At first, she didn't realize what she was doing. She went to the library often but had never really looked at the DVDs. She liked to read and enjoyed the feel of a book in her hands. Her friends had been urging her to get a Kindle or a Nook, but she wasn't interested. She preferred a good, old-fashioned, hard-cover novel, or a more compact paperback that she could toss into her bag to read on the subway or the bus. When she drifted into the DVD section, she told herself it was just curiosity. She walked among the shelves, her eyes scanning the titles, looking for a film that might catch her eye. It wasn't until she stopped in front of *Colonial House* that she realized she'd meant to come here all along. She reached for the DVD and turned it over to read the synopsis. A reality show about life in Colonial America in the seventeenth century. This was the closest she could come to learning what life might have been like for Valerie and her family. She'd added *The Scarlet Letter* for good measure and made her way to the checkout desk.

Several hours of watching the colonists toiling in the fields and women working in the primitive kitchens did little to raise Louisa's spirits. Life had been hard and joyless, especially when the religious leader was usually the only representative of the law in the colony. Church services had been the only break from hard work and were mandatory, with attendance taken at the door. Louisa turned off the program and picked up the best-selling thriller she'd checked out instead. What had she been expecting? She would return the DVD and forget the whole thing.

Several days later, Louisa attended a New Year's Eve celebration at the home of a friend. The city glittered with lights and pulsed with a festive spirit. Huge crowds had already gathered in Times Square, waiting for the ball to drop, and *Dick Clark's New Year's Rockin' Eve*, which was hosted by Ryan Seacrest this year, was on TV. A sense of excitement permeated the air, everyone waiting for midnight, when they could turn over a new leaf and forget the mistakes and disappointments of the previous year. It was a new beginning, but for Louisa it felt like the end.

Everyone at Tasha's party was well underway to being drunk and happy by the time Louisa made her appearance. The apartment was packed. She knew a good number of the guests, but many were strangers to her, and no one bothered to make the introductions. Louisa greeted some friends and accepted a glass of wine from her assistant, Billie, who'd come to the party with her new boyfriend. She glowed with happiness, and although Louisa was happy for her, her own loneliness weighed that much heavier on her heart. She wished Doug had come with her, but he was still in Montana, enjoying New Year's with his family.

Tasha muted the TV and slipped a CD into the stereo system. A soulful tune filled the room and couples began to dance, swaying to the music and canoodling in the semidarkness of the living room. It was past eleven, and Louisa felt a choking sadness at the thought of not kissing anyone at midnight, or having anyone to spend the first day of the year with. It had been her ritual to go see her parents on January 1st, to once again toast the New Year and spend the first day of the year with the people she loved. Last year, she had spent the day with her parents, Valerie, and Doug. This year she would be all alone.

Louisa grabbed her coat and slipped out of the apartment. Who'd miss her anyway? Most people were at the party with their significant others, old and new. Louisa would be just another person, sitting in the corner by herself at the stroke of midnight. She'd always felt bad for people who were on their own on New Year's Eve. It was just another night, but for some reason it carried such expectations. It was the end, the beginning, the past, and the future all rolled into one. It was an enchanted moment when all things seemed possible and the resolutions that had failed in the past would miraculously work out in the coming year.

The air outside was frigid and fresh, a brisk wind blowing off the Hudson River. Louisa wound her scarf around her neck and huddled into her coat, walking slowly toward her building on the Upper West Side. There was no reason to rush. She was walking down Columbus Avenue when the New Year found her. Revelers were all around her, but she felt far removed from their gaiety. She was completely alone in a city of millions, since the only people she wanted to be with were either dead or out of her reach. Valerie was dead too. She would have died in the 1600s, but Louisa's heart refused to accept that. Her sister was out there, living her life, and raising her children in colonial Virginia.

Doug returned from Montana just after the New Year, and broke the news that brought Louisa that much closer to a decision. He'd been negotiating a transfer to the Shanghai office and now all the details had finally been ironed out and a contract had been signed. He would be leaving at the end of January to settle into his new apartment and meet his team.

"Lou, come with me," he said. "It'll be good for you. A new city, a new start. It's only for three years. I'm sure the Met will hire you back when you return. Think of it. It'll be exciting, and fun, and completely new and different from everything you've ever known."

But Louisa stubbornly shook her head. "There's nothing for me in China, Doug. It's a wonderful place to visit, but living there for three years holds no appeal."

Doug looked hurt but didn't argue. Perhaps he understood what she was just been beginning to grasp. It wasn't the location that held no appeal, but the future. They'd been together since college, but their relationship was stuck in a rut. Unlike other couples of their acquaintance, they'd never moved in together or made plans to get married. Louisa had hinted numerous times that she was ready to take their relationship to the next level, but Doug had always sidestepped the discussion, clearly not as eager as she was to settle down.

He loved her, but saw no point in getting married, since he didn't want to have children. Louisa thought he might change his mind as he got older and his friends began to settle down and start families, but Doug remained unmoved. Their adorable toddlers and stories of the joys of fatherhood did nothing to sway him. In fact, she suspected that the move to China was a way to get away from her and make a new start. He'd asked her out of guilt and pity, but he didn't really want her to come. If he had, he would have discussed his decision with her long before it was made and not present it to her as a *fait accompli*.

By the time Doug left for Shanghai, Louisa began to prepare in earnest. She looked up historical information, started collecting seventeenth-century coins, and spent hours trying to imitate the speech patterns of the time. At first, she thought she sounded ridiculous, but after a while, the stiff turns of phrase came more naturally. Nothing would give her away like her speech, so she had to practice. There would be no more twenty-first century American slang.

What had Valerie told her husband of her past, or her future, in this case? Louisa wondered as she studied the fashions of colonial Virginia. She hadn't come to the past prepared. Surely, she'd had to make up some story to explain her origins, strange speech, and lack of family and possessions. Had she told him the truth? That seemed unlikely. Time travel was far-fetched enough in this day and age, when there were movies, books, and sci-fi conventions devoted to the subject. In the seventeenth century, the very mention of something so fantastic could have sent a person straight to the pyre. Being accused of witchcraft had been a very real danger.

James I, who would have been on the throne when Valerie arrived in the past, had been obsessed with witchcraft, and it had been during his reign in Scotland that a new Christian witch theory had come to be accepted. It held the belief that a witch made a conscious pact with the devil, and if there was one witch, there were others. There had been a full-scale persecution, which had resulted in the death of half of those accused. James's views hadn't been as readily supported once he took the throne of England in 1603, but the possibility of being accused had still been very real. Even healers had had to tread carefully, as anything that couldn't be readily explained might have been seen as the work of the devil. Valerie had obviously managed to keep her origins a secret, since she'd survived those first few years, but at what cost. Louisa couldn't begin to imagine how stressful and frightening those years must have been.

Louisa sighed and set the history book aside. No amount of preparation would help if Frederick Taylor refused to assist her. She didn't think the prickly old man would jump at the chance to send her into the seventeenth century. Two women had already vanished from his shop. A third woman going missing would prove to the authorities that the disappearances were down to him and weren't just some strange coincidence. Of course, if she went directly to the shop and didn't alert anyone to her presence there'd be no one to report her missing. That could work, but what really troubled her was the lack of an escape hatch.

If she went through with her plan, she would be trapped in the 1600s forever. There would be no way to return to the present if she failed to find Valerie. She would have to make a life for herself in the past, whether she wanted to or not. Valerie seemed to have done all right for herself, but she probably got lucky, if having your husband tortured to death in the Tower of London could be considered good luck. At this stage, Louisa was convinced that Finlay Whitfield had been Valerie's husband. She just couldn't see Valerie naming her son after a brother-in-law who'd been accused of treason. It would be a constant reminder to all who knew the boy that he was related to a traitor. The only logical reason to name a child Finlay would be to honor his father, consequences be damned. After Finlay's death, she'd remarried, and had another child, possibly more.

The thought of Valerie's children filled Louisa with longing. She'd stared at the portrait for hours and thought they were the most beautiful children she'd ever seen. She felt especially drawn to Louisa, who had obviously been named after herself. The little girl's amber eyes stared straight out of the painting and into Louisa's soul. Louisa longed to meet her, to trace the curve of her cheek and caress those dark curls. What she wouldn't give to see them in person and have them know her.

Louisa laid a hand on her own flat stomach. Would she ever have a baby of her own? She was nearly thirty; the clock was ticking. She wanted children, but the thought of having a baby in the seventeenth century was terrifying. Putting aside the obvious risks, there was also the question of a possible father. What kind of men would she encounter in the seventeenth century, and would she be able to love someone whose upbringing and views were so different from her own? Would they be able to love her? Would she ever be free to be herself or would she have to hide behind a mask for the rest of her life? Is that what Valerie had been forced to do?

Louisa shook her head in irritation. If she went on like this, she'd never take the plunge. There were a million reasons not to follow Valerie to the seventeenth century, and only a few compelling reasons to go. If she did this, it'd be the ultimate leap of faith. Was she brave enough to jump?

TWO

JUNE 2012

Summer sunshine filtered through the grimy windows decorated with threadbare green velvet curtains, casting a weak glow onto the dusty antiques and equally dusty proprietor. Time had not been kind to Mr. Taylor; he looked old and frail. His tweed jacket showed signs of wear, the horn-rimmed frames of his spectacles were scratched, and, at this moment, slightly askew. He was shocked to see Louisa again after their last meeting, since they hadn't parted on good terms and the old man thought he'd seen the last of the pesky American. Mr. Taylor had been even more shocked when Louisa had made her request, shaking his head emphatically and raising his hands palms up, as if to ward her off. He'd flat out refused to help, but Louisa wasn't taking no for an answer. She was going with or without his help.

"Louisa, please reconsider," Mr. Taylor pleaded with her. "This is madness. You'll be trapped in the seventeenth century whether you find your sister or not. Think about that. Are you prepared to take that risk?"

They'd been over the same ground several times, but Mr. Taylor wasn't giving up. Neither was Louisa. "Louisa, go home.

Your grief will lessen in time and you'll realize what a foolish idea this was. You'll thank me for talking you out of it."

"Mr. Taylor, I appreciate your concern; I really do. I know that everything you're saying makes perfect sense, and what I propose to do is absolutely insane, but my mind is made up. I'm going to find my sister. Now, I realize that you won't let me take the clock back to the States and transport myself somewhere in Virginia to make my search easier, but please, let me do it here. I'm ready. I've been preparing for a long time and if you don't let me go soon, I'll lose my nerve."

"That's what I'm hoping for," Mr. Taylor muttered to himself.

"Look, you owe me," Louisa announced. "I lost Valerie thanks to your carelessness. Had you had the sense to put that thing away, she'd still be here, where she belongs."

"Sounds like she belongs *there* now," Mr. Taylor replied. "She's adjusted to her new life, and so should you."

"I have no life," Louisa retorted. "It's been taken from me."

"Louisa, many people lose their loved ones. It's part of the human experience, but they find a way to go on."

"I *am* going on, straight to the seventeenth century," Louisa argued.

"You know I can't allow you to take the clock to America. If the hands were to move during transit, you could end up God only knows where and when. It must be here."

The old man was beginning to relent, and Louisa felt a strange tightening in her chest. This was it. There was still time to change her mind, but she wasn't going to. She'd planned for this for too long. She'd quit her job at the Metropolitan Museum of Art, had sold her apartment and most of her possessions, and had told her friends that she was going on an extended trip abroad. It was now or never.

"All right. When do you want to do this?" Mr. Taylor sighed in defeat. He took off his glasses and cleaned them with an old-fashioned handkerchief, avoiding eye contact. "Is there anything you need to do to prepare?"

"I just need to change into my gown and pack my valise. Are you sure I can take it with me?"

"Just grab on to it as soon as you turn the hands of the clock. I've been able to take things back with me. How do you think I've managed to come back to the present? Once you're in place, go up to the castle and tell them that you are Valerie Whitfield's sister. They will be sure to help you."

"Thank you, Mr. Taylor. I'll just be a moment."

"Take your time. You can still change your mind, you know."

Louisa stepped into the back room and leaned against the closed door. Her heart was hammering in her chest and there was a hollow feeling in her belly, but she was determined not to lose her nerve. She'd been planning this for months, and she wasn't going back. Louisa quickly stripped off her jeans and top and kicked off her shoes. She considered removing her underwear and bra, but changed her mind. No one would see them. She extracted her period clothes from her carry-on bag. Chemise, petticoat, stockings, overskirt, bodice, sleeves, and shoes. Her hands trembled as she pulled on the garments one by one. With each piece of clothing her resolve strengthened. She could do this. She would do this.

The gown was surprisingly well-made, since it'd come from the stores of the Metropolitan Museum. Louisa had 'borrowed' two gowns from the storage room, hoping no one would realize they were missing until long after she was gone. The gowns had been part of some exhibit but had sat in storage for years, waiting for their turn to see the light of day again. The first one was relatively plain. It was made of light-brown damask, its only embellishment a thin strip of lace at the neckline and sleeves.

The second gown was fancier. It was constructed of periwinkle-colored velvet and offset with a high collar made of stiff

lace. Delicate embroidery in midnight blue adorned the bodice
and the lower part of the skirt and tiny pearls were sewn into
the pattern, their luminescence glowing in the dim confines of
the back room. It was the gown of a lady, expensive and beautiful. Louisa would save it for later, in case she had an occasion to
wear it. For now, the brown one would do.

Louisa stepped out of the back room and found an old
cheval glass among the dusty antiques. She couldn't believe how
different she appeared, even to herself. She pulled a couple of
pins out of her valise and twisted her hair into a knot at the back
of her head, leaving a few tendrils loose to frame her face. The
woman who stared back at her might have been an actress
playing a part in some costume drama. She didn't think she
looked authentic enough to pass for the real thing, but this was
the best she could do.

"What do you think, Mr. Taylor?" she asked as the old man
came up behind her and surveyed her reflection in the mirror.
She did a slow pirouette, setting the fabric of the full skirt in
motion.

"I think you are as mad as a March hare," Mr. Taylor
answered gruffly. "Do you have your satchel?"

"Yes."

Louisa had carefully prepared her traveling bag, leaving
all her modern items in the back room of Mr. Taylor's shop.
She'd packed her second gown, a pair of shoes, clean underwear, a spare chemise, and a velvet cloak left over from a
Halloween costume. She'd dressed as a sorceress one year,
wearing the black cloak over her whimsical purple gown. She
hoped it would do. She'd also hidden several tampons in the
lining of the bag, along with some painkillers and a leather
pouch full of coins. Another small pouch was pinned to her
underskirt, in case she got robbed. She took a cheese sandwich wrapped in plain brown paper and a bar of chocolate
she'd purchased on her way to the shop and added them to

the valise before pulling it shut. She was as ready as she'd ever be.

Louisa followed Frederick Taylor to the front of the shop, where the clock sat on the counter in all its gaudy splendor. He'd locked the door and turned the sign on the door to read 'Closed', in case someone should come in. There was little danger of that, but Louisa appreciated the gesture. Mr. Taylor sighed, then turned the Cupid clock toward her, still holding on to it as if he might yank it back at any moment.

"I'm ready," Louisa said, feeling anything but.

"Open the glass cover and turn the hands with your right hand. Hold on to your satchel with the left. I wish you luck, Louisa, but most of all, I hope you'll never have cause to regret your actions. Goodbye. Give my regards to your sister, should you find her." Mr. Taylor finally let go of the clock and moved it slowly across the counter.

Louisa took a deep breath. She was so scared she could scarcely breathe. Her stomach was turning inside out and cold sweat broke out on her forehead as she reached for the clock. Her hand was shaking badly, so she pulled it back in order to steady herself, fixing her gaze on the chubby face of the Cupid. He was smirking, his round belly reflecting the morning light. Louisa shut her eyes and took a couple of deep breaths before trying again. This time her hand was steadier, so she pulled open the glass cover. She'd decided to go to 1610. Valerie's portrait had been painted in 1608, the portrait of her children in 1611. In 1610, Valerie was sure to be in Virginia.

Louisa reached out very slowly and turned the hands to 4:10. Her breath caught in her throat and her hand jerked involuntarily just as she was pulling it away from the clock, pushing the minute hand downward. She stared at the face of the clock, desperate to make sure she'd gotten the time right, but a wave of dizziness sidelined her. She began to fall, darkness enveloping her just before she hit the floor.

THREE

THE PAST

Snatches of birdsong drifted through Louisa's consciousness as her senses began to reassert themselves. The comforting scent of grass and sun-warmed earth filled her nostrils and a gentle summer breeze caressed her face. She opened her eyes. She had no idea what time it was nor how long she might have been lying there before coming to. The cloudless sky was an endless canopy of blue, and she wondered—in a detached sort of way—if seventeenth-century weather corresponded to the weather conditions she'd left behind in the twenty-first century.

Louisa sat up and looked around. The sun was riding high in the sky, so it had to be close to noon. She was momentarily distracted by the sound of buzzing as a pesky mosquito prepared to feast on her exposed neck. She slapped it away, then slowly got to her feet and turned in the direction of the castle, eager to see what it was like while still intact. The crumbling ruin it had become had attracted few tourists, more so because it had acquired a reputation for being a place where local hoodlums chose to congregate, to shoot up, and to hide from their worried parents.

The walls of the castle were bathed in the golden light of

the summer afternoon, the leaded windows reflecting the sunshine. It was strangely quiet, but then again, she was probably too far away from it to hear sounds of activity, especially since it was surrounded by a stone wall. Louisa turned around and gazed toward the river. She knew the village wouldn't be there any longer, but it was still a shock to find it gone. A few tumbledown cottages dotted the riverbank and a weathered dinghy lay overturned on the muddy bank, baking in the sun.

There were no houses, or shops, or the lovely café where Louisa had enjoyed breakfast while waiting for Mr. Taylor's shop to open. No sound of passing cars disturbed the silence, nor could she hear the laughter of children that had reached her from the street as she'd nursed her cup of coffee, her fingers clasped nervously around the mug, her gaze fixed on the door of the shop.

Several lazy seagulls circled above the shimmering water, searching for fish, but otherwise the place appeared to be deserted. Finally, feeling strong enough to face whatever awaited her, Louisa turned her steps toward the castle and began to walk. She rehearsed her speech as she walked up the hill, partly to make sure her story sounded believable and partly to calm her racing heart. As she approached the outer wall, she noticed that the massive, iron-studded door was slightly ajar, but heard no sounds of life coming from within. Was anyone even there?

Having finally reached the door, Louisa carefully pushed it open and peered into the yard. The first thing she noticed was the deafening silence. There were no people going about their business, no horses neighing in the stables, no dogs barking at the squirrel that raced up the tree by the wall. The place was deserted. Louisa looked up at the massive castle towering above her head. The door was padlocked against intruders, but several windows on the ground floor were broken, shards of glass poking out of their splintered frames at odd angles, birds flying in and out of the exposed rooms. The building that must have been a stable looked charred, as if a fire had been put out, but not quickly enough to prevent damage, and the water in the well was covered with a thick film of slime that lapped against mildew-covered walls. Louisa looked around. Where was everyone, and what was she supposed to do now? She'd expected to find people at the castle and had counted on them to help her and furnish her with information about her sister.

Louisa leaned against the well and sighed. She had to stop panicking and think rationally. There might not be anyone here, but there had to be people within walking distance. She'd studied the map as part of her research and knew that there was a village several miles to the north but going to the village would be her last resort. She needed to find someone from the castle, someone who could tell her about Valerie and her husband. The Whitfields had gone, but there had to be someone who'd lived at the castle before it had become vacant. Where would they have gone? Louisa bit her lip as she pondered this dilemma. Once finished here, she'd have to secure passage to the New World, but how did one go about such a task in the seventeenth century? It's not as if she could just book it on Expedia.

Sighing with frustration, Louisa walked back out through the gate. This was certainly a setback, probably the first of many, but she wouldn't give in to her fears. She'd walk down the track that led away from the castle and see where it took her. Maybe she'd come upon a cottage or a farm where she could ask after the Whitfields. Louisa looked to her right, then to her left. The path to the right seemed a little wider and more traveled, so she headed that way. Her shoes kicked up a cloud of dirt every time she took a step, instantly covering the hem of her dress with a layer of dust. Her throat grew dry and scratchy, as much from dust as from fear, and she wished she'd thought to bring some water.

Half an hour later, Louisa had yet to see signs of habitation.

She was first startled, then relieved, when a deep bark erupted behind her, followed by a black mastiff, who bounded toward her like a giant ball of fur. Louisa froze, terrified the dog would attack. The owner called out to the animal, telling it to sit, but didn't quicken his step. The man looked to be around sixty and was dressed in mud-colored pants and a leather doublet. His shirt might have been white at some point, but now it was yellowed with age and had been darned in several places.

"Good afternoon," Louisa said, praying the stranger would be friendly.

"And who might ye be, Mistress?" The man stopped a few feet away, cocking his head to the side and studying Louisa from beneath bushy eyebrows. The dog was still too close, and Louisa wished the man would take it by its collar and lead it away. She normally liked dogs, but this one was the size of a small pony and it intimidated her.

"My name is Louisa Jamison, and I'm looking for my sister, Valerie Whitfield."

"Are ye now? Ye'd best come with me then. Shall I take yer valise?" He reached out for the bag, but Louisa was reluctant to surrender her only possessions to this stranger. She held on to it, and made no move to follow him.

"May I have your name, sir? Do you know my sister?"

"My apologies, Mistress Jamison," the man replied with forced civility. He bowed stiffly from the neck. "I'm John Dobbs, and I'm the overseer of Yealm Castle, or what's left of it. I do, indeed, know yer sister and her husband. Will ye accompany me to my cottage? My wife will be glad to see ye."

The man held out his hand for the valise again and Louisa reluctantly handed it over before following him along the track. He seemed harmless enough, and, at the moment, appeared to be the only living soul in the vicinity. They walked in companionable silence for a few minutes before Louisa saw a small cottage with a thatched roof perched on the bank of a brook.

There were several chickens pecking at something in the dirt under the watchful eye of an orange cat, who pretended to snooze on a bench that stood beneath the window. A heavyset woman was hanging out some washing on a line, humming a tune under her breath.

"Mary," John Dobbs called out, "we have a guest. "This here is Mistress Valerie's sister, Mistress Jamison." The woman turned around, an expression of surprise on her round face. She studied Louisa for a moment before her face split into a smile of welcome.

"Oh, my goodness. Are ye really? Ye don't look much like her, do ye?" she remarked as she came closer. "Oh, wouldn't the mistress be glad to see ye if she were 'ere."

Mrs. Dobbs approached Louisa and held out her hand. "Come inside, my dear. Ye must be tired and hungry. A cup of ale will cool ye, and I have some freshly baked bread and cheese to tide ye over till supper. John 'as some chores to see to, but he'll join us later. Won't ye, John?"

Louisa got the impression that Mary Dobbs was instructing her husband to leave, since he looked surprised to hear he had chores to attend to. But he turned on his heel, tipped his hat to her, and headed back out after handing over Louisa's valise to his wife.

The cottage was small but clean, with red curtains at the window and a jug of wildflowers on the table to brighten the small space.

"Sit yerself down," Mrs. Dobbs said as she deposited Louisa's valise on the floor in the corner of the room.

Mary Dobbs set two pewter mugs on the table and filled them with ale. She kept sneaking curious glances at Louisa as she cut two thick slices of brown bread and then brought a covered dish from the sideboard. It contained a hunk of strong-smelling cheese. Louisa didn't blame the woman for being curious. She was curious herself and took the opportunity to discreetly study the room while Mary prepared her impromptu lunch.

Other than the table, which was flanked by two benches, some crude shelves, a trunk, and a curtained bed, there was nothing else in the room. There appeared to be a small loft, accessible by a wooden ladder that was propped against the wall. A few tools hung on nails hammered into the wall next to the ladder, and a bucket of slops stood near the door, filling the room with an aroma of decay.

"I'll just take that out, shall I?" Mrs. Dobbs clucked as she followed Louisa's gaze. "Tis for the pig," she added. She grabbed the bucket and disappeared through the narrow door. Louisa wished she would have left it open to allow some air to permeate the room. The window was firmly shut, and it was too warm. Mrs. Dobbs swept back into the cottage a few minutes later and took a seat across from Louisa.

"I hope ye don't mind bread and cheese. That is all I have at the moment. There'll be mutton strew for supper," she added in a reassuring manner. "Well, go on then."

Louisa reached for a slice of bread and set it on the wooden plate Mary had given her. She used the huge, heavy knife to cut a piece of cheese and laid it atop the bread, inwardly longing to eat her own sandwich. The cheese looked questionable, but she could hardly refuse. She took a sip of ale. It was bitter and unpleasant, but at least it was cool. After the long walk Louisa was hot and thirsty.

You'd better get used to this type of food, Louisa admonished herself as she took a bite of the bread. *And be thankful this woman is sharing it with you. She clearly doesn't have much to spare*. The bread and cheese didn't taste too bad despite their unappetizing appearance.

"Mistress Dobbs, what happened to the castle?" Louisa knew the woman was dying of curiosity but wanted to take the opportunity to question her first to see if Mary's answers fitted with what she thought she knew.

The woman shook her head in disgust. "It started shortly after the master and mistress sailed for America. There was no one left at the castle, just my John to look after it, and 'e didn't sleep there at night. Well, ye know how news travels. The looters came within weeks. They scaled the wall during the night and broke the windows to get in, taking anything that wasn't nailed down. They even took the horses and set the stables afire just to be spiteful. It was because of Master Finlay, ye see."

"Yes, I see," Louisa replied. The Whitfields were being punished for their role in the Gunpowder Plot. The people who'd looted the castle had to be tenants on the Whitfield estate, but with the master gone, there was no one to stop them or mete out justice.

"John was distraught. 'E had failed Master Alec. 'E took to sleeping at the castle with his musket to scare the ruffians off, but they did not bother to come back. They had what they'd come for." Mrs. Dobbs sighed and took sip of ale. "Not that the master is coming back, mind ye. They've gone for good."

"Why did they leave?" Louisa asked. "Was it because of Finlay?"

"'Twas such a bad business. Master Finlay died for 'is sins, but the infamy of 'is deeds lived on. The master suffered for it something awful, as did Mistress Valerie. Finlay left 'er widowed, and heavy with child. Heartbroken, she were. They'd only been married a few months," Mary added, giving Louisa a meaningful look.

Was she telling her that Valerie had already been pregnant by the time she married Finlay Whitfield? Had Valerie been in love with the man, or had he taken advantage of her and had done the honorable thing when he'd found out she was with child? Louisa wondered. She could hardly ask, but she had to try. She needed to learn as much as she possibly could about Valerie's life in the seventeenth century.

"Was it a happy marriage?" she asked carefully.

"As happy as a marriage could be," Mary Dobbs replied. "Master Finlay doted on Mistress Valerie. 'E were so excited 'bout the babe. Couldn't wait to meet 'is son. 'E did it for the child, I reckon."

"Did what?"

"Got mixed up in that awful scheme," Mary replied. "Wanted 'is son to know freedom. 'T was a foolish thing to have done, and dangerous. They've paid for it; all of them. Master Finlay was lucky to have been spared the axe, or worse. I'd loved 'im since 'e were a boy, but I'd say justice was done. Imagine, blowing up the king and the members of Parliament." Mary shook her head in disapproval. "'Tis murder, pure and simple."

"So, Master Alec and Mistress Valerie left England after Finlay's death?" Louisa prompted.

"Aye, soon after the babe was born, and they were wed. Gone to Virginia."

"Valerie married Alec Whitfield?" Louisa asked.

Mary nodded. "Master Finlay, 'e made the master swear before 'e died. Asked 'im to look after 'is wife and child."

"Does Alec care for her?"

Seeing Valerie's serene face in the painting gave Louisa permission to hope that Valerie had married for love, but Mary Dobbs was telling her that Alexander Whitfield married Valerie to fulfill a promise to his brother. Had Valerie gone along willingly, or had she married her husband's brother out of desperation?

Mary's generous mouth stretched into a wide smile, revealing several missing teeth. "Oh, 'e cares for 'er, all right. Master Alec lost 'is heart the minute yer sister turned up on 'is doorstep. 'E had been broken up over 'is first wife's death, but 'e forgot all about Violet as soon as Mistress Valerie showed up.

Too bad Master Finn beat 'im to it. 'E was like that, Finlay. A real charmer, 'e were, and so handsome. Master Alec is handsome too, mind, but in a different sort of way. Master Finn just had to look at a girl and she'd be lifting 'er skirts for 'im." She giggled like a young girl. "Finlay loved yer sister very much. I'd never seen 'im so besotted. Everything could have turned out so different."

Mary shook her head, recalling that time. "Mistress Valerie and Master Alec were beside themselves with grief after Master Finn died. They comforted each other, to be sure, but did not wed right away. She loves 'im, yer sister. Don't fret. She didn't just marry 'im to give 'er son a father. They were meant to be, those two."

Louisa felt something unclench deep inside her. So, Valerie had married for love after all. She was glad to know that. Valerie hadn't had much luck in the romance department, and Louisa was thrilled that Valerie had found two men who loved her and were able to give her the children she hadn't been able to conceive in the twenty-first century.

"And where have ye come from, dear?" Mrs. Dobbs asked, taking another sip of ale. She was watching Louisa from beneath her sparse lashes. She must have been dying to ask, and Louisa had her story all ready.

"I've lived in Flanders these ten years. My husband was Flemish, but he passed last winter. I prefer to use my maiden name in England, since people are wary of foreigners. It's easier on the ears than Van Horn. Valerie and I lost touch after I married. Our parents hadn't been in favor of the match, you see." Louisa cast down her eyes, hoping to discourage prying questions. The fewer lies she told, the better. Of course, her story didn't explain how she'd known that Valerie had wound up at Yealm Castle.

"Have ye no children?" Mrs. Dobbs asked, her eyes full of pity.

Louisa shook her head, still staring into her mug of ale. "The Good Lord did not bless us with any children."

Mrs. Dobbs patted Louisa's hand in sympathy. "There is still time, dear. There is still time. Ye are young and beautiful, and the Good Lord works in mysterious ways."

By seventeenth-century standards, Louisa was far from young. She was middle-aged and well beyond child-bearing age, but Mary Dobbs most likely assumed that she was much younger than she appeared to be, and Louisa saw no reason to disabuse her of that notion.

"Oh, I do hope you are right, Mistress Dobbs. I've always longed for a child." Louisa's eyes filled with tears as she looked at Mary Dobbs' sympathetic face. She did long for a child, but at present, she had other priorities.

"I need to find my sister," she whispered. "I've no one left in the world."

"Ye stay here with us tonight, and then on the morrow, John can take ye into Plymouth. Ye will find a ship there, although there is no telling how soon that might be. Do ye have the means to make the crossing?" Mary asked carefully.

"Yes. My husband left me well provided for." Louisa had no idea how far her money would go, but she was fairly sure she had a tidy sum. She wondered how much it would cost to make a trans-Atlantic voyage.

"Good. Ye'll need to find a girl, as well. John can help ye."

"What girl?" Louisa asked, confused.

"Why, a servant, of course. Ye cannot go on yer own. Maybe women go traipsing about on their own in Flanders, but not 'ere. Ye'll need someone to take care of ye and keep ye company on the voyage. John can help ye find a suitable person in Plymouth. There are many young women who are looking to sail to Virginia, especially since 1619."

Louisa stared at Mrs. Dobbs in horror. Sixteen-nineteen? She'd turned the hands to 1610. What year was this? Had her hand jerked so badly that she'd missed the mark and wound up much later than she'd expected?

"How long has it been since 1619?" she asked carefully. Mary Dobbs gave her a puzzled look.

"It's 1620 now, or have ye forgotten?"

Oh, dear God in Heaven, what have I done? Louisa thought miserably. Nearly ten years had passed since the last sighting of Valerie. What if she was no longer in Virginia?

FOUR

VIRGINIA JUNE 1620

Alec Whitfield pushed away the ledger in disgust and rubbed his eyes with thumb and forefinger. The numbers were beginning to dance in front of his face, but he still hadn't managed to make the columns balance. God, he hated doing the books. Alec leaned back in the high-backed chair and closed his eyes for a moment. A fragrant breeze was blowing through the open window, carrying the scent of flowers and freshly cut grass. He could hear the incessant buzzing of insects and croaking of frogs, but the house was quiet. The children had gone to bed hours ago, and Valerie had retired early, pleading a headache.

The thought of Valerie made Alec's chest constrict with anxiety. He couldn't forgive himself the momentary weakness that had resulted in another pregnancy. He'd been so careful, so controlled, but all it took was one mistake. That night, six months ago, he'd had a few glasses of brandy with Charlie before going up to bed. His brother enjoyed sitting before the fire, taking, and sharing a drink or two after the women had retired. He still lived with them, although it was time for him to be thinking of a family of his own. Alec was already married by Charlie's age, but Charles was in no hurry. He was itching to see the world, and he longed to do it before he settled down. Perhaps it was for the best, since there were virtually no women in Virginia. Ships had started coming last year, bringing brides for the colonists, but many were still unwed and longed for a woman of their own.

By the time Alec crawled into bed, Valerie was already asleep, naked and warm. She must have been waiting for him and dozed off. She never bothered to open her eyes as he came to her, just wrapped her legs around him in silent welcome. She had been so ready for him that Alec just plunged in, allowing his body to silence his mind. That had been his mistake. Valerie's legs were wrapped too tightly to pull out at the crucial moment, and he spilled himself inside her for the first time since Louisa's birth. He prayed there would be no consequences to his stupidity, but God hadn't been listening. When Valerie bolted out of bed to grab for the basin a month later, he knew. She was always sick in the first trimester, vomiting as soon as she opened her eyes in the morning. Alec had been so angry with himself he nearly killed his horse, galloping for hours to ease his fury.

It wasn't that he didn't want another child. He would have been happy with a dozen, but he would trade all the children in the world for his wife. Louisa's birth had nearly killed both mother and child, and Alec wasn't willing to take chances with Valerie's life. Finn had been born at Yealm Castle under the watchful, if baleful, eye of Dr. Marsh, but by the time Louisa came along they were already in Virginia, with Bridget being the closest thing to a midwife.

There had been a physician in Jamestown, but he had gone back to England along with some of the colonists who had chosen to return, and no one had taken his place. Alec hadn't worried too much, knowing that Bridget had delivered numerous babies and would be up to the task. After all, this wasn't a first child, and the second birth should be easier. Or so he thought. Louisa had been breech, and after three days of labor, Valerie had still not delivered. If the baby did not come soon, they would both die.

That night was still clearly etched in his mind. Three-year-old Finn had been crying for Valerie all day, unable to understand why he couldn't see his mother. Alec finally asked Charlie to take him into his own bed and comfort him. Finn adored his uncle, and was very happy to have Charles all to himself. Getting to sleep in Charlie's bed was a special treat and the little boy went off happily, kissing Alec and running off with his favorite toy clutched in his hand. His nightshirt trailed on the floor, making him look small and vulnerable. Alec prayed Finn would still have a mother come morning.

Bridget was already waiting for him by the time he walked into the bedroom and rolled up his sleeves. Valerie was lying in the middle of the bed, white and still. A few hours ago, she was still screaming, but by this time, she was so exhausted that the contractions came and went without a peep. Her eyes were closed, her face clammy to the touch.

"Val, it's me. I am going to help Bridget deliver this baby. Can you hear me?" Valerie gave a slight nod without opening her eyes.

"All right. Let's begin. We do not have much time. I will try to turn the baby from the inside, while ye push on her belly as hard as ye can when I tell ye. Can ye do that, Master Alec?" Bridget looked white as a sheet herself, her frizzy red hair doing its best to escape from the cap on her head.

Alec tried not to look at her bloodstained apron as he nodded. Bridget pushed up Valerie's shift and showed him what to do. She put her palms flat against the heaving belly, and moved them simultaneously to one side, trying to dislodge the child.

"Ready?"

Alec prepared for his task as Bridget pushed her hand

between Valerie's legs, the limb disappearing almost up to her elbow. Valerie's body went rigid with pain, but Bridget didn't stop. "Now!" Bridget's face was scrunched in concentration as she tried to maneuver the baby while he pushed on Valerie's stomach, ignoring her wail of agony. "Again." It took several tries before Bridget finally pulled out her arm. It was covered with blood, but she thought she had done it.

Valerie moaned as another contraction seized her. "Valerie, push. It won't be long now," Bridget promised as she positioned herself between Valerie's legs in preparation. "Push."

Valerie pushed and pushed, sweat pouring down her face as she marshalled the last of her strength.

"I see the head crowning. Just a little bit longer," Bridget announced after what seemed like hours. Valerie gave one more half-hearted push and collapsed onto the pillows, her face white as a sheet.

Alec never even bothered to look at his newborn daughter. All he cared about was Valerie. Her eyes never opened as the baby slithered into the world, her pulse so faint he was sure he'd lost her. He held her tight, trying to tether her to this world, praying silently that God wouldn't take her from him. The baby gave a lusty wail as Bridget cleaned it and wrapped it in a warm blanket.

"Take it away, Bridget," Alec growled. He didn't want Valerie disturbed. Alec sat by Valerie's side the whole night, giving her sips of ale and trying to feed her bits of bread soaked in beef tea. She needed strength to fight, but she hadn't eaten properly in days. He finally dozed off in a chair as Valerie sank into a fitful sleep, moaning with pain every time she moved. It was well past sunrise by the time Bridget entered the room carrying the mewling infant. "She is hungry, Master Alec. She needs her mother."

Alec watched as Bridget pulled down Valerie's shift and put

the baby to her breast. Valerie didn't stir, but the baby began to suck greedily, her tiny hand curled into a fist.

"Would you like to hold her?" Bridget asked once the infant stopped nursing and drifted off to sleep. Alec reached out for the little bundle, feeling its comforting weight in his arms. He peered into the little face, looking for traces of either Valerie or himself. He couldn't see any, but he felt a wave of tenderness as he held the baby close. "You have to bring her back," he whispered to the baby. "Only you can do it."

It took Valerie more than a week to recover from the birth. She was still terribly weak, but she was managing to eat and feed the baby. Alec had been right, the sight of her daughter was all Valerie needed to start coming around. Finn liked to come for every feeding, watching his mother put the baby to her breast. He was allowed to hold his sister for a few minutes after she fell asleep, before kissing Valerie and going outside to play. As the bloom came back into Valerie's cheeks, Alec thanked God that his family had been spared.

"Master Alec, can I have a word?" Bridget was standing before the desk in his study, nervously pleating the fabric of her skirt.

"What is it, Bridget? Is it the baby?" He had just seen Valerie, and she seemed much better.

"No, it is not the baby. I don't rightly know how to tell ye this, but I must say it, so please don't take offense, sir."

Alec watched Bridget's face turn a remarkable shade of scarlet as her eyes slid away from his face and toward the floor. "The mistress has suffered some damage during the birth. Another pregnancy might very well kill her. Ye must not get her with child again." Alec thought the poor woman would faint from embarrassment, but he couldn't let her go without asking.

"Are we forbidden marital relations then?"

"Not exactly forbidden, sir. Ye just have to ... ah ... ye know, not..."

"Thank you, Bridget. I think I take your meaning. I will be most careful." Bridget gave him a slight curtsey and bolted from the study, slamming the door behind her. At the moment, he didn't think he would ever dare touch Valerie again, but he knew time would change that. At least he could still make love to his wife.

FIVE

Alec was startled out of his reverie by Valerie's scream. It sounded shrill and desperate, and he bolted from the study and hurried toward their bedroom. He found Valerie sitting up in bed, her eyes wild, her arms wrapped around her middle, rocking back and forth. Alec sat down on the bed and drew Valerie into his arms.

"Again?" he asked softly. Valerie nodded into his shoulder, wiping tears with the back of her hand. "Do you want to tell me about it?"

"Only if you come to bed," Valerie replied, pushing the hair out of her face. Alec quickly removed his clothes and got in next to his wife, drawing her close. "Tell me."

"It's the same dream, but it gets more vivid every time. I notice details that I hadn't seen before, and it all seems so frighteningly real. I see my parents walking side by side. My father is wearing khakis and a white polo shirt, and my mom is wearing a burgundy dress with her favorite ruby necklace. They are walking down Fifth Avenue toward the Metropolitan Museum, laughing and talking. I can't make out what they are saying, but they seem happy. So happy. They must be going to visit Louisa and take her to lunch. They used to do that once a month when they came to the city from Connecticut." Valerie opened her mouth to continue, but a sob came out instead, making her sound like a wounded animal.

"Do you want to stop?" Alec wasn't sure if describing her dream would help, but she always seemed to want to talk about it.

"No. I need to tell you. I see them standing at the light, waiting to cross. They are about a block away from the museum now. It's a beautiful, sunny day, and there are lots of people on the sidewalk. The light changes, and they start to cross the street when a motorcycle comes flying around the corner, tires screeching. He plows right into them, and I see them going down, blood all over my father's white shirt."

Valerie shuddered with the memory of the dream. "My mom is lying on her back, her eyes staring at the sky above. She looks as if she's dead, but her hand is twitching, trying to reach my father. There is a crowd of people around them, staring in horror. Then there are the sirens of ambulances and police cars, and they're put on stretchers and taken to the hospital.

I can see the doctors working on them, but it's too late. My mom is gone. My beautiful mom. They pull the green hospital sheet over her face and turn away. My father is still alive. He is hooked up to all these machines. Their beeping is the only sound in room. He is so white and still. Doctors come and go, but there's nothing more they can do. He quietly slips away early the following morning. I can see Louisa crying as they tell her. She's with her boyfriend, Doug."

Alec held Valerie as she cried. He had a hard time picturing the dream since he'd never seen a motorcycle, ambulance, or a police car, but he could understand her grief. The dreams began a few months ago, and seemed to come more frequently as the pregnancy progressed. He was sure it had something to do with her anxiety over the impending birth. Maybe she was longing for her parents and sister. He still longed for his despite the fact that they were long gone, all dead except for his sister. Rose ran off years ago, shutting herself away in a French nunnery and severing all contact.

He still missed them all, especially Finlay. His brother had been his closest friend, and not a day went by that Alec didn't have a conversation with him in his head, telling him all about Valerie and his son. Finlay would have been so proud of his boy. Every time Alec looked into Finn's green eyes, so like his brother's, he felt a pang of sorrow that cut him to the quick.

"Alec, there was something else this time." Valerie looked up at him, her face pale and drawn. "I saw Louisa. She was dressed in an old-fashioned gown, holding the Cupid clock. Oh, Alec, what if she figured it out?"

"Val, I know it seems real, but they are just dreams, brought on by your anxiety. You are missing your family, that's all. Your parents are alive and well, doing whatever it is that middle-aged people do in the twenty-first century, and Louisa is most likely married with a baby by now. They are just dreams." Alec hoped that he sounded convincing, but Valerie wasn't having it.

"I see it all so clearly. I can feel it in my bones. They are dead, Alec."

"Sweetheart, I've known you for fifteen years now, and you've never had the Sight. You are just overwrought because your time is getting near. It will be all right, I promise. There is a physician in Jamestown now, and I will get him the moment you feel the first contraction. I will not let you die." Alec felt a lump in his throat as he spoke the words, knowing full well that he didn't have power over life and death. All he could do was pray, and beg God that he would spare Valerie and their child.

"Make love to me, Alec," Valerie slid her hand down his body, wrapping her fingers around him. "I need you."

"Val, please. You know we mustn't."

"It'll be all right." Valerie was stroking him, kissing his chest, and it would have taken a much stronger man than him to refuse her. Valerie lifted her shift and lowered herself onto him with a sigh of pleasure. She began to move slowly, deliberately, driving him to the brink. Alec cupped her breasts. They were heavy and swollen, but he liked them that way. He ran his thumbs over her nipples, making her throw her head back with a moan.

Alec tried to think of unbalanced ledgers to prolong the pleasure, but it proved to be in vain as he spilled himself inside her. Valerie collapsed on top of him, kissing him softly.

"I love you, Alexander Whitfield, and don't you ever forget it." Alec wrapped his arms around Valerie, holding her close. Some days he could almost feel Finlay in the room with them, but today wasn't one of them. Today she was his alone.

SIX

Louisa threw off the blanket and rose from the narrow cot. The loft was so dark she couldn't see her own hand in front of her face. Mrs. Dobbs warned her against opening the window during the night, for fear of letting in evil humors, but Louisa didn't care. She couldn't breathe in the stuffy, dusty space. She removed the wooden shutter covering the unglazed window, and let in the cool air. Weak moonlight flooded the room, dispelling the feeling of being buried alive. Louisa pulled a stool up to the window and sat down, peering into the darkness. She heard the brook gurgling somewhere to her right, and an owl hooting in the distance. The dark outline of the trees looked ragged against the night sky, the only light coming from the crescent moon and countless stars.

After living in Manhattan for eight years, the sounds of nature seemed almost like complete silence. Louisa longed for a car horn, or the sound of a TV from her neighbor's apartment. It would be lovely to put on her iPod and listen to some soothing music, but those things were lost to her forever. Her life would now be reduced to the basics, with no comforts or gadgets that she was so used to. Even running water seemed like a luxury after less than one day in the past. A shower would have been wonderful, but the closest she could come was the ewer and pitcher provided by Mary Dobbs. She could wash parts of herself if she chose, or get up early and go take a dip in the brook, if it was deep enough.

Louisa was so wound up that sleep simply wasn't possible. Silent tears slid down her cheeks as the pent-up emotions of the day finally caught up with her, drying quickly in the summer breeze. "Get a hold of yourself, girl," she whispered into the darkness. "It will be all right. One day at a time."

Over supper, John Dobbs had promised to take her into Plymouth come morning. He would leave her at a respectable inn, then go to the docks to inquire about a ship to Virginia. She wondered briefly if the *Mayflower* had already set sail for Massachusetts. It was right around this time that it left England, if she could remember correctly. She'd seen the replica of the ship at anchor in Plymouth, Massachusetts and had been in awe of the bravery of the colonists. There had been over one hundred people aboard, but the ship was tiny by modern standards.

There were only two cabins, one for the captain and the other for the first mate. The rest of the travelers shared an open space and slept on the floor, right next to overflowing chamber pots and domestic animals they were bringing to the New World. The sailors slept down below, in hammocks that left no room for privacy. John Dobbs said the voyage would take about two months, weather permitting. The idea of being trapped for such a long period of time aboard a small, wooden vessel in the middle of the ocean terrified Louisa, but she tried not to think about it. It was the only way to get to Virginia, and to Virginia she would go. Valerie made the trip with an infant, so her own crossing would be a piece of cake.

Louisa finally drifted off to sleep just before sunrise, exhausted and emotionally depleted, and didn't wake until Mrs. Dobbs came in and started chiding her about the open window.

It wasn't until Louisa finished her breakfast of ale and yesterday's bread that she realized she would be traveling to Plymouth on horseback. She'd mistakenly assumed Mr. Dobbs would take her in a wagon, but that luxurious mode of transportation wasn't on offer. She'd been on a horse only twice in her life, and didn't care to repeat the experience, but it seemed her ordeal was to begin sooner than she'd anticipated. As she mounted the horse with the help of Mr. Dobbs, she wondered what would be the bigger challenge, riding to Plymouth astride, or spending several hours with her taciturn companion.

SEVEN

The ride to Plymouth had been long and uncomfortable, with the unfamiliar muscles of the horse shifting beneath Louisa's butt and flies buzzing around her head. She was perspiring freely from the heat and the unfamiliar strain of keeping herself upright on the horse. Every time she began to relax, she felt as if she were sliding off to the side and would fall off, winding up under the hooves of the unfriendly mare. She was so tense she barely noticed the fields and villages they passed along the way.

John Dobbs was silent for most of the ride, as expected, and only perked up as they got nearer to the town, shielding his eyes from the sun and looking toward the harbor, where several masts could be seen rising above the roofs of the quayside dwellings. Was the ship that would take her to Virginia already in port? Louisa wondered as she followed Mr. Dobbs through the narrow streets of the city.

"There's a respectable inn near the docks, the Stag's Head. I'll leave ye there and go inquire about a ship. I know the proprietress, Mistress Fairley, and she'll do right by ye, don't ye fret."

Mr. Dobbs didn't really expect an answer, so Louisa just followed him to the inn, which was tucked away on a narrow side-street, a peeling sign of a stag's severed head swaying and creaking in the gentle breeze. Louisa slid off the horse, nearly falling down as her knees buckled from the long hours in the saddle. A young boy grabbed her by the elbow and supported her until she was ready to stand on her own. He then took hold of the reins and led the horse away toward the stables at the back. Louisa hoped she'd seen the last it, at least for today.

"Come on, then," Mr. Dobbs growled. "Time's a 'wasting."

Mrs. Fairley greeted Louisa with enthusiasm, and immediately escorted her to the 'best room' in the Stag's Head. The room faced the back of the house, thus being quieter and more private. It contained a bed, a small table with a single chair, and a chamber pot, discreetly pushed under the bed. Louisa set down her valise and sat down on the bed. Her behind was sore from riding for several hours, and she leaned back, grateful not to be on horseback anymore. Now she had to wait.

She extracted the cheese sandwich from the valise and sniffled it cautiously in an effort to determine if it was still edible. The cheese had melted in the heat and fused with the bread, so she decided not to risk it. The chocolate bar had melted as well, but Louisa would be damned if she would throw that away. She ate the chocolate, then licked the wrapper, savoring the last taste of home. Mrs. Fairley said supper would be served at seven and Louisa could partake of it in the main dining room with the other guests or have a tray sent up to her room. Louisa thought she might like to go to the dining room. She was curious about the people staying at the inn. But, in the meantime, she'd have a rest.

The knock on the door startled her awake. Mr. Dobbs entered the room, his hat in his hands, and stood awkwardly by the door.

"I found ye a ship, Mistress. The *Gloriana* will be sailing to the New World at the end of the week, so ye only 'ave a few days to wait, which is good luck indeed. Might 'ave been much longer 'ad ye come after she left. I cannot say when the next ship will be ready to sail." He shifted from one foot to the other.

"As it 'appens, Mistress Fairley 'as a niece who is eager to go into service. Shall I tell 'er to come see ye?"

Louisa nodded, uncertain how to respond. She supposed he meant that the niece wanted to apply for the position and needed to be interviewed. Louisa had no idea what to ask her, but she could hardly hire the girl without even talking to her. She would think of something.

"I will 'ave Mistress Fairley send up a tray for ye," John Dobbs informed her. "Rough crowd down there tonight. Best ye eat 'ere. I'll be on me way back now. Just present yerself to Captain Fellowes before noon. He'll be expecting ye and the girl. God speed, Mistress Jamison." With that, he bowed and left the room, leaving Louisa feeling strangely vulnerable. She was on her own now.

Louisa splashed some water on her face. It was hard to tell time without a watch and given that the sun set so late in June, it could have been anywhere between six and nine. She was hungry, but Mr. Dobbs had warned her against going downstairs, probably with good reason, so she sat on the chair and folded her hands in her lap. She hated waiting. Just then, there was a knock. Louisa unlocked the door and stepped aside to let the maid in. A young girl entered the room, carrying a tray laden with a bowl, a heel of bread, and a mug of ale.

"Good evening, Mistress Jamison. My aunt sent up yer supper. Oyster stew tonight. I hope it is to yer liking," the girl said as she set the food on the table.

She looked terribly nervous, so Louisa assured her that oyster stew would be wonderful, despite her own misgivings about eating oysters in a place like this. Her journey could end before it had even begun if the oysters were off. "I am the one looking to go to Virginia with ye," the girl added, staring at her feet.

"Oh. I see." Louisa sat down on the chair and faced the girl. "Tell me something about yourself then."

"I am called Agnes Crawley. Mistress Fairley is me mam's sister. I 'ave lived 'ere since me mam passed last winter. I can cook, clean, and mend clothes, if it please ye." Agnes snuck a peek at Louisa from under her dark lashes. Louisa suspected that the girl had more spirit than she was willing to show.

"How old are you, Agnes?" By the looks of her she couldn't be more than twelve, and a scrawny twelve at that.

"I am fifteen, Mistress."

"Why do you want to go to Virginia, Agnes? You seem to have a fine place here with your aunt."

"I would like to see something o' the world, and I would much prefer to serve one mistress to working as a skivvy at the inn." Agnes looked away again, her fingers pleating the fabric of her apron. "I'd like to be indentured to ye."

"Indentured?" Louisa hadn't expected that.

"Yes, ma'am. I would feel safer that way."

Louisa studied the girl. She supposed it would be all right if that's what Agnes wanted. The idea of actually owning the girl for several years was distasteful, but from Agnes's point of view, it probably guaranteed her a form of security. Louisa would be responsible for her well-being, and that would make Agnes feel less apprehensive about traveling across the Atlantic. If only Louisa could feel less apprehensive herself.

"All right, then, Agnes. The ship sails on Friday, so you have a few days to prepare."

"Aye, ma'am. Thank ye kindly, ma'am. I will bring up the contract when I come back to collect the tray. I know me letters, ma'am," she added proudly as she left the room.

Louisa lifted the lid off the bowl and studied the oyster stew. It smelled appetizing despite its thick, brown texture. She picked up the wooden spoon and plunged in. The stew was actually very good. Louisa finished it all and washed it down with the bitter ale Mistress Fairley had sent up. She had no idea what to do until bedtime, but it wasn't safe to leave her room. Tomorrow, she would have breakfast and go and explore Plymouth. She had four days until the ship sailed, and she meant to put them to good use.

EIGHT

Louisa feared the night. That's when the panic came. It began gradually as a tightening in her belly and the accelerated beating of her heart and progressed to a full-blown anxiety attack as the shadows of the early evening finally deepened into the impenetrable darkness of night. She would have given anything for the oblivion of sleep, but it wouldn't come. Instead, her mind buzzed with countless frightening thoughts, brought on by her forays into Plymouth. What would become of her if she failed to find Valerie?

Mr. Taylor had been absolutely right to question her sanity. No amount of books and movies could have prepared Louisa for the reality of life in the seventeenth century. She'd spent the past few days exploring the town, and grew more apprehensive with every passing day. She expected the poverty of the lower classes and the unsanitary conditions, but what she hadn't expected was the obvious lack of options. As she explored the streets of Plymouth, she paid particular attention to the women, eager to know what their lives were like.

As a woman born in the twentieth century, Louisa was used to the idea that she could do anything, be anything. The sky was the limit to what she could achieve, or the amount of money she could earn. She longed for a partner to love and eventually start a family with, but having a man wasn't a necessity. This world was vastly different. As a single woman, with no husband or male relative to protect her, Louisa was like a piece of driftwood afloat in an ocean of humanity. She didn't belong to anyone, and no one belonged to her, and sooner or later that would destroy her. If she didn't find her sister, eventually her money would run out, and she would have to make a place for herself in this cruel world.

As far as she could see, there were few choices open to women. A woman could get married, which was the most desirable outcome for most females, or she could work at some low-paying job just to make ends meet. The women who went into service worked long days, often in dismal conditions, and eventually died of disease or despair. Even if Louisa could find a job as a servant, she didn't have the necessary skills. Nothing she knew would be considered useful. She was a good painter, but who would allow a woman to paint professionally, in this day and age? She could sew on a button or cook simple dishes, but those would hardly qualify as job skills. She didn't even know how to start a fire in the grate without matches, or how to utilize the tools and ingredients of the day.

She supposed she could pour a mug of ale and work as a serving wench in a tavern, but she strongly suspected that most barmaids supplemented their income with other, less savory, activities. She hadn't gone into the taverns, since they were frequented only by men and she wouldn't get past the threshold, but she'd seen some of the women through the open doors. Their breasts spilled over the bodices in a way that invited the men not only to look, but to touch. They giggled as the men grabbed them and whispered lewd suggestions in their ear, and often perched in the customer's lap as they poured the ale in the hope of encouraging him to spend more coin that he'd intended.

Louisa couldn't begin to imagine such an existence. She'd been sexually active since High School, but she was no whore.

As off-putting as these options were, her choices would be even more limited in Virginia. What would she do in a struggling colony? The only choice open to women who came to Virginia was to marry a colonist. A single woman had no voice, no rights. Louisa flipped over onto her stomach, and pulled the blanket over her head, trying to stifle her thoughts.

What had she done? What would happen to her if Valerie was no longer in Virginia? She'd never been so scared in her life, and she wondered if that's why Valerie married Finlay Whitfield so quickly. She must have been terrified and alone, desperate for a man to offer her protection and security. But who would marry Louisa? She had been with Doug for years, and even he hadn't proposed. She chuckled to herself ruefully and turned back onto her back. What was she even thinking about? Marriage to one of these men would be more like a form of slavery, rather than a relationship based on love and respect. If she failed to find Valerie, her prospects were very dismal indeed. All the plans for survival she'd made back in the twenty-first century now seemed ridiculous and far-fetched.

NINE

Louisa tried to hide her smile as Agnes gave some poor sailor a tongue-lashing he'd never forget. The man had the misfortune of slipping on some filth and dropped a crate in front of them, prompting her maid's ire. Agnes had assumed her duties as Louisa's maid as soon as the contract was signed. It was too grand a name for the scrap of paper that bound Agnes to Louisa for seven years, but it was a legal document in this day and age. She was now responsible not only for herself, but for this young girl as well, and the knowledge weighed heavily on her. She wouldn't have the funds to send Agnes back to England if her quest ended in disappointment. The girl would have to share Louisa's fate, whatever it turned out to be.

Agnes was like no fifteen-year-old Louisa had ever met. There was no laziness or sense of entitlement so often present in the teenagers of Louisa's day. Although small for her age, the girl appeared to be the definition of efficiency. There was nothing she couldn't do, and Louisa was amazed by her work ethic and common sense. Agnes displayed a quiet maturity and seemed to miss little of what went on around her. After knowing her for a few days, Louisa could easily believe that Agnes had made the decision to cross the Atlantic all by herself. She obviously knew what she wanted.

The smell of the docks made Louisa's eyes water. It was a combination of dead fish, seaweed, muck, and stale sweat, occasionally punctuated by whiffs of tobacco. Not even the fresh breeze off the sea could mask the foul smells that seemed to be wafting from every available space. Louisa lifted her skirt a little higher in order to avoid soiling it on the assortment of garbage littering the stone walkway, and trod carefully behind Agnes, trying not to slip. Agnes was walking ahead of her, reading the names of the ships out loud, craning her neck in search of the one they needed. The ship would be leaving with the tide this evening, making it imperative for the women to find it soon.

"There it is, Mistress," Agnes exclaimed, pointing to a merchant ship some distance from them. Louisa could see the gold lettering on the side, and the carved figurehead of a young woman, her unnaturally red hair flowing behind her, her arms crossed beneath her bare breasts.

"Are we to assume that's *Gloriana* herself?" asked Louisa as she followed Agnes.

"I am sure I don't know, Mistress," Agnes replied in all seriousness. Louisa hoped she'd loosen up a bit. After all, they would be spending a lot of time together, and a sense of humor could sometimes be the only thing standing between her and despair. The ship seemed to grow larger as they approached, casting a slanted shadow. It was bobbing gently on the waves lapping against the dock, her crew buzzing with activity. Crates and barrels were still being loaded, and a reluctant goat was being led up the ramp onto the deck.

Mr. Dobbs had said the ship was a three-masted, square-rigged merchant vessel. There would be several passengers, but the primary purpose of the voyage was to bring goods and supplies to Virginia. Some vessels were crammed with passen-

gers bound for the New World, which made the conditions
unsanitary at best, horrific at worst, so this was as desirable a
situation as Louisa could hope for under the circumstances.

She looked up at the ship, suddenly noticing the gun ports
in the hull. There were six facing her, and probably six more on
the other side. Why did a merchant ship need so many guns?

"Do you require assistance, ladies?" Louisa turned to find a
tall, thin man standing behind her. His garb proclaimed him to
be a clergyman, his silvered temples and deep-set eyes giving
him an air of authority. "Allow me to introduce myself.
Reverend Blakeley, at your service." The reverend bowed to
Louisa, obviously expecting her to respond.

"I am Louisa Jamison, and this is my maid, Agnes Crawley."

Louisa suddenly felt a pang of unease. The Reverend
Blakeley was obviously Protestant, and might expect to conduct
services aboard the ship during the crossing. Although Louisa
hadn't been to church since her parents' funeral, she'd been
raised in the Catholic faith and knew little about the Protestant
religion, despite claiming that she'd been married to a Flemish
man.

King James I was Catholic, but there was still a lot of preju-
dice against Catholics, so Louisa felt no desire to advertise her
religious views. She hoped Reverend Blakeley wasn't a zealot.
She'd read enough about the religious beliefs of the time to
know that she'd be required to participate in whatever services
took place aboard the ship, keeping a low profile and guarding
her tongue against saying anything that might be construed as
blasphemy, heresy, or witchery.

That was another oversight on her part. She should have
attended Protestant church services before leaving for the
seventeenth century. Church services were mandatory, and
she'd have to adjust quickly in order to fit in, both aboard the
ship, and once she arrived in Virginia.

The deck was a beehive of activity, with sailors rolling kegs toward the narrow stairs and lowering them into the cargo hold. The captain was shouting orders, and a man Louisa assumed to be the ship's cook was supervising the storage of food supplies. She heard the goat bleat somewhere down below, shortly followed by the clucking of a hen coming from a cage to her left. How many animals did they have on board? Louisa jumped out of the way as a keg rolled toward her, nearly knocking her off her feet. A boy of about twelve muttered his apologies as he tried to redirect it toward the stairs.

"Be careful, boy!" the reverend shouted, as he escorted Louisa and Agnes toward the tubby man with bushy whiskers, who was issuing orders to the sailors. "Captain Fellowes, I presume." The tubby man stopped shouting and turned around to take stock of the new arrivals. "I am the Reverend Blakeley, and this is Mistress Jamison, and her servant."

"Delighted to make your acquaintance," the Captain replied, looking anything but. "I'll have the quartermaster show you to your cabins. Master Sheridan!" he hollered over the din of activity on the deck. A tall, dark-haired man, dressed in a navy-blue doublet and britches, appeared out of nowhere and gave them a stiff bow, sweeping off his hat.

"Reverend. Mistress Jamison. I am Master Sheridan, the first mate or quartermaster, if you prefer. If you would follow me, please."

Louisa couldn't help noticing that the man was very attractive, but he seemed annoyed by their presence, and didn't bother with the niceties as he led them to their cabins.

Louisa sat down on the narrow berth, taking stock. This would be her home for the next two months, give or take a few weeks. The cabin was tiny, with two berths bolted to the wall on opposite sides, and a small wooden table at the far end. There were two nails high in the wall for hanging clothes, and a bucket for their personal use. Without a porthole, the cabin was completely dark unless illuminated by a lantern. Luxury accommodations of the seventeenth century.

"'Tis quite nice, ain't it?" asked Agnes as she surveyed the small space, sitting stiffly on the edge of the berth.

"I couldn't have asked for more," Louisa replied with a genuine smile. If this was the worst of her hardships, she would gladly deal with it to get to Valerie. "I wonder who the other passengers are."

"I heard there was an older couple with their daughter, us, and the reverend. There ain't much room for passengers. What did ye make of the first mate, Mistress?"

"I haven't had enough time to form an opinion."

"'E is very handsome, I thought," babbled Agnes as she put away their few possessions.

"I suppose he is."

In truth, Louisa had forgotten all about him as soon as he left them to settle in. She was too nervous to pay attention to the crew. They'd be casting off soon, and she was excited and apprehensive all at one. From what she'd been able to see, the ship was bigger than the *Mayflower*, but it was still very primitive. How could this wooden box make it all the way to Virginia? What if there was no wind? She'd read something about the doldrums, which could last for weeks. Did that really happen? Louisa wondered as she tried to stretch out on the berth. It wasn't long enough to lie flat. She'd have to lie on her side and bend her legs. Agnes seemed delighted with the accommodations and couldn't stop talking.

"May I go up on deck?" Agnes asked.

"I don't think Captain Fellowes would appreciate having you underfoot," Louisa replied. "Maybe once we set sail."

"Shouldn't be long now," Agnes said. "Sounds like they've finished loading."

She was right, the sounds from above had changed. About

an hour later, the anchor was lifted and the wooden floor shuddered beneath their feet as the ship began to move out of the harbor toward the open sea. Louisa was truly on her way now. *Val, just stay put long enough for me to get there,* she thought desperately.

TEN

Valerie threw on her dressing gown and crept from the room. Alec was still asleep, his face peaceful in the milky light of dawn. It was the only time when he didn't look worried, and Valerie felt terrible guilt for the stress she caused him. She wished the horrible dreams would just go away. Alec was right, of course, she'd never had what people in these times called the Sight. If she had, she wouldn't have allowed Finlay to get involved with the murder plot that led to his death.

They never spoke of it, but Alec still bore the scars from the night Finn died. It took Alec all his considerable will to do what he'd done. It had been the only way to save him from an execution that would probably involve hanging, drawing and quartering, a gruesome fate reserved only for those guilty of High Treason. Finlay had been out of his mind with pain, bloody and broken after days of torture. He wouldn't have lasted much longer. Alec had given Finn last rites, a mercy he wouldn't have gotten from the Protest clergy present at the execution, before smothering him.

It had been a mercy killing, but Alec had never been quite the same. Valerie could see the pain in his eyes when he looked at young Finlay, the spitting image of his father. And now he was worried about this pregnancy. True, Louisa's birth had almost killed them both, but every time she looked at her beautiful girl she felt it had all been worth it. This baby would be worth it too. What were the chances of two breech births? Of course, she was now forty-one, and that was risky even in modern times, but Valerie tried not to dwell on the negative. Everything would be all right.

How easy it would have been in the twenty-first century. She would simply have gone to a hospital and had a C-section, performed by an actual doctor, in an operating room full of state-of-the-art equipment. But then she wouldn't have Alec, or Finn. Valerie had almost forgotten what modern life was like. For the first few years, she still missed the conveniences of life in the future, but eventually, the memories began to fade. She had always been the type of person to adjust to her surroundings and try to make the best of the situation, and she made a conscious decision not to dwell on the past, or in this case, the future.

The only thing she couldn't forget was her family. Not a day passed by that Valerie didn't think of her parents and Louisa. She sent them mental telegrams, telling them that she was alive and well, hoping that on some telepathic level they might somehow feel her vibe. She even had her portrait painted with the Cupid clock in the background, praying that Louisa, in her capacity as an art restorer, might somehow come upon it, but what were the chances of that happening? Absolutely none. The portrait now hung above the fireplace, mocking her desperate attempt to send a message through time. *Oh, Lou, what I wouldn't give to see you one more time*, Valerie thought.

She shut the door noiselessly behind her and started down the hallway, her feet silent on the bare floorboards. She'd surprise Alec by balancing the ledger. Amazing how the man had such a great head for business, but was a complete dunce when it came to accounting. Valerie smiled to herself. He'd been overjoyed to find that she had a head for numbers, and actually understood something about trade. Few women of the time would be able to grasp the concept, never having gotten any kind of an education. That had been before Alec found out about Valerie's past. It was their secret, one that bound them for life.

Her knowledge of the future came in handy sometimes, like right now. When John Rolfe introduced tobacco to the struggling colony of Virginia in 1612, Valerie advised Alec to start growing it on every inch of available land. He'd been skeptical of this new venture, but Valerie assured him that tobacco would be a huge export for the Colonies, and he believed her. The first two years didn't yield much, but by the third year, the plantation began to show a profit. He had to find more people to work the land and acquired a number of indentured servants, who were all too willing to work for a roof over their heads and food in their bellies.

Alec was a good master, who never raised a hand to any worker, even if provoked to anger. His Uncle Thomas might have been different, had he lived. He'd owned dozens of slaves on Tobago and thought Virginia would prosper if African slaves were brought over by the boatload. Sadly, his prediction recently came true, and more than a dozen slaves had already been acquired by the wealthier colonists. Valerie made Alec swear he'd never buy slaves, and he gave her his promise, although deep down, she wasn't sure he was really opposed to the idea. Slavery was common in the seventeenth century, and it was only her outrage that prevented Alec from considering it.

As it was, the tobacco planting paid off, and they were now one of the wealthiest families in Virginia. Rosewood Manor, which had been nothing more than a small cabin when they first arrived, was now a real home, with several bedrooms, a parlor, study, and dining room. It was small by modern standards, but by colonial standards, it was a palace.

Valerie was just about to turn the corner that led to Alec's study, when she heard a noise. There wouldn't be anyone in this part of the house so early in the morning unless they were up to something. She pressed herself against the wall and carefully peeked around the corner. The door to Alec's study opened slowly and a tall man stepped out into the shadows of the hallway. Valerie didn't need for him to turn around to know who he was. Charles was fully dressed, and judging by the state of his clothes, had been in the study all night. Valerie watched as he looked around furtively and made off toward his bedroom. She had just enough time to slip behind a curtain before he passed directly in front of her, and disappeared from view.

"What are you up to, Charlie?" Valerie whispered as she entered Alec's office. Nothing seemed out of place, but she had the distinct feeling that she was missing something.

ELEVEN

Louisa stood on deck admiring the endless vista of sky and sea. Today, the blue-gray water sparkled in the sunshine, seagulls screaming overhead as they dove for fish into the white-capped waves. Fluffy clouds chased each other across the aquamarine sky, periodically obscuring the sun, and providing some much-needed shade against the heat of the morning. She'd been terribly nervous the first few days of the voyage, but as the ship made its way toward the Atlantic, she began to relax. She liked the sound of the rigging creaking overhead, and the flapping of the sails as the wind filled them and propelled the vessel toward the New World.

Agnes had been suffering from seasickness, so Louisa left her in the cabin and came up on deck to enjoy the view. The tiny cabin made her feel claustrophobic, making it necessary to escape its narrow confines. If only she could find a place to hide. Despite the size of the ship, there was no place where she could find a bit of solitude. None of the sailors bothered her; it was the other passengers she wished to avoid. The Reverend Blakeley invited her to pray with him daily, and the Collins family were no better. Mr. Collins was a reticent man in his late forties, but

Mrs. Collins more than made up for her husband's pauses in conversation. She was full of comments, advice, and most annoyingly, questions. She kept asking Louisa about her life, making her nervous and upset.

Louisa decided not to tell the story of the Flemish husband for fear of being interrogated about Holland. Mrs. Dobbs had been easy enough to fool, but these people were more cosmopolitan. She was afraid to slip up and make some dreadful mistake that would make them suspicious of her. Louisa knew people in this day and age didn't need much proof to proclaim someone a heretic or a witch. The less she revealed the better. She became adept at avoiding personal questions by changing the subject, or paying a compliment to Mrs. Collins or her daughter. That seemed to work every time, setting Mrs. Collins on a whole new tangent that lasted a minimum of half an hour.

Louisa sighed in exasperation when she saw Reverend Blakeley making his way toward her, waving and smiling. She forced herself to smile and wave back. What a nuisance the man was becoming.

"Ah, Mistress Jamison. What a pleasure to find you here. I, myself, am a huge believer in taking the air. It does wonders for one's health. I was wondering if you might oblige me by reading with me today. I would love to share some of my favorite passages with you. There is one I particularly enjoy, about St. Paul on the road to Damascus."

Louisa had a brief vision of herself grabbing the good reverend by the ankles and tossing him overboard, but quickly dismissed the thought and put on a brave face. The reverend flipped the Bible open to the appropriate page, and was just about to begin reading when he was interrupted by the first mate.

"Mistress Jamison, a word in private, if you please," Mr. Sheridan called out to her. "It's about your servant," he hastily added when he saw the look of shock on the reverend's face.

"If you would excuse me, Reverend." Louisa watched as the disappointed reverend walked away, no doubt in search of another victim. She hoped he would find Anne Collins. The poor girl would probably appreciate some religious discourse. It might serve to fortify her, since the timid thing got the vapors if a bird so much as flew over her head.

"Is something wrong with Agnes, Master Sheridan?"

"Not a thing. You just looked as if you needed rescuing. I am afraid the reverend is concerned with much more than your immortal soul."

Louisa looked up, noticing his features for the first time. She was never close enough to him to take a good look, since he was frequently on the bridge or going about his other duties. Louisa wondered if Mr. Sheridan had a wayward Spaniard somewhere in his family tree. His wavy black hair was tied back into a neat ponytail, and his goatee framed generous lips that were stretched into a roguish smile. His best feature, however, was his eyes. They were slightly slanted and so black Louisa couldn't even see the pupils. At the moment, they danced with merriment, and she smiled back.

"I'm afraid you are right, Master Sheridan. I just hope he doesn't share St. Paul's views towards women." Oops, she shouldn't have said that. She glanced at the first mate to see his reaction.

"I doubt St. Paul spent much of his time pursing young women. If he had, it is not mentioned in the Holy Scripture. I think the reverend hopes to disembark in Virginia with a bride on his arm. Can a vicar marry himself, or would he require the services of the captain, I wonder?" The first mate gave her his arm. "Care for a stroll around the deck? I promise to refrain from theological discussions."

"Thank you, Master Sheridan. I will gladly take a stroll with you, if you promise to give Mistress Collins the elder a wide berth. I don't think I can stomach her this morning."

Louisa took the first mate's arm, grateful for his rescue. "Master Sheridan, I wonder if you might have something to read, other than the Bible that is. I long for something to pass the time."

"What type of literature do you enjoy? I have several volumes of poetry, and a play or two in my cabin. I also have some books on astrology and philosophy, if you are interested in that." The first mate skillfully maneuvered Louisa around some barrels and guided her toward the bridge.

"I would like to borrow them all, if I may. Now, if I could only find a place to read them undisturbed."

"I would gladly offer you the use of my cabin, but I fear Captain Fellowes would have my head for suggesting such gross impropriety."

He stopped by the steps to the bridge and gave Louisa a gallant bow. "I must leave you here, Mistress Jamison. I must begin my shift on the bridge. I will bring you the books after my shift ends. Have a pleasant morning."

Louisa watched as he sprinted up the steps to the bridge and took the wheel from the captain, who was smiling broadly having spotted her.

"Mistress Jamison," the captain called as he waddled down the steps. "Would you do me the honor of dining with me tonight? I have some excellent claret, and the cook promised some mutton chops." The captain was rubbing his pudgy hands together in delight. For some men it was women, for others, mutton chops.

"I would be honored, Captain," Louisa replied, eager to escape. The reverend was not the only one drooling over her cleavage, and she suddenly questioned the wisdom of joining the captain in his cabin. She would have to bring Agnes to chaperone. Every time she thought of that word she wanted to laugh hysterically, but she pulled her face into a polite mask and bid the captain a good day.

By the time Louisa got back to the cabin, Agnes was up and

about. She seemed to be feeling better, her pink cheeks a stark contrast to the pea-green they were earlier.

"You should eat something, Agnes. It might help settle your stomach. I brought you some goat's milk and bread from breakfast. I didn't think ale would be much help." Louisa sat down across from Agnes and looked her over. "I hope you like mutton chops."

"Who doesn't? Is that what cook is serving tonight?" She perked up at the sound of chops, which was definitely a good sign. The fare on the ship had been so basic and boring, mutton chops sounded like manna from heaven.

"He is to the captain, and we are to dine with him. I'm going to bring you along."

"I do not think the captain would much appreciate that, Mistress. I heard from the cabin boy that Captain Fellowes 'as been widowed these five years. Seems 'e is ready to marry again," said Agnes with a giggle. "So, who would ye say would make ye a more suitable husband, Captain Fellowes or Reverend Blakeley?" Agnes was really laughing now, and Louisa laughed along. It was nice to see her happy. She always seemed so pensive and restrained.

"If given the choice, I'll take the cook. At least he can guarantee me a supply of mutton chops," Louisa replied. "You should get some air. It will do you good."

"Yes, Mistress." Agnes was back to her serious self again, nervously pleating the fabric of her sleeve.

TWELVE

Valerie spread her blanket beneath a leafy oak and carefully eased herself to the ground. She lay back and closed her eyes, inhaling the soothing scent of pine and resin, and listening to the sound of the wind moving through the trees. Her face was dappled with sunlight streaming through the branches of the old oak, and sounds of birdsong filled the air, the birds oblivious to the turmoil in her heart. This was one of her favorite places, one she escaped to when she simply needed to get away. She made the best of her situation most of the time, but sometimes, it all just became too much. She could hardly tell Alec that she hated Virginia and wanted to go back to England. Their life was here now, and unfortunately, this is where her children would have to grow up.

Getting accustomed to life in seventeenth-century England had been difficult enough, but life in Virginia was positively savage compared to Europe. She'd learned to live without running water, heat, and the most basic medicine, but putting aside the living conditions, which weren't so bad at Rosewood Manor, what really bothered Valerie was the total lack of culture and enlightenment. Life had been reduced to the most basic of elements, most of those overseen by the overzealous eyes of the clergy. Punishments were severe and public, designed as much to humiliate as to teach a lesson. Watching someone get whipped, branded, or put into stocks was about the only entertainment most people could find in the harsh reality of their days.

Religion was mandatory, and services had to be attended regularly and twice on Sunday, with special individuals chosen by the minister to take attendance. The penalty for not coming to church was severe. As closet Catholics, this was even more of a burden for the Whitfields. Uncle Thomas had chosen wisely when he built Rosewood, since the house was far enough removed from Jamestown to attract little traffic. Not being part of the town or a settlement, the Whitfields had a little more freedom, but not much. They still had to attend church twice on Sundays, in order to avoid drawing attention to themselves.

They also held their own Catholic Mass at home, and Alec performed the necessary ceremonies, such as baptisms and funerals, being the head of the family. Valerie jokingly referred to it as the "Church of Alec." As in England, he had to do it discreetly, since not everyone at Rosewood Manor was a Catholic.

Alec frequently went to the docks and into the town, but Valerie chose not to accompany him. Her forays into Jamestown left her disgusted and depressed. On her last visit, she was forced to watch 'justice' being carried out as her path was blocked by the rowdy crowd, hungry for their entertainment. A man was dragged into the town square. It was difficult to guess his age, since he could have been anywhere between thirty and sixty. His clothes were filthy and torn, his hair so dirty and greasy it was impossible to even guess at its original color. He was obviously very poor, and shook with fear as the accusation against him was read. He had stolen some bread and an apple. The man tried to plead his case, but no one was listening.

Valerie closed her eyes and tried to fight the bile rising in her gullet as she heard the man's terrible scream, her nostrils filling with the smell of burnt flesh. The crowd roared its approval, thrilled to see the culprit punished, congratulating themselves on their good judgment and moral superiority. The man was quickly forgotten, and left in the square to clutch his branded hand as the gathering began to disperse. Valerie waited until there was almost no one left in the square and passed by the whimpering man, throwing a few coins into his lap. She was jolted by the realization that he was probably no more than eighteen, as he looked up at her in mute gratitude.

Valerie often thought of life at Yealm Castle before every-thing went awry. She could still remember Alec and Finlay teaching her the latest dances to the accompaniment of the lute played by John Dobbs. They had laughed and flirted, passing her between them, their eyes never leaving her flushed face. They'd been happy then, and alive. Finlay had taken her to London on a honeymoon of sorts. Valerie could still recall the thrill of driving through the streets of the London she'd only read about or seen in movies. The sights, sounds, and colors of the thriving metropolis overwhelmed her, and she bounced with excitement as she saw an advertisement for a play by William Shakespeare, which they had later attended. Finlay had taken her out on a pleasure cruise on the Thames, pointing things out to her as they sailed past Whitehall Palace and the Tower of London, having no inkling that just a few short months later, that would be the place where he'd come face to face with a horrible death.

Valerie heard a rustling noise and quickly sat up, looking around. The Indians rarely came this far, but anything was possible. They had been receptive at first when the settlers came to their shores, but relations were becoming distinctly more hostile between the Tsenacommacah Indians and the settlers, as the English took more of their land and food. Alec appeared between the densely growing trees and sat down next to Valerie, taking her hand in his and kissing her palm.

"Is it one of those days?" She simply nodded. "I just wanted to be alone for a while."

"Should I leave you in peace then?" He looked a little hurt, so Valerie assured him that she wanted him to stay, and Alec lay back on the blanket next to her, gazing up at the canopy of trees overhead.

"Tell me a story about the future," he said, pulling her head onto his shoulder. "I'd like to hear about space exploration."

Alec loved her stories, but as much as she enjoyed telling him things, she hated the way it made her feel. Being forced to recall the details of her modern life only reminded her of all the things she missed. Oh, what she wouldn't give for an outing to the movies or to the mall. Being surrounded by people who didn't care what her religious views were, or how often she went to church seemed like a version of Heaven. She hated the idea of her children growing up in these times of ignorance and intolerance, and felt a terrible frustration at not being able to do anything to change that. This was her life now, but truth be told, she wouldn't go back to the twenty-first century if it meant a life without Alec and her children.

Valerie got more comfortable and began telling Alec about the last space mission she could recall. His face was tense with concentration as he tried to picture a space shuttle and the image of earth as a blue sphere covered with oceans and continents, visible to the astronauts from their craft. Valerie kissed Alec's brow. He was so dear to her that no movie or shopping trip could ever compare to even one kiss from him.

THIRTEEN

Kit Sheridan splashed his face with a bit of tepid water and pulled on his boots. It was almost four in the morning and time for his shift. Most quartermasters hated the 4-8 shift, but he enjoyed it, especially on a warm, summer night like tonight. Kit went up to the bridge and took the wheel, inhaling the briny smell he loved. The moon hung low in the sky, silvering the tranquil ocean and illuminating the billowing sails. There was hardly anyone about and that's how he wanted it. It was the only time Kit could be alone on a ship full of people. The majority of the crew was fast asleep in the hammocks in the hold, snoring away and dreaming of land and the people they had left behind.

Kit hadn't left anyone behind. He was all alone, and being at sea, surrounded by people, kept him from being lonely. He dreaded going home to his silent, empty house, the house where Helena used to wait for him, flushed with happiness at having him back. The couple who took care of the house always welcomed him home, but retired as soon as they could, leaving him alone with his thoughts. He had grown up in that house, and could still remember his beautiful mother sewing by the fire or playing the lute, and his father coming back from months at sea and sweeping him up into a bear-like embrace, asking about all the things he learned while his old man was away. And there was always Caro, who loved him unconditionally. He'd been very sad when she married and went to live with her husband. He missed her dreadfully.

Kit thought all boys had such loving and gentle families, but he later came to realize that he'd been very blessed. He'd been surrounded by love growing up, and later, when'd he married Helena. That life had been so different from the life he was living now. He had no financial need to go to sea. He could live comfortably in his London house, or Essex country estate for the rest of his days, but he felt stifled at home and time weighed heavily on him.

It had been nearly seven years since his father died, and just over two since the Black Death took his wife and mother. He supposed he should think of marrying again, but the young women he met seemed shallow and calculating, their only desire to snare a wealthy, titled husband. Kit had both the title and the wealth, but his heart was at peace only at sea.

He was distracted from his thoughts by a slight movement on deck. He couldn't see the face, but he could tell from her gait that it was Mistress Jamison. Mistress Collins was too portly, and her daughter too timid to come up on deck by herself in the middle of the night.

"Mistress Jamison," he called out softly. "Are you quite all right?" She looked up at him, her face bleached of all color by the moonlight, and her eyes nearly black. "Would you like to come up?"

Mistress Jamison lifted her hem to avoid tripping and walked up the steps to the bridge. She looked anxious and tired.

"I couldn't sleep," she said quietly. "It's so lovely up here when no one is about."

"Yes. I like to be here at this hour, just before the sun starts to come up and everyone rises and reports for duty. Were you worried about something?" He had no business prying into her affairs, but he was curious to discover what was keeping her from her bed.

"I was worried about arriving in Virginia."

"Do you have family there?" The woman visibly tensed, and he felt terrible for asking.

"Yes. No. I don't know." Louisa looked out over the shimmering water toward the invisible line of the horizon. "I'm searching for my sister. I know she was in Virginia in 1610, but I've heard nothing since, and I'm terrified that she won't be there when I arrive. What will I do? Where will I go?"

"Would you return to England if you didn't find her or settle in the New World?" Kit thought, quite irrationally, that he would like her to return to England.

"I honestly don't know. Everything depends on what happens when I get there."

Mistress Jamison looked so scared he wished he could take her in his arms and comfort her, but he pushed the thought away. It would be bad enough if someone saw her up here alone with him, without him making matters worse. No one was allowed on the bridge, and he was breaking a cardinal rule by having invited her to come up.

"If there is anything I can do to assist you, you only need to ask. I will not return to England until I know you are safe with your sister and have no wish to return."

"Thank you, Master Sheridan. I appreciate your offer more than you know." With that, Louisa turned and left the bridge, bound for her cabin.

Kit looked up at the sky. The stars were beginning to fade, just a hint of light visible on the horizon. He loved the moment when the first fiery glimmer of the sun appeared above the water, painting the sky pink and gold. He suddenly regretted that he couldn't share the beauty of the sunrise with Mistress Jamison, and turned away.

FOURTEEN

"Oh, he is a fine figure of a man, isn't he? A fine figure, indeed."

Mistress Collins was eyeing the reverend as he emerged onto the deck. Louisa supposed that if the man remained silent for more than ten minutes, he could be labeled as attractive. With his shoulder-length dark hair, peppered with gray, and storm-colored eyes, he could be appealing to some. The reverend obviously took care to stay in shape, his tall form lean and graceful as he made his way toward the women.

"He is, Mistress Collins, and what a fine husband he would make for your daughter," Louisa agreed, smiling blandly.

"Oh, you've read my mind, my dear. How perceptive you are. My Anne would be most honored by a proposal from a man like dear reverend. If only she were more—what's the word I am looking for—coy, encourage him a bit. Might you have a word with her, Mistress Jamison, and sing the praises of the reverend?"

"I will do everything in my power," Louisa promised.

The reverend had become even more persistent, so she had to do something to discourage his advances without making an enemy of him. Anne Collins would actually be the perfect bride for him. She was shy and compliant, and hung on his every word as if he were the Oracle of Truth. Louisa was suddenly accosted by the unpleasant image of the reverend performing his husbandly duties. The man probably wouldn't even take off his nightshirt, just lift it enough to do the deed. Her gaze fell on Master Sheridan, who was standing on the bridge, his profile handsome and patrician. She suddenly wondered if he was married, and how he performed his husbandly duties.

Louisa turned away in embarrassment. What was she thinking? This wasn't the *Love Boat*, for God's sake. She was distracted from her thoughts by the appearance of Anne Collins. The girl came up on deck, her eyes firmly glued to the scrubbed planks beneath her feet. Anne would be a pretty girl if she wore something other than dark blue and gray and didn't scrape her hair into that severe bun. Reverend Blakeley didn't even turn his head when Anne came up, concentrating all his attention on Louisa, who seemed to inspire him despite her drab brown gown.

"Mistress Jamison, might I interest you in a stroll?" the reverend asked, offering Louisa his arm.

"Thank you, Reverend. I'm a little tired tonight, but I think Mistress Collins just came up for that very purpose, haven't you, Anne? Would you be so kind as to keep Reverend Blakeley company?" The poor girl blushed crimson, but nodded politely.

"I would be happy to, Reverend," she murmured, and took the reverend's arm.

"Well done, Mistress Jamison," a voice behind her said. "Well done, indeed." Louisa turned around to find Master Sheridan standing behind her, studying her with his head cocked to the side. A smile played about his lips, lighting up those bottomless eyes. "Are you enjoying the books I lent you?"

"I am. Thank you so much. I'm almost done with the second book of poetry. You mentioned you have a folio of *Macbeth*.

"Yes. I have several plays. Shall I get them for you now?" He made no move to leave.

"Tomorrow would be just fine. I wanted to stay up here a little bit longer. It's such a beautiful evening. I've never seen so many stars."

"The view is even more spectacular from the bridge. Would you like to see it?" Louisa was surprised. No one was allowed on the bridge unless specifically invited by the captain. Her previous brief foray onto the bridge was their secret. "My shift starts at ten. If you would join me on the bridge, I can show you how to steer the ship. Would you like that?"

"Yes. I would. See you then, Master Sheridan."

Louisa returned to her cabin. She felt unusually flustered, and wondered why she'd been so affected by the first mate's invitation. She had flirted with plenty of men in her life, but this felt different somehow. These men were different. They weren't like the men of her time who felt free to admire a woman, flirt with her, and even sleep with her, with no obligation. These men meant business, and to lead them on was dangerous. She had no idea what Master Sheridan's designs on her were, but she had to tread carefully.

It was easy enough to fob off the reverend on Anne Collins, or to be coy with the captain, but this man made her feel things she hadn't felt in a long time, not since she met Doug. His warm gaze left her breathless, and his smile gave her butterflies. She reached for the folio of poems, hoping it would distract her from her dangerous thoughts. She was just scared and lonely, trapped in a world so vastly different from her own. She longed for affection, and she was drawn to the first attractive, charming man she saw. He was simply being kind, nothing more, and it would make things easier if she didn't read anything into this invitation.

It was too dark to read, even with the candle, so she set the folio aside, turning to face the wall to avoid Agnes's prattling.

What had it been like for Valerie when she found herself in the past? Louisa wondered. Did she fall in love with Finlay because she was scared and lonely? Why did she choose him over the other brother? What drew her to him? Mary Dobbs said Finlay had been a bit wild, untamed. Did Valerie see him as a challenge, or did he take advantage of her fragile state and rush her into something she wasn't ready for? She had so many questions for her sister. She only wished she would get the chance to ask them.

FIFTEEN

Louisa waited until she thought it was past 10pm and slipped out of the cabin. Agnes was already asleep, and she hoped the reverend was asleep as well. She had no desire to see his eyes narrowed in speculation as he watched her go up on the bridge to join Master Sheridan. She suddenly wondered what his name was. Sometimes she was amazed by the formality ship life demanded. Everyone called each other by their surnames. Even the twelve-year-old cabin boy was called Master Willis. Everyone referred to her as Mistress Jamison, not Louisa, and the only person she called by her name was Agnes. Mistress Collins occasionally referred to her daughter as Anne, but everyone else called her Mistress Collins. The formality erected borders between people, which were perhaps necessary when confined to such a small space.

The night sky was pitch black, stars like jewels strewn across dark velvet. She liked the ship at night. There was hardly any activity, since most of the crew was already down below, resting up for another day of hard work. A lantern swayed gently from one of the beams, the candle inside throwing flickering shadows on coils of rope and barrels of tar. Several shadowy figures moved about the deck, but they were just sailors going about their evening tasks. She looked up at the bridge. The first mate was there alone, one hand on the wheel, eyes staring off into the distance. She walked up the steps and joined him.

"Good evening, Mistress Jamison. I hoped you'd come."

Louisa could see the moon reflected in those dark eyes as he took in her appearance. She hadn't bothered to put her hair up and it tumbled around her shoulders, gently blowing in the breeze. In her modern life, she used a flat iron to make it straight, but here, she had no choice but to let it dry naturally whenever she was lucky enough to actually wash it. The honey-blonde waves framed her face, making her look younger than her twenty-nine years. Most of the time she wore a linen cap that served the dual purpose of making her look modest and keeping her hair clean and vermin-free.

"Would you like to steer?" the first mate asked, his eyes never leaving her face. She nodded.

Master Sheridan moved away from the wheel, making room for Louisa. She stepped in front of him and put her hands on the spokes, enjoying the smoothness of the polished wood beneath her fingers. The wheel felt surprisingly heavy. She couldn't have turned it on her own even if she'd wanted to. The first mate came up behind her, putting his hands over hers, his body almost touching hers, but not quite. She could sense his warmth in the coolness of the night, suddenly longing to lean against him, to feel his arms around her, holding her tight.

"What's your name?" she whispered. She wasn't sure if he heard her above the rustling of the wind, but he had. He took a long moment to answer, no doubt startled by the question.

"Christopher, but the people who matter call me Kit. What's yours?"

"Louisa, but the people who matter call me Lou," Louisa replied playfully, trying to ignore the thudding of her heart.

"A beautiful name for a beautiful woman, but I prefer Louisa to Lou. It's more feminine."

Her name did sound nice in his mouth. Had he moved closer, or was her imagination playing tricks on her? Louisa gripped the wheel tighter, suddenly nervous. Her body seemed to be leaning back of its own accord, looking for the comfort of his. Christopher's hands covered hers, a strangely intimate gesture in this formal world where no one touched.

"Thank you, Master Sheridan. I'd better go back to my cabin now." She pulled her hands from beneath his and turned around. His face was only inches away from her own. Had he not been much taller than her, their mouths would almost be touching.

"Yes, you'd better. Good night... Louisa."

SIXTEEN

Louisa woke up sometime in the middle of the night. The air in the cabin was close and warm, the darkness impenetrable. She threw off the covers, lying there in her chemise. Agnes was sound asleep, obviously feeling better after a bout of nausea. Louisa wondered if the girl had reached puberty yet. Most girls did by the age of fifteen, but Agnes was small for her age, and might have been underfed her whole life. Lack of proper nutrition would forestall its onset.

The reason Louisa was wondering was because she needed some practical advice. Her period started a few days ago, and she had already gone through her stash of tampons. She had only two left and needed something to use in their place. She supposed women used some sort of rags, but she didn't have any, and had no idea what would hold them in place even if she did.

She'd been forced to part with her bra and panties as soon as they boarded the ship. Agnes went through her things and washed the undergarments as needed. It wouldn't do for her to see these items. Louisa didn't mind going braless, as much as she minded the lack of underwear. She felt strangely exposed despite the petticoat and long skirt, and kept pressing her legs together, conscious of her nakedness. She supposed she would have to get used to that, among other things, like not washing on a regular basis. The sailors provided buckets of seawater upon request, but the salt water made Louisa's hair feel coarse and brittle. What she wouldn't give for a hot shower and some good conditioner. A cappuccino wouldn't hurt either. She hadn't had a cup of coffee since her last morning in the twenty-first century, and she longed for caffeine.

The fare on the ship was horrible. They had biscuits and ale for breakfast, salted pork and bread for lunch, and a stew of some sort for dinner. The captain occasionally got a chop or a roasted chicken, which he frequently offered to share with Louisa, to the chagrin of the other passengers. She didn't want to encourage the captain's attentions, but at this point, she would do almost anything for a piece of chicken and a vegetable. She would probably have kissed him for a piece of fruit.

Agnes moaned in her sleep. She'd been tossing and turning all night. Louisa hoped it was close to morning. She couldn't stand being cooped up in this windowless box and was desperate to go up on deck. She dressed in the dark and let herself out of the cabin, taking a book with her. The light outside was beginning to change from inky blue to a misty gray, signaling the arrival of a new day. So far, the weather had been lovely, with a brisk wind that filled the sails and guaranteed a desirable speed. The captain was pleased with their progress and hoped to arrive in Jamestown by mid-August.

Louisa walked briskly to the bow of the ship and perched on a small barrel in the hope that no one would notice her presence. Rose-colored light spread across the water, the sun rising majestically over the calm waters of the ocean. Louisa remained perfectly still as she watched the sunrise. She'd seen the sun rise countless times, but it had never been as majestic as the sunrise on the sea. Once the sun was hovering above the horizon, Louisa opened Christopher Sheridan's book. It was a collection of sonnets, some of which she recognized. She was almost finished with it, but after last night, she was a little embarrassed to go ask him for another book.

Louisa flipped through the leather-bound volume, searching for her place, when a folded sheet of paper fell out onto her lap. Louisa picked it up and turned it over in her hand. It was bad manners to read other people's private correspondence, but she was curious about this man, and if it was that private, he would have removed it from the book. He probably forgot about it, in which case, she would read it and put it right back. Louisa unfolded the letter. It was written in an elegant hand, the ink slightly faded.

London

October 2, 1617

My dearest Kit,

No mere words can convey how much I miss you and long for your return. Your mother has been very kind to me, introducing me to London society and securing an invitation to Court for the Christmas festivities. I am a little intimidated by the prospect of meeting His Majesty, but I know you would want me to go, so I will put on a brave face and make you proud. Sometimes I sorely miss the peace and quiet of the country, but London is full of diversions, and I am doing my best to enjoy them.

There's a rumor going around that Thomas Edmondes is being recalled to England from his post as the Ambassador to France. Does this mean you will be coming home soon, my love? I hope and pray to see your face again before the end of the year.

Your loving wife,

Helena

Louisa refolded the letter and slipped it between the pages of the book. She felt crushing disappointment. Technically, Christopher Sheridan hadn't done anything wrong, but she was angry with him. Why was he being nice to her when he had a loving woman waiting for him back home? Of course, he was probably lonely, being away from home for months on end. The letter was dated 1617. She wondered how many years the man had spent at sea, away from home and his wife.

She had been a gullible fool to think that he was interested in her. He probably was interested, just not in the way she thought. The ship offered little privacy, but there was always a way. Christopher Sheridan had his own cabin, and likely hoped to lure her into it at a time when no one was about, like after his graveyard shift. Perhaps that's why he'd invited her up on the bridge, to see if she'd be willing to meet him at night. Louisa stuffed the book into the pocket of her gown and marched back to her cabin. She let herself in and sat down on her berth. The darkness seemed even more oppressive after the glorious sunrise, so she lit a candle and set the lantern on the small table before curling up on her berth. She was frustrated and angry.

Louisa was just beginning to calm down when Agnes sat bolt upright, startled out of a deep sleep. The girl looked around in a panic, then grabbed for the bucket and leaned over the side of the berth to retch into it. She wiped her mouth with the back of her hand, then lay back, breathing hard.

"Are you all right, Agnes? Shall I fetch you some water?"

"I feel better now," Agnes assured her. 'Tis just all this motion that's sickening me. I 'ave never been on a ship afore this."

"I would have thought you'd have gotten your sea legs by now. It's been two weeks."

Louisa had felt a little seasick for the first day or two, but then it passed, thankfully. She would hate to be as sick as Agnes had been. "Shall we get some breakfast? I'm famished, and there is nothing I'd like better than a hard biscuit and a cup of ale," added Louisa with a wicked grin.

"Ye go on up, Mistress. I will just tidy up and go to the 'ead, then join ye later. I am not ready to eat yet."

"All right. Suit yourself. Incidentally, I was just wondering if you might have some rags." Louisa looked away for a moment, unsure of how to verbalize her need.

"Ye mean for yer courses, ma'am? I 'ave prepared some for ye. They are just 'ere." Agnes pulled out several smaller rags and one large one, and handed them to Louisa. It wouldn't do to ask Agnes how to use these, since any woman of the time would be familiar with the process, so Louisa thanked Agnes and left the cabin. She would fold up the smaller rags and then use the bigger one to hold them in place, tying the ends at her hips and praying for the best.

SEVENTEEN

Agnes waited for the door to close behind her mistress before sinking back down on the berth. The nausea had abated, but she needed a few moments alone. She hadn't expected the sickness to last this long, or be so debilitating. She hoped it would pass soon. She liked Mistress Jamison, and prayed that she wouldn't sell her contract to someone else once they docked in Virginia. Agnes had never worked for anyone other than her aunt and uncle, but knew that Mistress Jamison was a rare find. She was kind and considerate. Agnes never expected a woman of quality to treat her with such care and compassion.

She did notice some strange things about her, but had no desire to question her betters. Mistress Jamison said odd things that Agnes didn't understand from time to time, and was almost too familiar with her, not like a mistress, but more like a friend. She supposed she was lonely on this ship with no one but the annoying vicar and the overbearing Collinses for company. Agnes couldn't help wondering if Mistress Jamison would consent to be wed. The captain was obviously smitten with her, as was the Reverend Blakeley. Agnes preferred Master

Sheridan herself. He was handsome and charming, and had lovely manners.

Agnes grabbed her stomach as another wave of nausea made her reach for the bucket, reminding her of her predicament. She wasn't sure how much longer she'd be able to hide her condition. She was about three months gone, and would begin to show by the time they reached the New World. Perhaps she should tell her mistress and beg for her understanding, but Agnes couldn't bring herself to utter the words. Mistress Jamison would feel duped once she discovered the truth and might punish Agnes. She couldn't imagine Mistress Jamison giving her a beating, but if she asked the captain, he might offer the services of one of the sailors for the task. Best to keep quiet for now, Agnes decided.

Agnes covered the bucket with the lid and curled into a ball on the narrow berth. Oh, how she wished she would miscarry. Why was it that the unwanted babies always lived on, while the wanted ones were taken away? She longed to love this child, but she simply couldn't. The way it had been conceived left her feeling soiled and angry. She knew it wasn't the child's fault, but she couldn't help the way she felt, could she?

EIGHTEEN

"You are an absolute gem," Alec said, kissing the top of Valerie's head. "That ledger nearly gave me an apoplexy last month, and I was dreading even looking at it this time." Alec settled himself across from Valerie and reached for a piece of bread.

"I thought as much. Glad to be of help." Valerie looked up as Charles walked into the dining room.

"Good morning, Charlie. How did you sleep?" she asked. Charles looked tired and drawn this morning, making Valerie wonder if he had been prowling the house again, lurking in Alec's study.

"Like a baby." Charles took a seat next to Louisa and winked at her, making her giggle. "How did you make out with the ledgers, Alec?"

"Valerie balanced them for me. I strongly recommend marrying a woman who can do the accounts. It doesn't matter if she is ugly as sin, as long as she can balance a ledger." Alec ducked as Valerie threw her napkin at his head.

Charles gave Cora a beatific smile as she set a bowl of porridge in front of him and poured him a cup of ale. The girl looked away, embarrassed, her cheeks turning a lovely shade of rose. Cora usually served them breakfast, and Valerie noticed that the girl always paid particular attention to Charles, who was without question, very handsome. Charles was tall, like his brothers, with the same wavy dark hair and thickly-lashed eyes, but his eyes were the color of jade, rather than the emerald green of Finlay's eyes, or the amber of Alec's. He was always charming, and had the talent of making the person he was talking to feel as if they were the most important person in the room. Cora flashed Charles a shy smile before taking the empty pitcher and leaving the room.

"I will take that under consideration, Brother. Speaking of marriage, I was thinking of going to visit Mistress Gaines today. Do you need anything from town?"

"Annabel Gaines? She can't be older than fifteen, Charlie." Alec set down his cup of ale and glared at his brother.

"And not that much younger than Violet was when you married her. Besides, I am in no hurry. I simply want to get there first, before somebody else does. You must admit, she has the face of an angel." Valerie was distracted from the conversation by the sound of Cora dropping something in the hallway.

"Are you getting married, Uncle Charles?" Louisa asked. "I've never been to a wedding."

"Not for some time, petal. I am simply staking my claim." Charles buttered a piece of bread and reached for the pot of honey, spreading his bread liberally.

"I am never getting married," piped in Finn. "I hate girls." Finn gave his sister a meaningful stare.

"Good, then you can stay here and take care of us in our dotage," Alec replied without missing a beat. "I intend to be a very cantankerous old man, and I am sure your mother will be simply unbearable. Just look at her now."

"Don't mock me, Father." Finn turned red, as he usually did

when he got angry. He had been difficult this past year, no longer a little boy, but not yet a man. Valerie strongly suspected he had been having some wet dreams, and was deeply embarrassed by his newly-discovered interest in the opposite sex.

"My apologies. I was simply trying to show you all the alternatives," Alec answered innocently.

NINETEEN

Kit pulled off his boots and stretched out on the berth, still fully dressed. He was tired after spending nearly all night at the wheel. Captain Fellowes had every right to delegate, but he was spending less and less time on the bridge, and more time guzzling his claret. Kit didn't mind being in charge, but it prevented him from interacting with others, such as Mistress Jamison. Louisa. She had been giving him the cold shoulder the last few days, and he needed to find an opportunity to get back into her good graces. He must have offended her that night on the bridge. He hadn't meant to caress her hands or stand so close, but she looked so beautiful, standing there in the moonlight, her hair curling around her face, her eyes full of wonder as she gazed at the night sky.

Kit closed his eyes and tried to picture Helena's face. It no longer came to him the way it did before. It had been too long since he'd seen it. He was still tormented by the same old regrets. How he wished he'd taken her away from London that spring. She might have still been alive. The outbreak of plague had been very minor that year, but it still claimed over one thousand lives, along with those of his wife and mother.

They had been married for nearly five years by the time Helena died, but, they'd spent little time together. He loved and desired her, but he'd known precious little of her soul. Having been sent to France with Thomas Edmondes, Kit spent long stretches abroad. The ambassador needed a trustworthy man to carry messages home and be there at his disposal should the need arise. Kit had captained his own vessel then, but that was before Helena died. He would have liked to take Helena with him to France, but it wasn't possible. He was in the service of the king and couldn't bring along his wife. He got to see her from time to time, when the ambassador sent him back to England with important messages for the king, but their reunions had been brief.

They never even had a child. At thirty-two, Kit was longing for a family, but he hadn't courted anyone seriously since Helena died. His sister, Lady Caroline Carew, harped on him incessantly about carrying on the family name and passing on the title, but he simply wasn't ready. She paraded eligible heiresses in front of him whenever he was in town, but no one caught his eye. They even argued when he visited her last Christmas.

All he wanted was to spend a peaceful Christmas with his only family, but it didn't turn out that way. The house was aglow with numerous candles, servants scurrying around as they brought out dish after dish to the already laden table. Strains of a festive tune played by a company of hired musicians floated from the hall, nearly drowned out by the hum of conversation. Caroline was dressed in a maroon silk gown, worked with gems and shot with gold thread, her dark hair piled high on her head and adorned with bejeweled pins. By the time Kit arrived, a dozen high-born couples were already seated around the table, eating and drinking. Caroline came over to greet him, her eyes sparkling with too much wine, and a satisfied smile playing about her rouged lips.

"You look well, Sister," Kit had said, kissing her smooth cheek.

"Burying a husband and taking a young lover can have that effect," she whispered in his ear. He was seated on her right, next to Lady Leticia Hawthorne. The young lover in question sat to his sister's left, openly devouring her with his eyes. Kit was surprised, but not shocked.

Caroline married Sir Arthur Carew when she was very young. Her husband had been much older and afflicted with gout, but Caroline had to have her way. He was as rich as Croesus, and had the ear of the queen, and later the king, making Caroline one of the most influential women at court. Now Arthur was gone, and Caroline was free to live life as she pleased, as long as she did it discreetly, which was something she needed to learn if she hoped to retain her position at court.

Kit had suffered through several endless courses, followed by hours of dancing, and a masque prepared especially for the occasion by some of the wives. He secretly thought that the only purpose of the masque was for the ladies to wear provocative costumes, but the performance was a great success, greeted with wild applause by the much soused husbands. It wasn't until close to dawn that the guests finally began to disperse, stumbling out of the house toward their waiting carriages, manned by sleepy coachmen who had been left to wait all night in the bitter cold.

Kit joined his sister in a glass of wine after her guests left. The house was quiet at last, the only sounds coming from the wind blowing outside, and the crackling of the fire in the hearth. Shadows danced across his sister's face, expertly hiding the little lines and blemishes of middle age. She didn't have much time left to enjoy herself, and she intended not to waste it.

"It is high time you were married, Kit," she said without preamble. "It's been nearly two years since Helena died. You need a good woman to wipe that look of misery off your face and give you a son and heir. What did you think of Lady Leticia?"

"I thought Lady Leticia was overly fond of Lord Gainsborough, who is your lover, if I am not mistaken." Caroline threw him a filthy look and took a sip of her wine.

"Don't worry about Lord Gainsborough. There are many more like him, if you know where to look. Now, let's get back to your solitary state. How long are you in town for before you hide yourself on some ship again? You're not even the captain anymore. What would father say?"

He hated when she invoked their father against him. He'd loved his father and wouldn't want to disappoint him or dishonor the family name, but he had his reasons. "I am leaving in a fortnight."

"Why don't you call on Lady Leticia tomorrow? She would be happy to receive you. I saw her looking at you. Kit, she is young, wealthy, and comes from a prominent family. All her female relations are very fertile."

"That must be very gratifying for them." Kit was quickly losing his patience. He didn't like Lady Leticia, and he liked his sister twisting his arm even less.

"Caro, I am not going to call on Lady Leticia, or anyone else. I have no wish to marry, but when I do, I will choose my own bride. I haven't met anyone who can take Helena's place, and I likely never will, so leave me alone and go back to your own sordid affair. I wonder what your sons think of your wanton behavior."

"My sons are too busy furthering their own ambitions to pay me any heed. They have no objection to me having a lover if he can elevate their position at court. They are their father's sons, after all. You are the only real family I have left, and I refuse to see you waste your life on mourning your insipid little wife."

"I've heard enough. Good night, Caroline."

Kit had risen from his chair, scraping it loudly against the stone floor, and strode from the room. He hadn't seen Caroline since, but he intended to call on her when he returned to England. She might be a meddlesome harpy, but she was still his sister, and he missed her.

What really set him off was not her matchmaking attempts, but the reference to his captaincy. Kit had been a captain of his own vessel, which he renamed *Helena* after his wife passed. It seemed that neither Helena was meant to survive. He hated thinking of that awful day nearly a year and a half ago, but Caroline reminded him of it, and it took over his mind, making his insides churn with grief and remorse.

He had set sail from Marseille only two days before the great storm hit. He should have seen the signs, should have set the course to avoid the eye of the storm, but he was eager to get home and thought they could ride it out. He was wrong. Dead wrong. The waves swelled to alarming heights as they battered the ship, nearly laying it on its side. The wind howled, sounding like a wailing woman, as the sky wept rain and sleet. The sailors cowered as thunder boomed with increasing frequency, the deck flooded by wave after wave crashing over the sides of the vessel.

They might have made it, had it not been for the lightning. The sky was nearly black, the jagged lines of lightning illuminating it with an eerie glow as thunder boomed frighteningly close. The air smelled of ozone, seaweed, and fear. A bolt of lightning struck the main mast. With a wrenching crack, the mast broke nearly in half and came crashing over the starboard railing, tearing the rigging, and upsetting the precarious balance of the vessel. Kit ordered the crew to saw off the mast to keep it from dragging the ship down, but it was too late. Wave after wave pounded the floundering vessel, filling it with seawater, and pulling it into a watery embrace. It sank fast, forcing the crew to jump into the roiling sea to avoid being sucked down with the ship.

The water was freezing as it rolled over Kit's head, filling his nose and mouth until he was choking. He struggled to keep his head above the surface, but the sea was a worthy opponent that day. He didn't stand a chance against the monstrous waves forcing him under. He wasn't sure who'd actually saved him, but when he came to, he was clinging onto a piece of wreckage that was bobbing on the heaving sea like a child's toy.

He'd lost seven men that day. The survivors had been lucky enough to be picked up by a passing ship once the storm abated and taken to England. They had been in the frigid water for hours and most of them were fevered by the time they were put ashore. Kit meant to go home, but he was closer to Caroline's residence, so he stumbled to her door, nearly falling as a servant answered his feeble knock.

Caro's manservant got him to bed and summoned his sister. Kit couldn't even remember Caro coming into the room. He was lost in delirium, fighting a high fever that threatened his life. Caroline had sat by his side throughout the night, applying cool compresses and trying to spoon water past his cracked lips. He must have been raving, since she kept telling him to calm down and rest. The fever broke by the fourth day, leaving him weak and confused. There were fresh bruises on his arms. He must have been bled by the physician, but he couldn't recall anything that happened after his ship went down.

"Welcome back to the land of the living," Caroline said as she took his hand, her face alight with relief. "I thought I'd lost you. How do you feel?"

"Like I've been in a shipwreck," Kit replied, his attempt at humor making him cringe. "Can I have something to drink?"

Caroline held a cup of tepid beef broth to his lips and helped him to drink. It tasted strange, but Kit tried to drink it anyway, knowing he needed nourishment to get better. Even this small task left him exhausted, and he sank against the pillows, drenched in cold sweat.

"Promise me you'll get better, Kitty, and I'll get you a girl," Caroline said with a meaningful wink.

"Caro, please don't call me that. I am no longer two years old."

"You will always be two to me," she answered and fluffed her skirts.

"Is that why you are offering to procure whores for me? I can barely hold a spoon, much less..." he trailed off, suddenly embarrassed to be having this conversation with his sister. She had always had a healthy sexual appetite, carrying on with his tutor right under their father's nose, but this was too much even for him. He knew his sister hadn't been faithful to her husband, but he truly didn't want to know, and he didn't want her bringing him harlots. Sex wasn't the answer to everything, at least not for him.

"Caro, I don't want a woman; I want my men back. It's my fault they drowned, entirely my fault."

"You did not cause the storm, and you did your best to save your crew and the ship. Stop talking balderdash."

She adopted her 'big sister knows better' look, forcing him to turn away. She didn't understand. He didn't cause the storm, but he could have avoided it had he not been an arrogant fool. Now his men were dead, his ship was gone, and he was lying here, barely able to move his limbs.

"Some mutton, I think," Caroline said, standing up and heading for the door. "You need meat. Try to sleep and I'll be back later. No whores, I promise." Kit gave her a weak smile, grateful that at least he still had his Caro.

Eventually, he went to sea again, but not as a captain. He signed on as quartermaster, still retaining a position of authority and respect, but shirking the immediate responsibility of being the captain. He wasn't ready to hold men's lives in his hands. He knew he would in time, but not yet. The voyage aboard the *Gloriana* was only his third trip since the shipwreck.

Meeting Mistress Jamison had been a surprise. When he heard about the passengers coming aboard, he'd been slightly annoyed. Passengers meant complaints, requests, and the need for patience. This lot was no different, except for her. When he tried to picture her face, it came easily enough, and so did the unbidden image of her naked body. Kit flipped onto his stomach. He was tired, frustrated, and aching with long-forgotten need.

TWENTY

Valerie set aside her sewing and stood up, easing her back. It was aching a bit, and she was ready to take a walk, but first she'd stop by the kitchen. She was getting awfully hungry between dinner and supper, and needed a little something to tide her over. This pregnancy was different than the last one. She wasn't as tired and sleepy, but boy, was she hungry.

The house was unusually quiet at this time of day since the children were outside, Louisa playing with the doll Valerie had made for her, and Finn was probably setting one of his traps for rabbits or foxes. He loved to hunt, and constantly begged Alec to take him shooting. Valerie was always nervous when they went off together, fearing they would run into a band of unfriendly Indians. There had been plenty of outbreaks of violence between the Indians and the settlers, and two white men carrying guns might appear to be enough of a threat to provoke an attack.

Valerie strolled into the kitchen, settling herself on a bench. "Hungry, Mistress?" Cook inquired, already knowing the answer.

"Famished. Is there any of that steak pie left?"

She hated calling the woman by her occupation, but as mistress of the house, she had to follow protocol. To call the cook Barbara would imply that they were somehow equal, and it wouldn't do. Barbara was one of the first women to come out to Jamestown, having lost her husband. She'd been lucky enough to come across Alec at the dock, and had found herself employed within the hour.

"I saved a nice, big slice especially for ye," answered Cook with a smile. "Shall I get it?"

"Yes, please. I wonder if there is any milk left." Valerie desperately wanted a glass of cold milk with her pie.

"I just used up the last of it. If ye'll wait a few minutes, I'll nip to the spring house and get some more. I sent Cora to fetch it earlier, but she got distracted. That girl can be so scatter-brained sometimes. I don't know how she doesn't forget her own name. And I have not seen Amelia since breakfast." Cook was already untying her apron, but Valerie stopped her.

"Don't trouble yourself. I'll go. I can use the exercise and the pie will still be here when I come back."

She took one last, longing look at the pie, and pushed away the plate, rising from the bench. It would keep, and she really wanted that glass of milk.

Valerie enjoyed the walk to the spring house, strolling through lush grass that spread like a carpet beneath her feet. The air was thick with the smells of summer, the hum of insects lulling the senses. Somewhere in the woods a lark was singing its heart out, its serenade nearly drowned out by the gurgling of the creek that ran under the stone structure of the spring house. All the milk products were kept in there. It was the closest thing the seventeenth century had to a refrigeration system. The cool spring water kept things fresh for a few days before they began to spoil.

Valerie pushed open the door, entering the dim interior and allowing her eyes a moment to adjust to the gloom before spotting the can of milk submerged in the spring. Her belly prevented her from bending down, so she got down on her knees to pull up the can. It wasn't until Valerie straightened up that she noticed something in the corner behind the empty, larger cans.

Valerie gasped as she came closer. She didn't need to touch the girl to know she was dead. Her eyes stared at the ceiling, wide and unseeing, her mouth was open, as if in surprise, and a pool of congealed blood glistened beneath her head. Valerie dropped the can of milk and ran toward the tobacco fields, calling for Alec.

TWENTY-ONE

Alec stood over the body, his face slack with misery. "She must have slipped and hit her head. That's the only explanation I can conceive of."

"Poor Cora. She was so young, no more than sixteen." Valerie closed the girl's eyes and looked away. It was such a waste. "We should bury her as soon as possible because of the heat."

"I'll get a few men to take her to the house. We'll hold a funeral tomorrow. I don't think Cora had any family other than her sister. I will speak to Amelia. I don't want you distressing yourself." Alec took Valerie by the arm, leading her from the spring house. Tears ran down her face as she followed him back to the house, mourning the sweet, young girl.

"Why don't you lie down for a while? I'll see to everything." Alec walked Valerie to their bedroom and pulled back the coverlet, inviting her to sit down. He got on his knees to remove her shoes and stockings, a worried expression on his face. "Just rest a while. I won't let the children disturb you."

Valerie tried to rest, but kept seeing Cora's face, frozen in death. She'd seen many people die since she'd left the modern world, but no one as young as Cora. She had been so sweet and full of life, always smiling and bringing treats for the children. Valerie had even suspected that Finn might have had a little crush on her, being only a few years younger. Amelia would be devastated by the death of her younger sister. They came over from England together, selling themselves as indentured servants, but only to someone who would take them on as a pair. Now Amelia would be all alone in the world.

Valerie turned her head toward the door, watching the handle turn slowly as the door opened just a crack, a sad little face behind it. "Mama, can I come in?"

"Of course, darling. Come and lie down with me for a bit. I could use some company, and you're just the person I was wishing for."

Louisa advanced into the room and climbed carefully onto the bed, snuggling next to her mother. She put her ear to Valerie's belly, listening intently. "Can I say something to the baby? Will he hear me?"

"Why are you so sure it's a he? Maybe it's a little girl, a sister for you to play with."

"No, it's a boy. I am sure of it. What will you call him? Will it be Alec?" Louisa looked up at Valerie, obviously expecting an answer.

"I don't know. Why do you think we should call him Alec?"

"Because you named Finn after his father, and you named me after your sister. There is no one named after Daddy. I think that's kind of sad." Valerie leaned over and kissed her daughter on the forehead.

"You are absolutely right. We should name someone after Daddy, so he won't be sad. Now, what about you? You seem sad." Valerie could see the unshed tears in Louisa's eyes.

"I liked Cora," she whispered. "I am sad that she is dead. I don't think Uncle Charles liked her very much."

"Why do you say that?" Valerie hadn't expected that, so she turned onto her side to better see Louisa's face.

"I saw them quarrelling in the woods behind the house last week. Uncle Charles seemed very cross, and Cora was crying."

"What were they quarrelling about?" What exactly had the child seen?

"I couldn't hear what they were saying, but they were there for a long while. I think I'll go play now. I'll see you later, Mama." Louisa gave Valerie a kiss and scooted off the bed, leaving her with her thoughts.

TWENTY-TWO

The funeral was a somber affair, with Alec reading the service from the Bible to the mourners gathered around the grave. The Whitfields had their own cemetery some distance away from the house, already home to Uncle Thomas, and one of the indentures who died of a fever. Cora's grave would be the third. Amelia cried quietly as Alec spoke the words. There were only a few people, since Cora worked at the house and didn't really interact with the field workers. Charles stood off to the side, looking pale and miserable. He kept toying with a button on his doublet, his hand jerking nervously.

Could he have done it? Valerie couldn't believe Charles would kill anyone. He was an enigma to her, but she couldn't imagine that he would murder a young girl. Charles had been twelve when they arrived in Virginia, having lived with his aunt and uncle since his own parents died of the bloody flux when he was six. He'd been a sweet boy, but Valerie consistently saw something furtive and underhand in him. He was always charming and polite, always quick with a compliment, but he didn't seem sincere.

He disappeared from time to time, but she had no idea

where he went or what he did, and she was reluctant to question Alec about it. They shared a nice bond, which Alec cherished, Charles being the only sibling he had left. There had been a lot of them at one point, but death claimed a few children in infancy, Rose ran away to a convent, and Finn died by Alec's hand. Now it was just Alec and Charles, and Alec wouldn't let anything come between them.

Alec finished with a heartfelt 'Amen' and closed the book before picking up a shovel. The sound of dry earth hitting the pine coffin drew an agonized wail from Amelia, then everything went quiet as the men filled the yawning grave with dirt. Louisa placed a bouquet of wildflowers on the freshly filled grave, slipping her hand into Amelia's as they filed out of the cemetery in silence. They would go back to the house, where Cook had prepared some refreshments to serve as a wake for poor Cora, but no one was particularly hungry.

Valerie took Alec's arm and allowed him to lead her back to the house, her mind still on Charles. Should she say something to Alec? After all, she had no idea what Louisa really saw, and to accuse Charles without any concrete evidence would surely cause a terrible rift between them. He'd never done anything to arouse her suspicion, except for that morning when she saw him coming out of the study. Maybe he was just looking for something. He didn't have anything in his hands when he left, so it didn't seem like he took anything.

"You are awfully quiet. Is there something on your mind?" Alec gave her arm a squeeze, startling her out of her reverie.

"I'm all right. It's nothing. Just grieving, that's all."

"As am I. She was a very special girl." Valerie looked up at Alec. His comment surprised her. He never seemed to notice Cora and to call her a 'special girl' seemed a little out of character.

TWENTY-THREE

Louisa finished her meal before going up on deck to take a little exercise. She hoped she wouldn't run into Master Sheridan. She'd been giving him a wide berth since finding his wife's letter, preferring to keep her distance. It was easy enough during the day, but at night, when the ship was quiet and her mind unoccupied, thoughts of Christopher invaded her brain. She missed his company and good humor, and the look in his eyes as she turned in his arms on the bridge still haunted her. He had wanted her—badly. Almost as badly as she wanted him. She found herself searching for him every time she came up on deck, hoping to catch a glimpse of him as he went about his duties.

Louisa wondered if he'd ever been unfaithful to his wife. He was a sailor after all, and that saying about a girl in every port probably wasn't too far off the mark. She thought there was something honorable about the man, but she barely knew him, so it was probably just wishful thinking. In this time, men went to brothels to satisfy their urges. Christopher might not have a mistress in ever port, but that didn't mean he went without.

Once on deck, she sensed tension among the sailors. They

stood in small groups, talking quietly among themselves. Louisa looked up at the sky. Clear and blue, so no storm was brewing. Captain Fellowes was looking at something on the horizon, his spy glass gripped tightly in his pudgy hands. Louisa followed the direction of his gaze. She could just make out a ship. It was hard to tell how big it was from a distance, but she was close enough to see the captain's unease. He said something to the first mate, who glanced in her direction, before replying quietly, his mouth tense, his eyes anxious. What was going on? As far as she knew, England was not at war with anyone, so it couldn't be an enemy ship.

Louisa turned to Mistress Collins, who was huffing and puffing after climbing the stairs. The older woman was white to the roots of her hair, her hands shaking with nerves.

"What's happening?" she asked.

Master Collins was headed toward the captain. He seemed awfully agitated, gesturing toward the ship in the distance.

Mistress Collins put her hand on her ample bosom. She was panting, either with exertion or fear. "It appears to be a pirate ship, Mistress Jamison. They'll know more once the ship gets close enough to see its colors."

"Pirates? That's ridiculous." She hadn't come across anything about pirates in the Atlantic in her research. Her idea of a pirate was Johnny Depp, sashaying on the deck of the *Black Pearl*, slurring his words from too much rum, but that was just for entertainment. Surely, there were no actual pirates sailing the high seas.

"I must go see to Anne. She is in a state, poor thing."

Mistress Collins lumbered back down to her cabin, leaving Louisa to await answers on her own. The reverend stood back, observing the scene, but didn't approach. He seemed to have finally realized that Louisa wasn't interested in his attentions and had been keeping his distance. Suddenly, Captain Fellowes bellowed a command, and all the sailors within hearing sprang into action, running down to the cargo hold, and reappearing some time later with barrels. Christopher Sheridan descended from the bridge and walked over to Louisa.

"What's in those barrels, Master Sheridan?" Louisa asked. She had a sinking feeling in her belly, knowing that whatever he told her wouldn't be good.

"It's gunpowder, Mistress Jamison, but please don't be alarmed. At this stage, it's just a precaution. We must be ready."

He was looking down at her with an intensity she hadn't noticed before. Usually, there was a smile playing about his lips and a twinkle in his eye, but today Christopher Sheridan looked positively grim.

"Ready for what?"

"That vessel in the distance looks like a Barbary pirate ship. Once they spot a merchant vessel, they are not likely to leave it alone. They seem to be changing course and heading directly toward us." His hand reached for hers and held it for a moment before letting go. "I must return to the bridge."

"Wait. Who are they, and what do they want?" Louisa had never heard of Barbary pirates.

Christopher Sheridan drew her aside as Master Collins walked right past them, angry and agitated. "Barbary pirates are Corsairs, who sail mostly out of North Africa. They use the ports of Tunis and Algiers as their base. Their cruelty is legendary. Their main goal is to seize a ship and its cargo, and take as many Christian prisoners as they can." The first mate looked away as he said that, gazing out over the calm ocean, clearly avoiding eye contact.

"What do they do with their prisoners?" Louisa whispered, horrified.

"They take them back and sell them at the slave markets. If a prisoner happens to be a wealthy individual, they might allow him to write a letter asking his relatives to raise money for a ransom. Most captives are never heard from again, especially the women. They disappear into the harems of the Ottoman Empire, or end up being serving girls or kitchen maids. I won't let them harm you, Louisa. You have my word." With that he walked off toward the bridge, leaving Louisa openmouthed and terrified.

Was this really happening? Only a month ago she was still working at the Metropolitan Museum of Art, surrounded by priceless paintings and civilized people. Today she was on a seventeenth-century merchant vessel, about to be attacked by Corsairs, who might either kill her, or take her captive and sell her into slavery. She let out a hysterical giggle. At this point, she wasn't sure which fate was worse. She would have to go down and break the news to Agnes. Did the word 'barbaric' come from Barbary? she wondered as she descended into the bowels of the ship.

TWENTY-FOUR

Valerie looked anxiously out the window. She hadn't seen Finn for hours, and was beginning to worry. The first stars were beginning to twinkle in the twilit sky, the mosquitoes coming out in full force to feast on anyone foolish enough to step outside. Finn had gone to set some traps after completing his lessons, but he hadn't come back for supper, and no one had seen him since dinnertime. She hated to be a worrywart, but the boy was only fourteen, and alone in the wilderness. Having made up her mind, she went to get Alec. He'd know what to do.

As Valerie approached the study, she heard raised voices. She couldn't make out what was being said, but it sounded as though Alec and Charles were in the middle of an argument. She was just about to knock on the door, when their words began to sink into her worried brain.

"Do not lie to me, Alec. I saw you with her. She followed you into the stables and didn't come back out for some time. Did you enjoy her?" Charles sounded angry and accusing.

"What are you saying, Charlie? I hardly noticed the girl. She brought me a bottle of cider sent by Cook. I don't know what she did afterward."

"Look, I understand, your wife is with child, and you have your needs, but did you have to kill her? Did she threaten to tell your wife you were having it off with her? Or was she with child as well?" Valerie leaned against the wall, her heart hammering wildly in her chest.

"Pray, allow me to understand you correctly. Not only are you accusing me of adultery, but you're also accusing me of murder. Is that right?" Alec's voice came out in a snarl, angry beyond belief.

"Yes, that's right. I bet she was a rare treat. Young and pretty, with those lovely little tits and nice arse. I know you love Valerie, but she's over forty now, and what man isn't tempted by someone sweet and innocent. Hey, I don't blame you. I noticed her too. She was so much jollier than that sour sister of hers." She could hear the glee in Charlie's voice. Why was he goading Alec like that?

"Get out, you little bastard, and stay out of my sight. If any of this reaches Valerie's ears, I swear, I'll kill you with my bare hands." Valerie heard something crash as Alec shoved Charles out the door and slammed it behind him.

"Ah, Valerie. I hope you are having a pleasant evening." Charles adjusted his doublet and walked past her, smiling and whistling a merry tune. Valerie felt the ground shift beneath her feet as the floor rushed up to meet her.

TWENTY-FIVE

"Valerie, wake up. Valerie. Bridget, do something. She's fainted." Alec was bending over her, cupping her cheek, a look of worry in his eyes. "Can you hear me?"

"I can hear you, and I heard Charles. Now leave me alone and go find Finn. He hasn't come home for supper, and I'm worried about him."

Valerie covered her face with her hands. She couldn't bear to look at Alec. Did Charles know something? Had Alec slept with Cora? Was Alec turned off by her? She was big and ungainly, and she was in her forties. Cora had been lively and flirtatious, too flirtatious for a girl her age. Valerie had seen the signs, but had chosen to ignore them. Cora had definitely been carrying on with someone, she just never imagined it might be Alec.

Valerie shook her head. No, it wasn't possible. Alec had always been faithful to her. She'd never even seen him so much as glance at another woman, but he did refer to Cora as a 'special girl.' What had he meant by that? Would Alec kill Cora if she threatened to tell? Valerie pushed the unwelcome thought from her mind. Alec was the most decent human being she'd ever met. The idea of him killing an innocent girl to silence her was absurd, but Charles put the awful thought in her brain and now it refused to leave.

Valerie allowed Bridget to help her up and take her to her room. Alec still stood there, frozen with shock, but Valerie waved him away. Finding Finn was a priority. Everything else would come later. Alec finally sprang into action and ran down the stairs, calling for a torch. He would get a few of the field workers and organize a search party. They would find Finn. They had to.

Valerie allowed Bridget to take off her gown and slip a linen shift over her head. She needed to lie down, but she was too agitated. Her head ached, and her belly felt tight and heavy.

"Let me brush out yer hair, Mistress. It will soothe ye." Bridget picked up the brush and began to brush Valerie's hair gently, singing some lilting Irish tune about lost love and missed opportunities. Valerie tried to relax, but she simply couldn't. This was too much. The idea that something might have happened to her son and that her husband might be an adulterer, and a murderer was simply too much to bear. She dissolved into tears, burying her face in Bridget's shoulder.

"Oh, hush now. They'll find 'im. Ye just wait and see. Master Finn is a smart lad. He wouldn't let anything happen to 'im. Hush." Bridget stroked Valerie's head, trying to calm her down. "Why don't ye lie down and get some rest? Ye have to think of the baby."

"Lie down with me, Bridget. I can't be alone right now."

For a brief moment, Valerie considered confiding in Bridget, but stopped herself in time. Whatever happened, Alec was her master, and she had no right to undermine his authority in Bridget's eyes. She didn't think such a thing were possible anyhow. Bridget worshipped the ground Alec walked on and wouldn't believe such slander against his character. Valerie rested her head on Bridget's shoulder. She didn't believe it either. Charles was just being spiteful. He'd wanted to provoke Alec, and he'd succeeded, but what was the reason for his anger? As they used to say in the future, "Where there's smoke, there's fire."

Valerie shut her eyes as Bridget stroked her hair and sang to her. She was so tired, and so worried.

TWENTY-SIX

Every minute felt like an hour as the afternoon began to turn into evening. The wind had dropped, leaving the sails limp and sagging above their heads, and eliminating any chance they had of outrunning the pirate ship. Louisa felt strangely worn out despite the fact that all she'd done was pace the deck in her agitation. The captain was on the bridge, spyglass in hand, which was just a charade since everyone could see the pirate ship clearly eye now. Their ship was different from the *Gloriana*. It was longer and lower, with only two masts and long oars that extended from the hull. The oars moved in mesmerizing unison as the vessel drew closer and closer. She could see the pirates moving on deck, watching the *Gloriana* as they prepared to attack, and there was no doubt they would attack. Their gun ports were open, black mouths of cannon yawning, ready to rain fire on their vessel.

The crew of the *Gloriana* was ready too. Everyone was in a heightened state of excitement, especially Mistress Collins, who ran around like a chicken without a head, clucking non-stop. Anne Collins was down below, lying down, with her father for company, and Reverend Blakeley kept trying to organize a group prayer to beseech God to spare them. No one paid him any attention, as everyone went about the business of preparing for the attack. Christopher left the bridge and came toward her.

"I want you to go to my cabin. It's on the side facing away from the pirate ship. I think it might be safer than yours. Take Agnes and stay out of sight until the fighting is over."

Louisa looked at the sword at his side. He hadn't been wearing one before. A pistol was tucked into his belt.

"I have a dagger in my boot as well," he said, following her gaze. "We are as ready as we'll ever be. Just do your best to stay hidden. Promise me you'll stay safe."

Louisa nodded. She had no idea what staying safe entailed when being fired upon by cannon, but it's what he wanted to hear, so she promised. Whatever was going to happen was going to happen. She had no control over the situation, and couldn't do anything to help. The least she could do was follow orders from someone who presumably had been through something like this before. She was about to tell him that when he lowered his head and kissed her tenderly.

"Please, stay safe. I couldn't bear it if something happened to you." She watched him walk away, the taste of his lips still on hers, then went down to get Agnes.

The first shot was fired just as dusk melted into a moonless night. Louisa felt the ship shudder as impact was made and closed her eyes in prayer. She hadn't prayed like this in a long time, but her lips moved silently, begging God to help them. Agnes was crying and hugging herself, rocking back and forth, her eyes huge in her face, and her cheeks wet with tears.

Time stood still as they waited for the second blast to come. Louisa felt the floor go out from under her as she fell against the berth, hurting her shoulder. Agnes fell on top of her, screaming in terror. The shots came regularly after that, but Louisa couldn't tell if they were from the pirate ship or from their own guns. The booming of cannon was so loud, she couldn't make anything out. The cabin was like a separate universe where only the two of them existed, clinging to each other and praying for deliverance. It went on and on, the ship shuddering violently every time it took a hit. The wood creaked, and the floor rolled beneath their feet, making it impossible to keep their balance. Louisa and Agnes climbed into the berth and held on to each other, burying their heads in each other's shoulders to drown out the noise.

Louisa wasn't sure how much time had passed, but it seemed like hours. Suddenly, all fell quiet. She could smell smoke, and then she heard it—sound of numerous feet hitting the deck.

"Oh, Lord Jesus," wailed Agnes. "We've been boarded."

The clash of steel and the screams of wounded men came from above as the fighting intensified. It was now hand to hand combat, and it sounded brutal. Louisa bolted the cabin door, but the lock wasn't nearly strong enough to keep anyone out. She didn't know how long they sat there, huddled in the berth.

A loud noise just outside the cabin brought Louisa back to her senses, prompting her to unlock the door and open it just a crack. One of the *Gloriana* sailors was lying at the bottom of the steps, a jeweled dagger protruding from his chest. His shirt was soaked with blood, which appeared black in the dim confines of the narrow passage. The man was still alive, moaning pitifully and mouthing something to her. Louisa wanted to help him, but had no idea what to do. She couldn't see anything from her spot at the bottom of the stairs, but she could hear the clashing of swords and the occasional shot being fired. Who was winning?

She should have stayed put, but she had to see what was going on. She had to know. Louisa stepped over the now dead sailor and climbed a few steps to get a view of the deck. She froze with shock when she saw the carnage unfolding above her head. The deck was swarming with pirates, more coming over the side at an alarming rate. The crew of the *Gloriana* appeared to be vastly outnumbered.

Men in turbans and embroidered kaftans were everywhere, their faces indistinguishable from one another in the darkness of the night. The deck was littered with the dead and wounded from both sides, bloodstains black and slick on the scrubbed wooden surface. Louisa frantically searched for Christopher. She couldn't find him, but she knew he was out there some-where, in the thick of it. Captain Fellowes was up on the bridge, deftly wielding his sword as he repelled two Corsairs who were advancing on him with their deadly weapons. He was pretty agile for a man of his girth, but he couldn't hold them off indefi-nitely. Louisa turned away, unable to look, as the pirates backed him up against the railing of the bridge.

Narrowed black eyes were watching her when she turned her gaze back to the deck, a sly smile spreading beneath the thick, curled moustache of the pirate. He made for the stairs, his sword reflecting the meager light of the stars. All thoughts fled Louisa's head as she nearly fell down the steps and raced back to the cabin. Her hands shook so badly she could barely slide the bolt into place, but eventually she got it. Agnes was in the corner, moaning softly and hugging her middle.

"They'll kill us all, I know they will," she wailed.

The door heaved as the man put all his considerable weight against it. Louisa looked around desperately for some kind of weapon. Didn't Christopher Sheridan keep anything in his room? She should have pulled the dagger out of the dead sailor, but she hadn't been thinking, just feeling. The only thing of any use she saw was a pewter candlestick. Much good it would do her. Louisa tightened her fingers around the candlestick, raising it above her head. A candlestick against a cutlass. Her chances couldn't be worse.

The door gave way with the sound of splintering wood, revealing the men behind it. There were two of them now, their swords raised high above their heads as they examined their find. One man murmured something to the other, and they lowered their swords, slowly advancing into the cabin. They wouldn't hurt them for fear of ruining the merchandise. Louisa backed away, still clutching the candlestick. Her heart seemed to have stopped beating as she took in the sharp swords and evil smiles of the men who were obviously very pleased with their discovery.

Agnes was still wailing in the corner, while Louisa inched away from the men toward the back wall. She wanted to scream, but her lungs felt empty of air, her throat parched and constricted. She had never known such overwhelming fear. One of the men pulled out a length of rope from his trouser pocket, probably to tie their wrists with, and advanced further into the room. He showed Louisa the sword and then ran his finger across his throat, indicating that he would kill her if she resisted. The whites of his eyes and his teeth were the only things that Louisa could make out in his dark face, but she could smell him. The pirate reeked of stale sweat mixed with something like cumin and mint.

Louisa was so fixated on the cutlass, she barely noticed the man whip around in panic. The second pirate, who'd stood just behind him, suddenly let out a gurgling noise as the tip of a sword protruded from his belly. Louisa must have screamed, but her voice was drowned out by the animal cry of the dying man. Blood poured over the embroidered kaftan and onto the floor of the cabin as the man fell to the floor face down, dead as a doornail.

Christopher Sheridan yanked his sword out of the dead man and lunged at her attacker. She ducked out of the way just in time as the pirate swung his sword, bringing it down on the first mate's shoulder. Christopher's sleeve turned black as blood soaked the fabric, but he was still fighting, his eyes blazing with fury. Louisa watched in horror as the pirate backed away from

Christopher toward her, his cutlass raised high above his head. She stepped back and tripped over Agnes. Louisa tried to break her fall by grabbing on to the table, but the pirate let out a horrible scream and fell backward, knocking her sideways. Louisa's head met with the side of the table, and the world went quiet and dark.

TWENTY-SEVEN

Alec sat down on a fallen log, trying to get his bearings. The forest around him felt sinister and alive, the leaves rustling above his head as an owl hooted somewhere in the distance. Small animals darted here and there, breaking twigs or moving branches. Alec heard a howl somewhere not too far off. There were wild animals in the forest, ones that wouldn't hesitate to pounce on a boy and tear him to shreds. The wolves never came near the house, but they were out there, in the darkness, waiting.

They'd been searching for hours, but there was no sign of Finn. If they'd set out during the daytime he would have been able to track him, to follow his path, but right now, whatever trail Finn left was lost in the darkness and trampled by numerous feet. Alec had two men with him, as did Charles. He refused to go with his brother after the accusations he'd made. Alec felt a wave of fury build up inside him. As if it wasn't bad enough that his brother thought him a fornicator and a murderer, Valerie heard the whole thing. Did she really believe he was capable of such things?

She watched you kill Finlay, a voice inside his head reminded him. That had been completely different, but killing was killing. Alec still mourned his brother every day. He would have never let him die had he thought there was even the slightest chance of clearing him of the charge of treason. "I wish you were here, Finlay. I miss you so much," Alec whispered into the silence of the night. "If you are out there somewhere, please help me, and lead me to the boy."

Alec got up and joined the other two men. They'd taken advantage of the short break and relieved themselves against a tree before continuing with the search.

"I think we should continue north," Alec said.

"Master Whitfield, if we go any farther north, we will be entering Indian Territory. You know full well how they deal with white men." The two men hung back, looking fearful and unsure.

"You're probably right. Finn wouldn't have come this far anyway. We need to spread out so we can cover more ground. Stanley, you go east and I will go west. Bixby, retrace our steps and see if we missed anything. Search under every bush, in every ditch, and look up at the trees. Maybe he climbed up to get away from something." Alec turned and walked off into the trees. He had to find Finn, and he had to find him alive. If anything happened to him, Valerie would never recover. She was probably going out of her mind, desperate for news. He hoped they'd find Finn soon.

Alec searched in vain for another couple of hours, but found nothing. He was tired and thirsty, and his heart was aching with worry and fear. He wasn't Finn's biological father, but he loved the boy from the moment he first held him in his arms when he was born. He was his beloved brother's son, and he would gladly lay down his own life to save his. Where could he be? He must be hurt. Alec began walking again, calling out every few minutes and listening for an answer. All he heard were the sounds of the forest coming back to life with the arrival of dawn. The sky was beginning to grow lighter in the east and soon the sun would be fully up. Valerie would be frantic by now. Alec hoped she'd managed to get some sleep, but knew better.

TWENTY-EIGHT

Louisa opened her eyes and lay without moving. Her ears were ringing, her vision slightly blurred. The ceiling seemed to be strangely close to her head, every whorl and nick in the wood visible to the naked eye. She tried to remember what happened, but nothing came to mind. Her thoughts were disjointed and confused. She saw movement out of the corner of her eye and then Agnes's anxious face came into view. The girl was saying something, but all Louisa saw was the opening and closing of her mouth. The girl looked dreadful, her hair tangled, and her bodice ripped and soiled.

Louisa closed her eyes again and waited for the ringing in her ears to subside. It was replaced by another sound that she couldn't quite place. It was the sound of quiet drumming.

"What is that?" she asked, finally finding her voice.

"'Tis rain, Mistress. It's been raining for a while now. 'Tis really coming down. Can ye move? I was afraid to move ye." Agnes gripped Louisa's hand, as if trying to tether her to reality.

Louisa slowly realized that her head was, in fact, under the table where she fell and tried to sit up without hitting it again. Agnes brought a cup of water to her lips, urging her to drink.

She took a sip and looked around. Slowly, memory began to return and Louisa shot upright as she remembered the dead pirate. There was no one there now, but there was a dark stain where the man had fallen, and her own dress was stained with ugly brown splotches of dried blood. She was about to ask Agnes what happened when Christopher Sheridan appeared in the doorway. His hair and face glistened with rainwater, his upper arm was bandaged with a dirty blood-soaked cloth, but the look of relief on his face was unmistakable. He sank to his knees next to Louisa, caressing her face.

"You are all right. Thank God. You hit your head hard when you fell. How do you feel?" he asked gently.

It must have been the genuine concern in his eyes that undid her. Louisa began to cry. She clung to Christopher as she sobbed into his chest, afraid she might not be able to stop. All the fear and uncertainty she had felt since leaving the twenty-first century combined with the terror of the past few hours came pouring out. He just held her close, his lips warm against her cheek. "You are safe now."

Christopher lifted Louisa off the floor with one arm and sat her on the berth, taking a seat next to her. She leaned against him, letting him hold and comfort her. Christopher drew her to him with his good arm and kissed the top of her head. "It's all over. We beat them off."

"How? There were so many of them."

"We were overrun and outnumbered, but men do heroic things when fighting for their lives. Our sailors fought bravely, but we were losing, and fast, until Master Willis had an idea. He is a clever lad, that one. The Corsair ship was very close to ours, but lower in the water, so Master Willis and Master Coyle tossed several barrels of burning pitch onto their deck. The barrels smashed as they hit the deck, and the fire spread. Master Willis said he got the idea from fire ships.

The fire created confusion among the pirates. They weren't

sure if they should continue with the attack or try to salvage their ship. Their momentary indecision turned the tide in our favor and we were able to drive them off. The reverend's prayers must have been answered, since the wind began to pick up, and we were able to gain speed, leaving them behind to put out the flames. Captain Fellowes has been seriously wounded. He's in his cabin with Master Willis."

Christopher winced as he moved his injured arm, but his eyes never left Louisa's face. "Does your head hurt? Can you see clearly?"

"I think I'm all right. Just a bump. It's a little tender, but nothing more. Are you in pain, Kit?" She realized what she'd called him as soon as the name escaped her lips, but she didn't care; she'd wanted to call him that since the night on the bridge.

"Not anymore." His kiss was gentle and sweet, full of longing and promise. Kit pulled away and smoothed a stray lock away from her face, caressing her cheek with his thumb. "I must tell you something, Louisa. There were many casualties, but the worst part, by far, is that they took Anne Collins and her mother. The women ran up on deck during the fighting, and were gone before anyone could stop the pirates. They just dragged them to the other ship. They're gone."

"Kit, we must get them back. We can't just leave them to their fate."

"I'm afraid we must. Captain Fellowes is not in favor of pursuit. We lost a lot of men, and will be sailing with a skeleton crew as is. The ship suffered a lot of damage. The carpenters will do what they can, but we'll have to stop for repairs in the West Indies. We'll never make it to Virginia in this condition. We'll be limping into port."

"We can't just give up on them. They must be terrified. Those poor women. What will happen to them?"

"They will be sold to the highest bidder at a slave market, but I doubt they'll be killed."

"Will they be raped?" Louisa asked, horrified.

"Most likely, but their fate will still be better than that of the captured men, who are either assigned to hard labor, or turned into galley slaves. There is no fate worse than that. The slaves are chained to the benches, forced to row for years without leaving their spots. They hardly sleep, and are given just enough food to keep them alive. Their life expectancy is very short once they are sold to the galleys."

"That's absolutely barbaric." Bitter tears slid down her face. The thought of the Collins women on that ship was terrifying. She couldn't even begin to imagine what they must be feeling, or if they were even still alive. If the Corsairs couldn't put out the flames, the ship would sink.

"We have to go back for them. Please." Louisa was pleading with Christopher through tears.

"I agree with you, but it isn't my decision to make. I am not the captain. Captain Fellowes must do what's best for the passengers and crew, and in this case, it's to sacrifice a few to save many. I must go up, Louisa. The men will be ready for the burial at sea. Do you wish to come up and pay your respects?" Kit rose unsteadily to his feet, holding out his hand to her. Louisa took it and followed him out of the cabin and up the steps.

Forty-two bodies were laid out on the deck, ready for burial. About thirty were Corsairs, dressed in colorful kaftans and flowing pants. Their white turbans were still on their heads, a stark contrast to their dark skin. The bodies of the English sailors were stitched into sacking and laid out separately. Louisa looked around, but couldn't tell who was missing. The rain was coming down hard, the sails overhead taught and flapping in the gusty wind that was taking them further and further away from the pirate ship and their captives.

Louisa watched as Reverend Blakeley stepped forward, his prayer book in his hands. He waited silently while several

sailors tossed the corpses of the pirates overboard before beginning the funeral service for the English sailors. It was brief and
poignant, bringing nearly everyone to tears. The bodies of the
sailors were consigned to the sea one by one, as their names
were called. Louisa wiped the tears from her eyes, saying her
own prayer and asking God to have mercy on their souls. Her
dress was soaked, her hair plastered to her face, but she didn't
care. At this moment nothing really mattered.

Her eyes found Master Collins. He stood alone at the edge
of the crowd. He looked haggard, and his shoulders were
stooped, as if he'd aged decades in the past few hours. His gaze
was blank as he stared at the shrouded bodies, his mouth open
and slack. His fingers kept pulling at a button on his doublet
until it came off in his hands. He looked down at it in surprise,
as if he'd never seen a button before.

Louisa was about to go over to comfort the man, when his
head jerked up and he looked around wildly, as if he'd heard
someone calling him. But no one had called his name. No one
was paying any attention to him. Master Collins pulled himself
up onto the railing of the deck and sat there for a moment, as if
unsure of what he was doing. His eyes met Louisa's for a brief
moment before he fell backward into the roiling sea. Louisa's
scream was lost in the chaos that erupted, sailors shouting to
Master Collins to stay afloat. It took mere moments for the
waves to swallow the man, leaving an empty space where only
seconds ago a human being had been.

TWENTY-NINE

Kit Sheridan stood on the bridge, swaying slightly. His arm was on fire, the skin uncomfortably tight and swollen. His sleeve was soaked with blood, despite the driving rain that soaked his shirt and plastered it to his body. The gash was much deeper than he'd originally thought, and he'd bound it with linen strips in an effort to stop the bleeding. He should have wrapped it tighter, but it wasn't an easy task to accomplish with only one hand. Kit used his teeth to hold the bandage as he tried to tie it. Giant swells tossed the ship from side to side, making it difficult for him to keep his balance. He used his good arm to steer, spreading his feet further apart to give himself more leverage against the heaving wood beneath his feet.

Captain Fellowes was in his cabin, tended to by young Master Willis. The boy showed incredible courage and ingenuity last night, earning the respect of the crew, but his actions hadn't come in time to save Captain Fellowes. The captain had fought like a lion, killing pirate after pirate, but at one point found himself outnumbered on the bridge. He'd been stabbed in the back with a dagger, the blade piercing his lung, instead of finding the heart. The pirates left Captain Fellowes lying in a pool of his own blood as they moved on to their next victim. Now, the captain lay in his bed, gasping and wheezing, his eyes closed against the light, his face waxy and pale as he waited for death to claim him. Once the captain succumbed to his injury, Kit would be in command.

Kit hadn't been completely honest with Louisa when he agreed that they should have returned for the captives. He felt profound pity and regret, but to risk what was left of the crew to rescue the women would not be practical. Even if he could go back and find the pirate ship in this storm, they would still be outnumbered, turning a rescue mission into a suicide attempt. Their best bet would be to head for Jamaica or Trinidad, restock, make repairs, and continue on to Virginia.

You would go back for Louisa, his mind whispered. Yes, he would go back for her. He'd risk everything and everyone to get her back; he'd do anything. The thought of Louisa being dragged onto a platform at a slave market, stripped to show her assets, made his blood boil. He knew full well what happened to white women who were sold into slavery. They didn't last long. Few of them were ever ransomed. Most ended up in the brothels or harems, used by countless men until they died a lonely and awful death.

Mistress Collins might have a chance of survival since she was older and less desirable. She might wind up working in the kitchens or the laundry. Anne, on the other hand, was doomed. The girl was young and fair, and presumably still a maid. She would fetch a lot at auction, and her owner would most likely not be kind or considerate.

Kit was distracted from his morbid thoughts by the appearance of Louisa. She was dripping wet, the bodice of her dress clinging to her breasts, leaving little to the imagination. Kit tore his gaze away and focused on her face. Louisa's hair hung loose, raindrops sparkling on her eyelashes.

"Go down, Louisa. You're soaked." Kit didn't really want her to leave, but he didn't want her to get ill.

"I came to check on you. How's your arm?" Her look of concern made him feel a little warmer, and he tried to give her a reassuring smile.

"I am well. Please don't concern yourself."

"You don't look well." Louisa stood up on her tippy toes and reached for his forehead. "You're burning up. You need to be in bed, and your wound must be cleaned and disinfected."

"Disin-what? It's just a flesh wound. It will heal in no time." Kit was lying through his teeth, but he didn't want to alarm her.

"Disinfected so that it doesn't fester. Come with me, and that's a direct order. Who's next in command on this ship?" She looked so determined that Kit nearly burst out laughing. It had been a long time since anyone cared enough about him to show this kind of spirit.

"Master Prescott is the second mate. He's next in command," he answered reluctantly.

"Call him to the bridge then."

"I don't know where he is at the moment," Kit lied. "Louisa, if you're in the mood to play nursemaid, perhaps you should see to the captain. His need is greater than mine."

"There's nothing I can do for the captain," Louisa replied ruefully. "The captain needs a skilled physician. But I can help you. I expect to see you in your cabin in less than five minutes. I'll find Master Prescott and send him to the bridge," she added.

With that, Louisa disappeared down the stairs, leaving Kit bemused and overruled.

THIRTY

Louisa had no trouble finding the second mate. He was below decks with several other sailors, drinking to the memory of the departed and cursing the Corsairs, using some very colorful language. His eyes opened wide with shock when she ordered him to the bridge, leaving before he had a chance to comment or refuse. She had to do one more thing before tending to Kit. Louisa knocked lightly on the door of the captain's cabin, so as not to disturb him.

The smell of imminent death hit her as soon as she walked into the room. Master Willis sat by the captain's side, his childish face full of worry and fear. Captain Fellowes looked deathly pale, his face clammy, horrible wheezing sounds coming from his chest. The captain's lips were cracked and bleeding, moving soundlessly in an effort to either pray or say something to the cabin boy.

"Master Willis, I wonder if I could have a cup of claret," Louisa whispered.

"Certainly, Mistress Jamison. It's over there on the desk. You must be quite shaken."

Daniel Willis looked quite shaken himself, but he was

trying to put a brave face on his fear. Louisa gave him her warmest smile, wondering how long he'd been at sea, and where his parents were, if he had any.

"I heard of your bravery, Master Willis. You are a very impressive young man. You will make an excellent captain someday."

The boy's face turned pink with pleasure and Louisa had the most overwhelming desire to give him a motherly hug. He was just a child, after all. Instead, she took a cup and filled it with claret. She would have liked to drink the wine. She was shaken, but she had things to do before she could tend to her own feelings. She thanked the boy and left the cabin.

Kit was already in his cabin by the time she got there. He had managed to pull off his boots and lay wet and dripping on his berth, his eyes partially closed. Louisa set down the cup of claret and the basin of rainwater she carried under her arm, and went to shut the door. She nearly laughed at his expression of shock. Unmarried women didn't go to a man's cabin, much less shut the door behind them. The fact that the man in question was barely conscious didn't diminish the impropriety of the situation.

"Can you take off your shirt, Master Sheridan?"

"So, it's Master Sheridan again, is it?" he mumbled, as he tried to sit up without moving his injured arm.

"Let me help you." Louisa helped him sit and started to pull off his shirt, leaving the sleeve of the wounded arm for last. She peeled off the wet fabric from the filthy bandage and helped him lie back down. At least the shirt wasn't stuck to his arm. The linen bandage was soaked with blood and covered his arm from elbow to shoulder.

"Let's have a look at that, shall we?" She tried to sound soothing, but he just laughed.

"The last time someone spoke to me like that I was five and

had skinned my knee. Help yourself, Angel of Mercy. I am at your disposal."

Kit closed his eyes and let her untie the bandage. Louisa tried not to stare at the jagged wound that gaped open to reveal torn muscle and a glimmer of bone. Right. It was deeper than she expected, but it didn't look infected. Not yet. Louisa dipped some clean cloth into the rainwater and began to cleanse the wound. She was glad it had rained, since salt seawater would have been the worst thing to use. The salt would have burned, causing Kit a lot of unnecessary pain. The cloth was quickly saturated with blood, needing to be washed out every few minutes.

"I'm going to disinfect your wound by putting some claret on it. It will probably sting, but it will kill any infection," she informed him.

"Are you mad, woman? You're going to waste good claret on my arm? Give it here. It will do more good." Kit was staring at her as if she'd taken leave of her senses, reaching for the cup. Louisa reminded herself that he knew nothing of germs or infections, and was lucky if he washed his hands from time to time.

"I know what I'm doing, Master Sheridan," she snapped, pressing the claret-soaked cloth to his arm. He stiffened as the alcohol met his tortured flesh, but remained quiet, watching her.

"Have you cared for wounded men before? And how much good wine have you wasted?" he asked with a slight smile. She could tell he was in pain, but he had to have the last word.

"Don't concern yourself with that. Just drink the rest of the claret and try to sleep." Louisa handed him the cup and watched him drain it in one gulp. He lay back, still watching her.

"May I ask you something?"

Louisa nodded, afraid of what he might ask. She knew the question would be very personal, and had to figure out how to answer him without arousing suspicion.

"Why did you never marry?" he asked softly.

"How did you know I never married?"

"I heard Mistress Collins telling Anne that if she didn't get her priorities straight and find a husband, she'd end up like you, still unmarried in her twenties."

"I see," Louisa replied, suddenly feeling just a little less pity for Mistress Collins. "The truth is, no one ever asked."

It was the truth. Louisa had been with Doug for nearly eight years, but he never asked her to marry him. He seemed happy with the way things were, and told her he loved her without needing to make it official. His love for her didn't stop him from leaving though, did it?

"I don't believe that. You must have had dozens of offers."

"No. There was a man I loved, but he never asked me to marry him." Louisa turned away, embarrassed by Kit's direct gaze.

"He was a fool to let you get away," Kit replied, taking her hand in his. "I am asking."

"Asking what?" Louisa could feel the heat coming from his hand. He was burning up with fever.

"I am asking you to marry me."

"Master Sheridan, Christopher, you are fevered and you don't know what you're saying. You are married already."

"Why would you think that?" He looked a little confused, making Louisa wonder if she had been wrong.

"I didn't mean to read it, but it fell out of the book. There was a letter from your wife."

"That was the last letter she ever wrote to me. There was an outbreak of plague that spring. She died, as did my mother."

"I'm terribly sorry. I didn't know. I assumed she was waiting for you at home. Please forgive me." Louisa felt ashamed of herself, first for snooping, and second for jumping to conclusions.

"There is nothing to forgive, which brings us back to my question."

THIRTY-ONE

Charles's unease grew as the sun began to make its ascent into the summer sky. The forest was still shrouded in shadow, darkness pooling between the trees and in shallow depressions, but the tips of the trees were already bathed in the pink glow of the coming dawn. He had been searching all night, and he was bone-tired and hungry. Charles hadn't fully realized until last night just how much he loved his cousin. Finn could be annoying and whiny sometimes, but he was Finlay's son, and that made him special.

Charles had adored his brother, and wanted nothing more than to be just like him when he reached adulthood. Finlay had been the 'fun brother.' Alec was always busy with the business and his own life, devoting most of his time to Violet. Charles hadn't been jealous; he'd loved Violet as well. She had been beautiful and sweet, unlike his sister Rose, who was always crying and praying. Finlay had already been in his teens when Charles was born, but he never treated him like a baby. He took him hunting and fishing, and taught him to ride. Once, he even took him into a tavern in the village.

Then everything changed. The bloody flux wiped out most

of the Whitfield family within a few days. Charles lost his parents, Violet and her newborn son, his uncle, and several servants. Only Finn, Alec, and Rose had been spared, leaving Charles scared and bewildered. Rose ran away to a convent, and Alec spiraled into a drink-fueled depression that only worsened his horrible grief. Only Finn took the time to comfort the little boy and ease his terrible pain. Charles didn't blame Finlay for bringing him to Uncle Thomas and Aunt Lottie. Finlay wanted what was best for him, and his aunt and uncle became his surrogate parents until Uncle Thomas took him to Virginia, where Charles was eventually reunited with Alec.

He'd been overjoyed to see Alec again. He missed both his brothers terribly, not really understanding that Finlay was gone. He kept imagining him back at Yealm Castle, riding his spirited stallion and flirting with tavern wenches. Eventually, it sunk in that his beloved brother was dead, buried in a lonely grave by the abbey ruins. He wasn't even in a proper graveyard. His resting place was probably overgrown with weeds and flowers that grew tall enough to obscure the stone bearing his name. It had been Alec's idea to bury him by the abbey, away from prying eyes, and those who might wish to desecrate the grave of a traitor.

Charles had been happy when Alec and Valerie came. He liked Valerie, and enjoyed playing with little Finn. He had been adorable, toddling everywhere after Charles like a devoted puppy. It wasn't until one night the following November, when Charles was thirteen, that he'd overheard the conversation that changed his life. He wished to say goodnight to Alec and Valerie, but heard them talking and stopped outside their door. They were speaking of Finlay. It was the anniversary of his death, and he heard Valerie crying softly.

"Oh, Alec, I know you had to do it, but sometimes I still dream of it. I can still see him in that horrid cell, beaten and bloody, shivering with cold. He was just barely alive, but he was still with us. I have dreams of you holding that coat over his face, his legs twitching and his fingers clawing at the floor, fighting death with everything he had. I will never forget that moment as long as I live."

"I dream of it too. May God forgive me for what I've done."

Alec's voice was very low, but Charles heard the words loud and clear. He ran to his room and was violently sick. Alec had killed Finn in the Tower. He suffocated him until he was dead. How was it possible? Alec loved Finn. They'd shared an unbreakable bond. And then he understood. Alec coveted Finn's wife. No wonder he'd married her less than six months after Finn's death. It even said in the Bible that you shall not covet thy neighbor's wife. Well, this was worse. Finn hadn't been a neighbor; he'd been Alec's brother, his friend and ally since they were boys. Alec was a murderer and a sinner, and Charles would never forgive him. Never. He would bide his time and avenge Finlay's death, no matter how long it took.

Charles had to learn to live with his resentment, but life wasn't finished with him yet. When Uncle Thomas died, he left all he possessed in Virginia to Alec, not to Charles, who had been his ward since the age of six. Alec had not only killed his brother, but had stolen his inheritance. He was now the wealthy landowner, while Charles would have whatever Alec chose to give him. At the time, he'd been too young to do anything about the circumstances, but he was no longer a child. He was old enough to fend for himself, and could contain his resentment no longer.

Charles had been happy to see Valerie outside the study last night. He meant for her to overhear his accusations. They were both guilty, and they should both pay, one way or another. Sowing the seeds of doubt was only the beginning. Charles rubbed his tired eyes and continued on through the forest, calling out Finn's name.

THIRTY-TWO

Valerie stood by the window, staring out into the half-light of morning, searching for any sign of movement outside. Bridget was sound asleep, snoring lightly. With every hour that passed without any news Valerie felt more panicked. Horrible scenarios ran through her head, becoming more vivid with every passing minute. Oh, how she wished she had the Sight now. She would know exactly where to look for her son. Valerie rubbed her eyes with her palms. They burned from lack of sleep, and her back ached from all the pacing she'd done. Soon Louisa would be up and would start asking questions about her brother.

She also felt terrible about Alec. She'd sent him off last night with barely a kind word. She'd been scared and angry, but she knew in her heart that Alec was innocent. She knew him too well. Even if he had strayed and slept with the girl, he would never have killed her. Alec wasn't a murderer. A mercy killing was not the same as killing someone in cold blood.

As Valerie paced her bedroom in the dead of night, she had to ask herself the question. Would she be able to forgive Alec if he had cheated on her? Would she still love him and allow him to make love to her? The answer was yes, she would. She would be hurt and angry for a long time, but she would forgive him. She loved him so fiercely that nothing would make her stop. She had to trust him in order for their marriage to survive, and she would. She had always trusted him in the past, and her faith in him had never led her astray. All she wanted was for him to bring Finn home and then come to her, so that she could tell him that she didn't believe a word of Charles's accusations.

Valerie heard the creaking of stairs as Cook made her way to the kitchen to start breakfast. She'd get dressed and go have a cup of warm milk. Everyone thought she was mad for drinking milk instead of ale, but she was afraid to consume too much alcohol, and milk had calcium, which her baby needed. She needed it as well. The child would take what it needed from her body, leaving her depleted. Many women lost their teeth during pregnancy, but she wouldn't be one of them. She'd managed to hold on to her teeth with both Finn and Louisa.

Valerie slipped off her dressing gown and reached for her skirt. Just as she was tying the laces, something warm gushed between her legs, rooting her to the spot. For one mad moment, she thought her bladder had let go, but the puddle on the floor wasn't urine. It'd be better if it had been.

Valerie reached out a trembling hand and shook Bridget awake. "Bridget, my waters broke."

THIRTY-THREE

Louisa waited until Kit fell asleep before letting herself out of his cabin and going back to her own. Agnes was sound asleep, her hands folded over her belly. Louisa was tired, but she knew she wouldn't sleep. She took off her damp dress and climbed into her berth in her chemise. Her skin became instantly covered with gooseflesh, so she pulled the blanket to her chin in an effort to get warm. She smiled to herself in the darkness. Her first marriage proposal. The man was delirious with fever, but still. She didn't think he'd remember it in the morning. Funny that she'd made it to almost thirty without ever being proposed to, despite the numerous guys she'd dated, and all she had to do was land in the seventeenth century to get an offer of marriage. Is that how it had been for Valerie?

Louisa had to admit, albeit reluctantly, that the thought of marrying Kit wasn't as unwelcome as she wanted to believe. There was something about him that made her feel safe and desired. It wasn't just the physical attraction between them, it was more than that.

Louisa had been with Doug for years, but she always felt that he'd held something in reserve. There was a part of him that was off limits. He gave her as much as he was capable of giving. Louisa suspected that Kit would give all of himself once he declared his love, and would expect all of her in return. Once, she might have found that a little off-putting, but right now it seemed like exactly the right thing. Wasn't that how love was supposed to be? Maybe that's why letting Doug go hadn't been as painful as she'd expected. She had held something in reserve as well, and her heart was cracked, but not broken. She put Doug out of her mind and allowed her thoughts to return to Kit.

Louisa closed her eyes. She could see Kit's face in front of her, his gaze glazed with fever, his lips so full and soft. His stomach muscles had tensed when she touched him in the course of changing his bandage, and he seemed to be holding his breath until she removed her hand from his hot skin. Louisa wondered if he truly felt as drawn to her as she did to him. She tried to imagine what it would be like to have him make love to her, and felt a familiar warmth in the nether regions. She wanted him—desperately. Louisa slid her hand slowly down her body, finding the source of her desire, and let her mind drift. She pictured Kit's naked body on top of hers, and what it would be like to have him inside her, moving slowly and deliberately until he couldn't hold himself back any longer, his thrusts becoming hard and fast. Louisa quivered as her body found release, and drifted off to sleep, still smiling.

THIRTY-FOUR

Kit woke up later than usual. He couldn't remember the last time he'd actually slept through the night. His shift was usually from 4-8pm, and then again from 4-8am, but lately he'd been putting in a lot more hours due to Captain Fellowes' fondness for drink. Kit tried to stretch, but the sharp pain in his left arm reminded him of the reason he got to sleep late in the first place. He put a hand to his forehead. He was still a little warm, but not as fevered as last night. Louisa's ministrations must have helped. His arm was still on fire, the wound swollen and oozing blood, but the linen bandage wasn't soaked, just stained. Definitely better. Kit was about to get up, but decided to give himself a few more minutes. No one had come to summon him back to the bridge, so things must be under control for the moment.

He'd been enjoying a most pleasant dream before waking. He closed his eyes, trying to recapture the image of Louisa moaning beneath him as he sheathed himself in her body. Had he really asked her to marry him last night? He had. And he'd meant it. It was time for him to stop grieving for Helena and get on with his life. Louisa was the first woman to capture his interest in a long time. There was something different about her, something he couldn't name. An independence of spirit, perhaps.

Most women her age were either married or widowed, but few women of her loveliness remained unwed. How old was she? he wondered. It was hard to tell. She had clear eyes and smooth skin, but there was something about her knowing gaze and bearing that suggested she was older than he imagined. Perhaps she was around twenty-three, he concluded.

He failed to believe that no one had wanted to marry her. Nonsense. She was too beautiful not to have had suitors. There was something else there. Something he would discover in time. She seemed very guarded sometimes, almost tense, but at other times she allowed herself freedoms that most women would find improper, like wearing her hair down, or touching his arm when speaking to him.

Kit's thoughts returned to his dream. As an unmarried woman, she would be expected to be a maiden, but he had his doubts. Louisa looked like a woman who'd known love, physical love. She'd mentioned a man last night. Maybe she had been his mistress. Kit shifted on the berth, suddenly uncomfortable in his snug breeches. He hadn't had a woman in a long time.

"Enter," Kit called out as a timid knock sounded on the door.

"Begging your pardon, sir, but you are wanted on the bridge. Master Prescott is organizing a service for Captain Fellowes. He passed during the night." Daniel Willis looked forlorn as he handed Kit a cup of ale. "I thought you might be thirsty."

"Thank you, Master Willis. I am. I will be up shortly. Have you seen Mistress Jamison this morning?" Kit swung his legs over the side of his bed, looking around for his boots. He needed a clean shirt too.

"No, sir. I haven't seen her. May I assist you?"

"Yes, get me a clean shirt, and help me with my boots. I am actually famished this morning. Are there any biscuits left?" Kit allowed the boy to help him with his boots and pushed his arm carefully into the sleeve of the shirt.

"I'll go check, Master Sheridan. I mean, Captain."

"Daniel, you acquitted yourself well, son. You took good care of him. It's not your fault." Kit could see the relief on the boy's face.

"Thank you, sir. I appreciate that. Now, let me see about those biscuits."

Kit drained the cup of ale and shrugged on his coat before going up on deck. He was the captain now, and he had to take charge. *I have a battered ship, a skeleton crew, and a long way to go*, he thought. *At least the cargo is intact, for now.*

Most of the crew was already on deck, gathered around the reverend who stood on a crate, Bible in hand. Captain Fellowes' body was laid before him, sewn into sacking and ready for his final journey. Kit went up to the front to pay his respects, the sailors parting silently to let him pass. The rain had stopped, but the sky was still the color of dirty laundry, everything damp and dripping. The reverend took a deep breath and began, his voice quivering with emotion.

Man that is born of a woman hath but a short time to live, and is full of misery. He cometh up and is cut down like a flower; he flieth as it were a shadow, and never continueth in one stay. In the midst of life we be in death: of whom may we seek for succor but of thee, O Lord, which for our sins justly art displeased. Yet, O Lord God most holy, O Lord most mighty, O holy and most merciful savior, deliver us not into the bitter pains of eternal death. Thou knowest, Lord, the secrets of our hearts, shut not up thy merciful eyes to our prayers: but spare us Lord most holy, O God most mighty, O holy and merciful savior, thou most worthy judge eternal, suffer us not at our last hour for any pains of death to fall from thee.

Kit bowed his head, listening to the words. He'd miss Captain Fellowes. He had been a good man and a great captain, when he was sober. It wouldn't be easy to fill his shoes. The reverend finished the funeral service and asked for a moment of silence, before several burly seamen heaved the body overboard, the captain's remains parting the water with a mighty splash. Kit turned and walked toward the bridge. It was time get on with things.

THIRTY-FIVE

The sun was fully up now, warming Alec's shoulders and lighting the way. He had become completely separated from the other men, but hoped that they'd signal him if they found Finn. They all had hunting horns to use for communication. One long blow meant that they'd found Finn. Two blows meant they needed help. Alec hadn't heard anyone blow their horn, so he continued his search. He wished he could check on Valerie, but he couldn't lose precious time and return to the house.

The sound of a waterfall caught his attention, and he decided to investigate. At the very least he would get a drink. Alec stepped out of the dense woods into a lovely glade. There was a small waterfall rushing into a pool of water that looked like an oval mirror in the middle of the forest. The surface of the pool sparkled in the sunshine, reflecting the pristine sky and wispy clouds lazily floating overhead. Alec sank to his knees and swallowed a few handfuls of water. It was cold and sweet, reviving him instantly. He stood up, looking around carefully, his gaze sliding over every surface, looking for clues.

Alec saw something closer to the waterfall. It was worth checking. He touched the surface of the rock and examined his fingers. Blood. He stood still, taking in every detail of the ground before him. There it was. More blood and a trail of flattened grass. Something large had been dragged toward the waterfall. Alec loaded his pistol and began to follow the path on silent feet. He wasn't sure what to expect, and didn't want to startle a wounded animal, if that's whose blood he'd found. There were more smears of blood as he got closer to the water's edge, then they disappeared. The mist from the waterfall was making his face damp, but he got closer and closer, looking through the gushing water, and then he saw it, the narrow mouth of a cave hidden behind the waterfall. Alec pressed himself against the stone, inching through the narrow tunnel between rock and water toward the opening. It was dark and dank inside the cave, but Alec thought he heard ragged breathing.

"Finn! Finn!"

"Oh, Daddy." He heard the boy calling as he sidled through the narrow opening. Finn lay on his side, wet and shivering. His teeth were chattering from the cold, his leg at an odd angle. Alec finally got to his side and set the pistol down to examine Finn.

"I think my leg is broken. I can't move it, and it hurts so badly. I thought I would die here." Finn was sobbing like a baby, his arms around Alec's neck. "I want to get out of here. I want to go home."

"I'm going to move you very slowly." Finn gave Alec a pitiful look in the darkness.

"Is it going to hurt?"

"Most likely, but you have to be strong. There is no other way for me to get you out. Ready?" Finn nodded and let out a shriek as Alec moved him a few inches. "Finn, you have to help me. Push off with your good leg. It will go faster that way." Alec tried again. By the time he got Finn to the mouth of the cave the boy was nearly insensible with pain, screaming and crying for

Alec to stop. "I have to get you to the bank, and then we'll figure something out. Just a little bit longer, son." Finn nodded, and Alec began to pull him again, ignoring his pitiful whimpering.

At long last, he deposited Finn on the grass, letting the sun warm him and dry his wet clothes. "How did you come to be in that cave?" Alec asked. Finn was still crying softly, but he blew his nose on Alec's handkerchief and tried to answer.

"I went out to set the traps, and I just kept going. I wanted to explore this part of the forest. I heard the sound of the waterfall and thought I'd have a swim. I was hot, and the water looked so cool and inviting. I swam for a while. It was wonderful. After I got out and got dressed, I started walking on the rocks. That's when I slipped and fell, and hurt my leg. I didn't know what to do. I was far from home, and no one knew where I was. I just lay there for a while, thinking about my options when I heard them in the distance. I think there were three of them."

"Who was it?"

"Indians. They were talking and laughing, and making no effort to stay quiet, so I thought I must be on their land. I didn't know what they would do if they found me, so I crawled into the cave. I'd seen it while I was swimming. The Indians stopped by the water and had a drink, but they left soon after. It was getting dark, and I was afraid to come out. My leg was hurting even more after crawling into the cave, so I knew I wouldn't be able to walk home. I thought it was safer to stay in the cave through the night, and then try to get home in the morning. I was thinking of making a crutch out of a sturdy branch." Finn took Alec's hand and squeezed it.

"I am so glad you found me, Daddy. My leg became so swollen during the night that I couldn't get out of the cave. I thought I was going to die."

Finn was crying again. Alec stroked his hair and tried to comfort him. He'd obviously been terrified. Now Alec had to figure out how to get him home. They were far away, and it would be difficult, not to mention painful for Finn, to carry him all the way home. Maybe he could call the men, and they could make some sort of stretcher. On the other hand, if there were Indians nearby, it probably wasn't wise to announce their presence.

"Finn, I'm going to have to carry you. It's going to hurt, but that is the only way for me to get you home. Your mother must be sick with worry by now. We need to hurry." Finn nodded miserably.

"All right, Dad. I'm ready."

It took Alec nearly three hours to carry the boy home. They stopped periodically for Alec to take a rest and for Finn to catch his breath. The boy was nearly unconscious by the time Alec finally caught sight of the house. He didn't want to alarm Finn, but he felt as if he might drop him. The boy weighed more than he thought, and Alec was barely managing to hold him after such a long walk. He had blown his horn once they got closer to Whitfield land, but no one came to help him. Alec wondered if they went back some time during the night.

Alec was just approaching the house when he heard Valerie scream. Oh, God. What now?

THIRTY-SIX

In the days after the pirate attack, the mood on the ship was morbid, to say the least. Empty hammocks swayed with the motion of the ship, relieved of their human cargo. The Mess was half-empty, and the deck was practically deserted as silent sailors, some of them wounded, went about their work, mourning their fallen friends and captain. As if by some unspoken agreement, no one mentioned the Collins family. Louisa tossed and turned for hours every night, unable to get to sleep. Thoughts of Mistress Collins (she didn't even know her first name) and Anne permeated her every waking moment. There was nothing more to be done for the captain or the dead sailors, but the women were still alive somewhere out there, suffering God only knew what. Luisa hoped they were together, but even if they were, they wouldn't be for long.

Louisa gave up on sleep and went up on deck. Some fresh air always helped, and at this hour of the morning there would be almost no one about. Master Prescott was now the first mate, so he would be on the bridge instead of Kit, and Louisa was grateful for that. She wanted to be alone for a while, and as much as she yearned for Kit's company, he couldn't help her come to terms with the events of the past few days.

The wind whipped Louisa's skirts as she emerged on deck, making her glad she'd worn her cap. The sails above her head snapped as they filled with air, white-capped waves covering the surface of the ocean like a wooly quilt. The sun would just be coming up, but the morning was misty, the sky overcast and angry looking. Louisa hoped there wouldn't be another storm. Her face was damp from the morning mist, and she absent-mindedly tucked a stray curl under her cap to keep it from getting wet.

She nodded to a passing seaman, and made her way toward the prow of the ship. She liked the spot behind the figurehead. For some reason, it made her feel calmer to see the carved body of the woman, staring straight ahead to their destination, unper-turbed by anything that happened on board. Her hair gleamed with moisture, and her bare breasts were unnaturally pink. Louisa thought of her as Gloria, named after the ship.

She was surprised to see the reverend sitting on an over-turned crate, his eyes closed in contemplation. Louisa thought of turning back, but he called out to her and waved a hand in invitation. Normally, she would have been annoyed, but today she welcomed the reverend's company. He was the only passenger left, besides her and Agnes, and Louisa hoped that in his capacity as a cleric he might help her deal with the after-math of the attack.

"Good morning, Reverend. I didn't expect to see you up so early." Louisa sat down next to him, keeping a proper distance, and folded her hands in her lap.

"I never got to sleep, Mistress Jamison. Like you, I haven't been able to come to terms with what's happened." The reverend sighed and looked at Louisa. She could see the dark shadows beneath his eyes, and the fatigue etched into his features. He looked tormented, and Louisa felt sorry for him.

"Shall we pray together?" She never expected those words to leave her mouth, but she thought it was what the reverend needed and was willing to do it for his sake. Truth be told, she needed the comfort of prayer at that moment.

"Thank you, Mistress Jamison, but to tell you the truth, I'd rather talk, if you don't mind."

Louisa nodded mutely, stunned by the reverend's sudden need to treat her as a confidant. "Of course, Reverend." She sat back quietly, letting him unburden himself. The reverend looked out over the deck, fixating on the seagull perched high up in the rigging.

"I wanted to be a clergyman since I was a little boy. Some boys dream of being great soldiers, while others long for a life at sea, but I always wanted to dedicate myself to God. My brothers laughed at me and called me a weakling when I didn't want to join in their games and preferred to sit by myself, contemplating the miracles of our Lord's creation. I never doubted my calling, never wavered. I know that some people don't share my faith, or love Our Lord Jesus as much as I do, but I'd always hoped that I could show them the way and lead them to the path of righteousness." Louisa groaned inwardly, but remained silent and let the reverend speak.

"I can't make sense of any of this. For the first time in my life I am lost and confused, and can't find the answers in Holy Scripture. I watched countless men get butchered, but that's not what undid me. It was the fate of the Collins family."

Reverend Blakeley sighed loudly and bowed his head. "Men have died to protect their freedom and possessions from the beginning of time, but the kidnapping of two helpless women, and the suicide of that poor man, haunt me. Master Collins chose a path forbidden by the Church, knowing full well that his eternal soul would face damnation, rather than go on without his wife and daughter. To be perfectly honest, I don't blame him in the least. I know that as a man of God I should condemn his act, but I simply can't. I feel pity for him, and want to beg God not to judge him too harshly."

"That's very commendable of you, Reverend," Louisa said, hoping she was helping.

"Now, when I think of the women, my faith is tested even more severely. Our Lord is merciful and just. Why would he subject those two poor lambs to such an ordeal? The fate they face is worse than any death. They will be abused and humiliated at the hands of their heathen captors, and dwell in a hell on earth before they even meet their Maker. I can't make sense of it. I simply can't. Maybe I am not fit to be a religious leader. How can I preach the word of the Lord when I sit here questioning his judgment?"

Louisa reached out and took the reverend's hand without thinking, surprised that he didn't yank it away. She held it for a moment, thinking of what to say. She had never been a very religious person, but she could understand his confusion and emotional turmoil. Most people in the future questioned the existence and ways of God early in their lives, but in this place and time, this would be considered heresy. People accepted God the way they accepted that the sun rose and set each day. For a man who'd been steadfast in his faith all his life to doubt his beliefs at this stage would be earth-shattering.

"Reverend, we are not meant to understand the will of God, simply to follow it. It's your duty as a clergyman to help what's left of this crew find solace, and accept the terrible loss we've all suffered. I'm tormented by thoughts of Mistress Collins and Anne as well, but I hope that by some miracle, they won't suffer too much at the hands of their captors. They are good, pious women, and the good Lord will protect them."

Louisa hoped the reverend couldn't see through her lie. She didn't believe for a moment that the Collins women would be spared, but she couldn't do anything to help them, so she had to help the reverend instead. She didn't particularly like the man, but she could see that he was genuinely suffering, and wanted to do what she could.

"Are you saying that there was some divine purpose to this attack?" Reverend Blakeley turned his gray gaze on Louisa, studying her as if seeing her for the first time.

"I am saying that I don't know the will of God, and neither do you. We must accept what's given to us, and allow our faith to help us overcome our grief and confusion. I look to you, Reverend, for guidance and comfort." Louisa allowed her eyes to slide away from the reverend's face, unable to bear the intensity of his gaze.

"I thank you, Mistress Jamison. I knew the good Lord wouldn't let me doubt him. He has spoken through you, and I will redouble my efforts and lead this crew in spiritual healing. I must admit that I had my doubts about you, but I see now that you are a very pious woman indeed. I must return to my cabin at once and prepare a sermon on the power of faith. God bless you and keep you."

With that, the reverend rose from his perch and practically ran along the deck in the direction of the stairs leading down to the cabins.

"Glad I could help," Louisa muttered to his retreating back and got up, turning her gaze to Gloria. "And what do you think?" She had about as much faith in God as she had in the carved woman in front of her, but she was glad that she'd been able to help the reverend. She had no idea where the sentiments had come from, but they seemed to offer him comfort. Louisa genuinely wished she had more faith. At the moment, things seemed very bleak, and she would have liked to know the will of God, if he was up there somewhere.

THIRTY-SEVEN

Valerie felt another contraction sink its teeth into her as she heard the commotion downstairs. She needed to know if the searchers had found Finn. She tried to rise, but Bridget stopped her. "I will go. Ye're in no condition to be walking down the stairs."

She sprinted out the door and left Valerie alone with her pain. The contractions began shortly after her water broke, getting closer at an alarming rate. Valerie gritted her teeth, waiting for the pain to subside. This was her third labor, and still she couldn't believe the severity of the pain her body could put her through. She tried to focus on what was happening downstairs, rather than allow her mind to roam free. She had spent all day and night worrying about Finn, but she was also terrified for her baby.

She wasn't due for another two months. Many premature babies survived, but the chances were diminished in the seventeenth century. What if the baby's lungs weren't developed and it needed to be on a respirator? Valerie tried to push the frightening thought away. Bridget said that everything was going well and reassured her repeatedly. She didn't know exactly how many weeks along she was, but she was closer to eight months, based on the date of her last period. The baby might be small, but it would be fully formed by now. Another contraction drove all thought from Valerie's mind, making her ball her hands into fists and grind her teeth. Sweat broke out on her forehead, and her legs shook as the pain tore through her mercilessly, indifferent to her fears.

The door opened and Alec walked in. He looked awful. His hair was all tangled with bits of leaves and twigs in it, his clothes were filthy and damp. There were scratches on his face, and he looked near collapse. Valerie raised herself on her elbow. "Did you find him?"

Alec nodded before sinking into the chair vacated by Bridget. "He's going to be all right. His leg is broken and needs a splint, but he is all right. He had a terrible fright."

"I want to see him," Valerie moaned.

"I'm afraid you are going to have to wait until you've delivered."

"No. This might be my last chance to see my son. Please, Alec, bring him here." Valerie gave him a stern look just as the next contraction took her breath away.

"Sweetheart, don't talk like that. You're not going to die. Bridget said everything is progressing normally." He looked scared, so Valerie softened her tone.

"Nevertheless, I need to see him. Please."

"All right. I'll bring him to see you. He's lying down on his bed, eating hot buns." Alec got up, ready to go back down again.

"Alec, are you all right? You look dreadful." The pain subsided, giving Valerie a momentary break.

"I just need to sleep for a day or two and I will be right as rain. I'm getting old, Val." He gave her a searching look, trying to figure out if she was still angry.

"Alec, I don't believe what Charles said. I never did."

"It's not true, Valerie. I swear to you on everything that's holy that I never touched that girl. Never. I don't know who killed her, if anyone at all, but I will find out. Just not today." Alec kissed her tenderly on the forehead and left the room.

THIRTY-EIGHT

Kit looked around his new home. He'd moved into the captain's quarters a few days ago, and was still getting used to his new accommodation. This room was a far cry from the cabin of the first mate. It was much larger, with an actual bed hung with crimson velvet curtains, and a trunk for his clothes. The windows spanned the entire width of the stern, making it appear light and spacious. The walnut desk, placed before the windows to capture the light, held a naval log, inkwell, and several sharpened quills, as well as various nautical instruments. A bookshelf, containing texts on navigation, astronomy, and geography, was built-in below the row of windows to maximize the use of space. A round table in the center of the cabin, which was used only for dining and entertaining company, completed the decor. Every available surface gleamed with polish, painstakingly administered by the steward every day.

Kit finished shaving and tied his hair back with a thong. His company would be along shortly. He had invited Louisa to dine with him, and had to admit that he was a little nervous. His arm felt much better, thanks to her, so he had no trouble getting dressed. The table was set for two, and the steward would bring up the first course as soon as Louisa arrived. Kit wondered if she would bring her maid along. She had when she dined with Captain Fellowes, but he fervently hoped she would come alone.

He answered the knock himself, inviting Louisa into the cabin. She looked lovely, with her hair piled high on her head, and obviously recently washed. Kit could still smell the lavender soap she used and took a discreet whiff, enjoying the fragrance. He pulled out a chair, inviting her to sit down. Cook had promised some soup and roast fowl, which would be a welcome break from the salt pork and hardtack everyone had been having for days. She deserved a decent meal and some good wine. Captain Fellowes made sure his cabin was well stocked. Kit poured Louisa a glass of claret and sat down across from her. They made small talk while the steward served the soup, waiting for him to depart.

"How is your arm, Christopher?" Louisa asked. She appeared to feel a trifle self-conscious under his intense gaze. She took a spoonful of soup and snuck a peek at him from under her lashes.

"I am much improved. Thank you. How is the soup?"

"Delicious."

"You never gave me an answer."

She looked up, startled. "How did you go from soup to marriage in three seconds?" she asked with a smile.

"I'm not one for wasting time. I hope to convince you to marry me between courses. We have about ten minutes until the next course arrives." She blushed and he smiled, gratified by her reaction.

"Kit, we barely know each other."

"Many marriages are built on less. Why don't you tell me about yourself? Where were you born?" The question seemed to fluster her further, and she looked away from him, focusing on the soup.

"Why don't we start with you? Where were *you* born?"

"I was born in London in 1585. My father was a ship's captain, and had sailed with Sir Francis Drake before taking command of his own ship. He fought against the Spanish Armada, and was awarded a title by Queen Elizabeth for his bravery." Kit took a sip of wine and smiled at Louisa. "What else would you like to know, my sweet?"

"What about your mother? Do you have any siblings?"

"I have an older sister from my father's first marriage. My father was nearly forty-five when I was born, and my mother nineteen. I am their only child." She seemed to completely miss the bit about a title being bestowed on his father, and he was glad. He didn't want her to think he was trying to impress her with his lineage. She obviously hadn't heard of Lord Robert Sheridan.

"How did you meet your wife?" *She must be concerned that I still love my wife*, Kit thought. *That's why she's reluctant to give me an answer.*

"Helena was my mother's second cousin. My mother took her in when her parents died. I suppose my mother was lonely with my father away at sea for at least six months out of the year. Helena was the daughter she'd never had. I went to sea when I was ten years old as a cabin boy. I sailed with my father, who tried very hard not to show me preferential treatment. Helena was always there when I came ashore."

"Did your father succeed in not showing you favor?"

"Not even close. He was stern in front of the crew, but when we were alone together he was very affectionate and fatherly. He always saved little treats for me and bought me presents when the ship came into foreign ports. It was a good life." Kit still missed his father desperately. The old man suffered horribly for many months before he finally died, leaving a terrible hole in Kit's heart.

"Is he still alive?" Louisa asked, as if reading his thoughts.

"He had a tumor in his stomach. It took its time killing him. He died when I was twenty-five."

"I'm sorry. It sounds like you two were close." Her eyes suddenly filled with tears and Kit reached over and took her hand.

"I take it you lost your own parents." She nodded, a tear sliding down her cheek.

Kit let go of Louisa's hand as the steward pushed open the door, balancing a heavy tray. The chicken smelled heavenly, making his mouth water. He waited for the steward to serve them and leave.

"So, have you made up your mind?" he asked, suddenly nervous.

She looked up at him, a smile playing about her lips, and pushed away her plate. Louisa walked around the table and sat in Kit's lap, wrapping her arms around his neck. Her lips came down on his, taking his breath away, and he pulled her closer, kissing her hard. Her mouth opened under his, her tongue sliding into his mouth and exploring him shamelessly. Kit felt himself grow hard against her thigh, and shifted a little to avoid shocking her, although at this point he wasn't sure she'd be shocked. Louisa obviously knew what she was doing. She slid her hand downward, but Kit grabbed her wrist and broke the kiss. Louisa drew back in shock and looked to him for an explanation.

"Louisa, I can't. You must see that."

"See what?" She seemed genuinely confused.

"I don't know what kind of men you've known in the past, but I am an honorable man, and I will not lie with you without marrying you first."

Kit was confused by the expression on her face. What had he said that surprised her so? Most women longed for marriage, but Louisa seemed willing to take him to bed without accepting his proposal. She slid off his lap and went back to her seat, obviously perplexed.

"Louisa, I don't understand. Have I offended you in some way?"

"I'm sorry, Master Sheridan, I think I'll take my leave now."

Kit watched in helpless confusion as Louisa walked out the door.

THIRTY-NINE

Louisa couldn't bear to go back to her stifling cabin, so she decided to take a walk on deck and prayed that she wouldn't run into Reverend Blakeley. Her cheeks burned with humiliation, but she willed herself not to cry. She wasn't sure why she was so upset, but she felt as if Kit had just kicked her in the stomach. She had never been rejected by a man before and although his reasons were honorable, it still hurt her terribly. She'd been thinking with her twenty-first century brain, and she made a terrible mistake. She just wanted him to love her, to touch her. She couldn't contemplate marriage without knowing what it would be like to kiss him and feel him.

She wouldn't be contemplating marriage at all if she wasn't so scared. She had always thought of herself as being strong, but at the moment she felt anything but. She'd never truly been alone before she went back in time and she desperately wanted to belong to someone and have someone care of her. She had to admit that the idea of marrying Kit Sheridan gained appeal with every passing minute. He made her feel safe and protected. Nothing bad would happen to her as long as he was there, and the fear that constantly gnawed at her stomach was almost gone when she was with Kit.

Of course, there were also drawbacks to getting married. She was still trying to understand this world she'd landed in, and she was terrified of doing something that would ruin everything. This wasn't 2012. In 1620, her husband would become her lord and master, and would be able to control her in every way that mattered. She didn't think Kit would be a dominating or cruel husband; she simply wasn't ready to make that kind of commitment to him. She needed to find Valerie, first and foremost.

Louisa was shaking with frustrated desire as she stomped around the deck, trying to calm down. What had she done? What possessed her to act like that? Now he would think her a wanton hussy and treat her accordingly. She should have known better than to be forward with a man like Kit. All he wanted was to give her his name and protection, and she threw it back in face and insulted his honor. What a fool! What would their relationship be like now?

FORTY

Kit stared at the door of his cabin, still reeling from Louisa's rejection. What had he done wrong? Should he have declared his love for her? Was that what kept her from accepting him? She seemed very willing to let him take her, so why refuse his proposal? Maybe she wasn't free to marry. She seemed very secretive about her past. Could it be that she was running away from an abusive husband? It didn't seem that way. God, what a fool he'd been. He'd humiliated her by rejecting her advances, and now she would never forgive him. He'd ruined everything.

Kit stood and headed for the door. He would go find her and apologize. He wasn't sure what he would be apologizing for, but an apology seemed to be in order, and he didn't want to put it off and create tension between them. He would give her a little time and try again. They still had several weeks until they reached Virginia. He would pursue her more carefully and give her time to reconsider. She was like a skittish horse; she simply needed to be reassured and gentled.

Kit knocked on Louisa's cabin door, surprised to face a startled Agnes. "She is not 'ere, sir. I thought she was dining with ye tonight."

"Ah, we had a slight misunderstanding. I'll go look for her."
Kit went up on deck. Where else would she be?

He saw her standing alone behind the figurehead. She'd let
down her hair and it was blowing in the evening breeze, silvery
in the moonlight. Kit could see by her posture that she was
tense and upset, and cursed himself yet again for being a
complete idiot.

"Louisa?" She spun around at the sound of his voice. She'd
been crying. "I am so sorry. I didn't mean to offend you. I
believed I was doing the right thing." At this point, he had no
idea what the right thing was, but he'd be damned if he didn't
figure it out soon.

"I can't imagine what you must think of me." She turned
away from him, obviously embarrassed.

"I think I want you more than I've ever wanted any woman
in my life."

She looked up at him, her eyes full of confusion. What did
she want? He had no idea, but knew damn well what he
wanted. He took a step toward her and pulled her into his
arms, kissing her hard. If this was what she wanted, he would
give it to her. Louisa stiffened in his arms for a second, but then
kissed him back, matching his ardor. Her body relaxed against
his, her arms going about his neck, pulling him closer. She
tasted so good. He pushed her up against the railing, cupping
her breast and grinding his body against hers. He was so
enflamed he could have taken her right there, but he couldn't
jeopardize Louisa's reputation or undermine his authority as
captain.

Kit let her go reluctantly and studied her face. She was
looking up at him with such longing that he strongly considered
throwing her over his shoulder and taking her back to his cabin,
but he took a step back and willed himself to behave.

"Kit, I can't marry you. I've sacrificed more than you can
possibly imagine to find my sister, and that's what I must do.

Valerie is the only family I have left. I can't make any commitments until I find her. Can you understand that?"

"Do you think I would prevent you from looking for your sister?" He seemed taken aback by her insinuation.

"No, but if I was to become your wife, my first responsibility would be to you, and I can't give you that right now. Besides, you live in England and my sister is in Virginia, at least I hope she is."

"What about a compromise?" Kit asked, feeling more hopeful. "Let us become betrothed, but we won't marry until you are ready. I will help you find your sister when we get to Virginia, and ask her for her blessing."

"You really want to marry me that much?" Louisa seemed surprised, but he could see the beginning of a smile.

"Louisa, I loved my wife, but I'm done with grieving. I yearn for you the way I haven't yearned for anyone in years. I don't care where you come from or what you've done. I simply want you to be mine. I know I sound like a besotted fool, but that's the truth."

"Would you still want me if you found out something about me you didn't like?"

Kit was momentarily thrown by the question, but the answer came from his heart and not from his brain. "Yes, I would still want you." He went down on one knee, taking her hands in his. "Louisa Jamison, will you do me the honor of becoming my wife whenever you are ready to do so?"

"Yes, Christopher Sheridan. I will."

Kit kissed her hands and got to his feet. "Do you still want to seduce me?"

"Only if it won't offend your girlish sensibilities."

"I think I'm past that. Come back to my cabin," he whispered to her. Louisa nodded and followed him back wordlessly. Kit locked the door behind them and turned to Louisa. She was standing by his bed, unsure of what to do. Kit removed his coat and threw it over a chair as he approached her. She just stood there, watching him, her eyes full of desire. Kit took Louisa by the shoulders and turned her around. He unlaced her bodice and undid the ties of her skirt as he kissed her neck and bare shoulders. The skirt pooled around Louisa's ankles, leaving her in her chemise.

Helena had never allowed him to see her naked, but he had a feeling Louisa didn't share Helena's inhibitions. Kit pulled the garment over her head, leaving Louisa naked, her back still turned to him. He wrapped his arms around her, inhaling her scent and enjoying the feel of her warm skin. She turned around then, letting him look at her. She was so beautiful. Her golden hair tumbled over her shoulders, her breasts were full and creamy, and filled his hands perfectly when he cupped them. She gave him an enigmatic smile and pulled his shirt over his head, careful of his wounded arm. Her fingers undid his laces. She pushed down his britches, looking at him, her mouth slightly open and her lips moist.

Kit pushed her onto the bed, spreading her legs. He needed to see her, to taste her, before he allowed himself the pleasure of taking her. Louisa moaned and arched her back as he slid his fingers inside her. She was so ready. The fact that she was unashamed aroused him, and he got on top of her, drawing her nipple in his mouth. Louisa took his hand and pushed it back down between her legs, not wanting him to stop what he was doing. Her fingers wrapped around him, stroking and teasing until he thought he would explode with desire.

Kit pulled her to the edge of the bed and grabbed her hips as he plunged into her. She wrapped her legs around him, her hips meeting his thrust for thrust. Kit had just enough sense left to pull out before he spilled his seed onto her stomach. She wasn't his wife yet, and he didn't want to get her with child. He slid down to his knees, resting his head against her thigh, his gaze locked on the rosy flesh between her legs. Louisa was still panting and her eyes were closed, but there was a satisfied smile on her lips.

"Do you still want to marry me, Master Sheridan?" she asked playfully.

"Yes," he said simply. He did. He had no idea where she came from or who she'd been with, but he was bewitched by her. No woman had ever loved him like that before.

FORTY-ONE

Louisa woke up sometime in the middle of the night to find the bed empty and cold. Kit wasn't due on the bridge until 8am, so he had to be around somewhere. She pulled aside the heavy bed hangings and looked around the dim cabin. Kit was sitting with his back to the desk, facing the row of windows, his feet propped up on the low bookshelf built into the wall beneath the windows. He was bathed in moonlight, his skin silvered by its glow. Louisa couldn't see his face, but she could see the tension in his posture. He didn't look like a man simply enjoying the beautiful view of a moonlit ocean.

"Kit? Are you all right?" Louisa threw her legs over the side of the bed, ready to go to him, but his words rooted her to the spot.

"Who was he, Louisa?" His voice was low, angry. She knew this would come up. No man of this time could overlook a lover.

"Who are you referring to?" She knew full well, but needed to hear it from him.

"The man you loved so dearly that you were willing to lie with him without the benefit of marriage." He didn't look at her, but continued to stare out of the window, tense and cold.

"He was someone I knew when I was very young. It was in a different place and a different time. Why does it suddenly matter, when only a few hours ago you said you didn't care about my past?" Louisa felt a heavy weight drop into the pit of her stomach. Her modern mind wanted to rage at him, to tell him to mind his own business and just get over it, but her heart suddenly felt very fragile. His opinion of her mattered greatly, and she wanted to go to him and tell him that the past, or in this case, the future, didn't matter. That Doug was out of her heart, and he was the only one she wanted. She admired his sense of honor and wanted him to think of her as an honorable woman, not some cheap trollop who would fall into bed with any man she found attractive.

Kit slowly turned around, his eyes bottomless pools of blackness in the moonlight spilling from the window. His face was bleached of all color, nearly as white as his shirt.

"It matters because I've never felt what I am feeling now. Helena loved me since she was a child. I never had cause to doubt her. I had been her first and only lover. I never knew what jealousy was until tonight. My insides are twisted into a knot, burning and writhing, leaving me breathless with my own helplessness." He made no move to rise, but Louisa could sense the coiled tension emanating from him.

"Kit, I can't take back the past. I understand if you wish to withdraw your offer of marriage." Louisa got out of bed and bent down to lift her gown off the floor, but Kit was next to her in a moment, grabbing her by the shoulders and turning her to face him.

"Louisa, you misunderstand me. I am not withdrawing my offer. I am simply consumed with doubt that you will ever love me the way you loved him, and that he'll always be uppermost in your heart. I want you to love me that way. I need you to love me that way." His eyes were pleading with her, filling her heart with tenderness. He was insecure, not angry. What babies men were, in any age.

"Kit, you needn't compare yourself to him. He's gone from my life, and from my heart. He might've been my first, but I want you to be my last. I love you." She hadn't even known it herself until she spoke the words out loud, but they felt so right, so true. She lifted her face to his kiss, tasting relief and joy on his lips.

FORTY-TWO

Alec watched as Master Thorpe applied the planks to Finn's leg and bound them with linen strips to hold them in place. Finn screamed like a girl when the man set the bone, but it had to be done. Thankfully, his leg was broken in only one place and would heal cleanly. Master Thorpe was one of the indentured servants who worked the land, but he had been a barber-surgeon back in England and was the closest thing Alec could get to a physician on such short notice. Once Finn's leg was seen to, Alec wanted to ride into Jamestown to get Doctor Gideon, but Bridget assured him that wasn't necessary. The labor was progressing normally, and despite Valerie's periodic screams, there was no cause for alarm.

"I am all right now, Father. You should get some rest."

Finn lay back against the pillows, his gaze already far away in dreamland. He was exhausted by his ordeal. Alec thought it was interesting how he went from calling him 'Daddy' in the cave, to 'Dad' on the way back, and now went back to 'Father.' Sometimes he wished Finn was a little more affectionate toward him, but he was almost a man, and probably felt awkward about calling him 'Daddy,' as he had done when he was a little boy.

Alec kissed him on the forehead and left the room. He needed a bath, a meal, and some sleep, but the latter would have to wait until he knew that his wife was delivered safely.

Alec didn't feel like waiting for Amelia to heat and bring water for a bath, so he walked down to the pond and stripped off his clothes. He was far enough from the house not to shock anyone with his nudity. The water felt wonderful and he allowed himself a quick swim before he took the bar of soap from the bank and washed away the grime and sweat of the past few days. He would stop by the kitchen on his way back, then check on Valerie. She had been in labor since morning, and he hoped her ordeal would be over soon.

Alec got out of the water reluctantly, pulled on some clean clothes, and scooped the filthy garments off the ground. The cool breeze ruffled his wet hair as he walked back to the house, oblivious to the chirping of crickets and the croaking of frogs. Mistress Dolly, or Cook as everyone called her, took the dirty clothes from him, dished out some leftover rabbit stew and cider to tide him over until supper, and sent him on his way.

Alec could hear Valerie moan as he approached the bedroom door. He sent up a silent prayer and crossed himself before knocking on the door and poking his head in. "May I come in?"

"She is nearly there, Master Alec," Bridget replied. "Ye should stay. Yer presence always calms 'er."

Valerie looked tired and flushed, but she smiled when she looked at him. "Help me, Alec. Get behind me and hold me while I push."

Alec did as he was told and held Valerie against him, feeling the tension coursing through her body. He was instantly trans-ported to the night of Louisa's birth, but he put the memory from his mind. This was different. The baby was in the right position, and it would be just a matter of time before it was born. It took another hour of pushing, but Bridget finally eased the infant out of Valerie and laid it on the bed to clean. Valerie slumped against Alec, exhausted and relieved.

"Is it a boy or a girl, Bridget? Why isn't it crying?" Valerie raised her head to peer at the baby and gasped. The baby was the size of a loaf of bread, wrinkled and bluish. No sounds came from its small form as Bridget worked on its tiny body, trying to breathe some air into its lungs and rubbing it briskly. She looked up at Valerie, her eyes full of sorrow, and shook her head. Alec tightened his hold on Valerie as she let out a horrible wail that tore through his heart.

"I am so sorry, Mistress," Bridget said through her own tears. "He just came too early. He wasn't ready for this world."

Valerie was crying softly, her hands covering her face. Alec's vision blurred as the tears came. He couldn't help wondering if the baby would have lived had Finn not chosen this particular time to worry his mother.

"I want to hold him, Bridget," Valerie said quietly. She reached out her arms for the baby, taking him carefully from Bridget and holding him close.

"He looks like he's sleeping, doesn't he?" she asked Alec. "So peaceful." The baby did look peaceful. His lips were stretched into a little smile, as if he didn't just go through the ordeal of birth. He was small, but perfectly formed, with rounded cheeks and a button nose that never drew air. Valerie cupped his head, which was covered in dark fuzz.

"I wonder what color his eyes were," she said. "Now we'll never know."

"Valerie, let Bridget tend to him. You need to rest," Alec knew it was useless, but he had to try.

"No. I want to be with him for a while before he's taken from me. I want to remember what he looks like."

FORTY-THREE

They buried the baby two days later. Alec was devastated because the baby hadn't been baptized, but Valerie did not believe in Limbo, Heaven, or Hell for that matter, but she couldn't tell him that. Having grown up in the seventeenth century, Alec's faith was much stronger than her own. There'd been a resident priest at Yealm Castle, who tended to the family's spiritual needs despite the terrible discrimination against Catholics. The family went to Protestant Mass on Sundays, then held their own Mass at home. There was no Catholic priest in Virginia, but Alec did his best to keep the traditions alive. He was usually the one to perform the funeral services, since he was the head of the family following Thomas Whitfield's death.

Alec read the funeral service, but had to stop several times to regain his composure. They named the baby Alexander Thomas, and his pine cross looked very small and forlorn as Alec drove it into the ground. Finn cried as he stood by the tiny grave, supported by Charles. Valerie knew he felt responsible for his brother's death, but there was nothing she could do to soothe him. She didn't have any comfort to give at the moment.

Bridget wanted to prepare Alexander for burial, but Valerie wouldn't let her. She held him for hours before finally washing him clean and putting a white gown with a matching bonnet on him. She'd been planning to use the gown for his christening, but now he'd be buried in it instead. She wondered when exactly he died, since he was still moving in her womb the day she went into labor. *My poor little boy*, she thought. *How I would have loved you*.

Valerie looked over at Louisa, whose eyes were puffy from crying. Louisa clung to Bridget during the funeral service, but broke away and hurled herself at Valerie, burying her face in Valerie's skirts. Valerie wrapped her arms around her daughter, holding her close. This was the first death that really mattered to her. She had been fond of Cora, but she didn't take it as badly as the loss of her baby brother.

"Come on, darling. Let's go back to the house. Baby Alexander is with God now. He is happy. I promise you." Valerie couldn't say she really believed that, but she knew it would make Louisa feel better.

"Are you sure, Mama? He hadn't been baptized. Father said it was important."

"Don't worry. God loves babies, even if they weren't baptized. Alexander is with the angels now, looking down on us and wishing for us not to be sad." Louisa nodded in agreement. She wanted to believe that, and she did.

FORTY-FOUR

Charles accepted a glass of brandy from Captain Smith and took a sip, enjoying the aroma of the liquor. The *Morning Star* would be sailing on the morning tide, its cargo hold full of timber for His Majesty's Navy. Trade with England had decreased at one point, but things were picking up again since England needed wood to build ships. The vessel would return in a few months, bringing back much-needed supplies for the colonists. The *Misty Dawn* now sailed between Virginia and the West Indies, bringing back spices, molasses, and rum.

Charles enjoyed going to the docks to oversee the loading and unloading of the vessels. Finlay used to do that a lot when he was alive, and Charles felt like he was following in his brother's footsteps. He always took a glass of port or brandy with the captains, catching up on the latest news and gossip. Alec had been devoting more of his time to the planting of tobacco, delegating more of the shipping to Charles. The tobacco had been planted in spring and was now flowering, leaving Alec free, but the death of the baby took its toll, so Alec left Charles take care of business.

"How have you been, Captain Smith? Any adventures on this last voyage?"

The captain was tall and thin, with a pointy white beard and rheumy blue eyes. He looked more tired every time he came into port. The man had to be in his sixties by now. He had been a captain for at least thirty years, and a first mate for several years before that. He'd been at sea since he was a boy of eight.

"Not on this voyage, thankfully. I tell you, Master Whitfield, sailing has become a very dangerous business. The Barbary pirates used to pillage the Mediterranean Coast, but they're now coming as far as the North Atlantic. They've learned shipbuilding techniques from those damn Dutch and are building stronger, faster ships. There are more attacks than ever. The slave trade is booming in North Africa."

"Yes, I know. Captain Horace of the *Misty Dawn* tells me that it's booming in the West Indies as well. The slave markets are a huge draw for merchants from all parts of the world. I fear it won't be long before there's a slave market in Jamestown. There are already some Negro slaves in Virginia." Charles had heard detailed accounts of the slave auctions on the islands and was partly curious, partly horrified.

"I can't see that happening, Master Whitfield, not here. Who could afford them anyway? Most of these colonists are barely scratching out a living as is. Sure, there are some wealthy people, but they seem content with indentured servants. It profits both servant and master, and at least they gain their freedom at the end of their contract. What would happen if the Negro slaves were set free? Would they be free men? It doesn't bear thinking about."

"I take your point, Captain Smith. Now, how are things in England?"

"Much the same, Master Whitfield, much the same. The king is at odds with Parliament, but at least he hasn't dragged us into any wars recently. I tell you, I am getting weary in my old age. I have a small cottage near Plymouth. My widowed sister keeps it for me. I long to retire there, maybe find a good woman to marry. I've been a widower these past fifteen years. Might be time to find a companion for my old age." The captain finished his drink and stood, ready to return to his duties. It was a signal that it was time for Charles to leave.

"I hope your dream comes to fruition, Captain. I'll just let myself out."

"Please pass on my condolences to Master Alec and his lady."

"I most certainly will, Captain Smith. Good day to you."

Charles retrieved his horse from the public house and set out for home. He considered paying a visit to Janet, but changed his mind. He was in no mood to deal with her little brat. If he visited now, the child would be up and about, and full of energy.

Janet was one of the first women in Jamestown to become widowed, after being married for only a few short months. Other newly-arrived brides urged her to marry again as soon as possible, but Janet decided to wait. She'd be severely punished by the law of the colony if word got out, but she supplemented the income from the farm by taking unwed men to her bed. The arrangement seemed to work out for everyone, and when Janet's son was born, everyone chose to believe the child was her husband's. Perhaps it was, Charles mused. It didn't matter to him as long as the brat wasn't his.

Charles adjusted his hat to shield his face from the hot sun and trotted down the road to Rosewood. He was in no rush. It was a beautiful day, and he had no reason to hurry home. There was nothing waiting for him there, except gloom. He wished Cora was still alive. He really missed her. Cora came to Rosewood Manor a year ago with her sister, Amelia. Charles noticed Amelia first. She was like a paler version of Annabel Gaines—

blond and blue-eyed, with a lovely figure. He tried to talk to Amelia or give her the occasional trinket, but the girl would get spooked and run from the room, her eyes averted, her cheeks flaming. After a month of two Charles gave up. He had no desire to force his attentions on anyone.

Cora was different from her sister. She was dark-haired and dark-eyed, with an impish smile and quick wit. She always had a sweet smile for Charles, and gladly accepted a ribbon for her hair or a bunch of wildflowers. Charles enjoyed their flirtation and waited for the right moment to make his move. At sixteen, Cora was undoubtedly a maiden, and he didn't want to frighten her off. There was time aplenty. He enjoyed the chase as much as he enjoyed the conquest.

Cora came to him soon enough. It was last autumn. She waited for Amelia to fall asleep, then crept to his room in her shift, a shawl over her shoulders. Charles was excited. He'd never had a virgin before, and took his time getting her ready. He kissed her and caressed her until she was melting like butter on warm bread. She whimpered sweetly when he took her maidenhead, and didn't carry on or cry. Their meetings became regular after that. Cora took to fornication like a fish to water. She couldn't get enough. Sometimes she actually managed to shock Charles. She would come into a room when he was alone and flash him a breast or grab his cock. Once she actually turned around and lifted her skirts to her waist, shaking her sweet little bottom at him. Charles nearly lost it there and then. He followed her to the spring house, where Cora sank to her knees and sucked him until he spilled himself into her mouth.

Yes, he missed Cora. He had been crazed with jealousy when he saw her follow Alec into the stables, and then again into his study a few weeks ago. He snuck into the study that night, to see if he could find any evidence of their tryst, but there was nothing that he could see. Was he sharing her with his brother? He had never known Alec to trifle with the maidservants, but then again, with his wife pregnant, he was probably living a monk's existence. Charles had enjoyed Janet numerous times while she was with child, but figured Alec was too much of a gentleman to trouble his wife while she was expecting.

Charles showered Cora with little gifts and always took care not to get her pregnant. He didn't want to bring disgrace upon her or ruin her life. She would want to marry someday, so it'd be cruel of him to ruin her reputation. He wasn't sure if Amelia knew of their trysts, but he hoped not. She wouldn't approve, that was for sure.

Charles jumped off his horse and picked some wildflowers that grew on the side of the road. He would stop by the cemetery and lay some flowers on Cora's grave.

FORTY-FIVE

Agnes pretended to be asleep when her mistress crept back into the cabin and lay down on her berth. Agnes didn't need to see her face to know that she was smiling. So, it happened then. Master Sheridan must have found her all right. *On her back, he found her*, Agnes smirked. Agnes put her hands on her growing belly. Would he marry Mistress Jamison, or was he just taking advantage of her vulnerable state? He didn't seem the type. Master Sheridan was a real gentleman.

She sighed with worry. Agnes had gotten to know her mistress relatively well over the past weeks, and was beginning to think that she wouldn't be too hard on her when she found out about the baby. This changed everything. If she married the captain, he would become Agnes's master, and he might not take kindly to her disgrace. If only she would miscarry. Agnes had been so terrified during the pirate attack she thought she might lose the baby right there and then, but nothing happened. The blasted child hung on. She thought it was curious that the Collins women, who were righteous and godly, were abducted, while Agnes, who had sinned and deserved punishment, had remained unmolested. The Lord certainly worked in mysterious ways.

Agnes listened to Louisa's even breathing. Had this been the first time she had lain with the captain? She might be with child as well. Agnes pondered the implications of that idea as she finally fell asleep.

FORTY-SIX

JULY 1620

Valerie forced herself to get out of bed. She had been so lethargic lately. Her body was getting back to normal after the birth, but her mind still reeled. She went to the cemetery every day, gazing at the freshly carved cross with her son's name on it. If only things could have been different. Her breasts ached with milk despite being tightly bound, a sad reminder of the child she would be nursing had he been alive. Valerie put her hands on her empty belly. He should still have been in there. Instead, he slept in this sad little cemetery.

Valerie glanced at Cora's grave. Someone had left a bunch of wildflowers on the mound of earth. It must have been Amelia. The poor girl had been floating around the house like a ghost since her sister's death. They had been so close. Valerie turned to leave the graveyard and made her way back to the house. She would go talk to Amelia. Maybe she could find something out about Cora's activities in the days before her death. Alec was still agonizing over Charlie's accusations; it would help if Amelia could shed some light on the matter.

Amelia was cleaning the children's bedroom when Valerie finally tracked her down. She was pale and drawn, dark circles beneath her eyes. Amelia didn't even bother to greet Valerie, just went about her business.

"How are you, Amelia?" Valerie pretended to be looking for something, not to put the girl on her guard.

"I am well, ma'am." Amelia continued to dust, her eyes averted.

"You must miss your sister very much."

"I do, ma'am. I miss her every moment of every day." Amelia turned to Valerie, her eyes swimming with tears. "I want to know who done it, ma'am."

"So, help me find out. Did Cora have a young man? I've never seen her with anyone, but maybe there was someone among the workers."

"She snuck out several nights a week to go meet someone, but I don't know who it was. She never said."

"Did she seem happy or frightened? Do you think someone was forcing her?" Amelia thought about that for a moment, dusting forgotten.

"She was as she should be, ma'am. Not scared or anything. I suppose she was enjoying whatever they were doing." Amelia hastily averted her eyes and went back to her task. She'd said everything she was going to say on the subject.

"Thank you, Amelia. Let me know if you need anything."

Valerie left the room and went down to the garden. She needed to think, and she found the peace of the garden to be soothing. So, she now knew that Cora probably had a lover. Amelia said that she snuck out at night, so it couldn't be Alec, not that she ever really thought it was. Alec usually went to bed with Valerie and stayed in bed all night. Valerie was a light sleeper, especially during pregnancy, and she would have known had he been sneaking out.

Cora might have been meeting one of the field workers. There was a loft over the stables that could be used for assignations. No one slept there and it was a nice, private space that was warm and dry. Valerie took a mental inventory of the male workers. Most of them were older men who showed very obvious signs of wear. She couldn't imagine that a young, pretty girl like Cora would be attracted to any of them. There were two younger men who could be called handsome. She would have to go and speak with them.

Valerie didn't think Alec would approve of her questioning the workers, but she needed to find out if Cora died an unnatural death. Besides, it took her mind off her darling baby, if only for a short time. Valerie headed to the barracks that housed their laborers. They had been built especially for that purpose, and were some distance from the house. There were two buildings, housing twenty men. At this time of day, the workers would be having their midday meal. By the time Valerie got there, they would be nearly finished eating, ready to return to the fields.

The men were just coming outside when Valerie approached the building. She was glad to see that they all looked fit and well fed. They might be indentured, but they were treated with kindness and respect. Valerie knew all of them by name, and had spoken to them all over time, finding out their stories and their goals for the future. The workers greeted Valerie warmly as they shuffled by, stepping aside to let her pass.

Valerie spotted the two young men she wanted and called out to them. "Martin. Richard. May I have a word?" The men looked startled. The lady of the house didn't normally single them out.

"Certainly, ma'am. How can we help ye?" Martin was close to twenty, tall and lean. He had cornflower-blue eyes and flaxen hair that any girl would find appealing. Richard was his exact opposite—short and stocky, with curling dark hair and pitch black eyes. He was not as handsome, but there was intensity in him that some girls might find appealing.

"Richard, would you mind waiting outside while I speak to

Martin alone? I would like a word with you after." Valerie led Martin back inside and sat down on a bench, but Martin remained standing, his hat in his work-roughened hands.

"Please, sit down, Martin. I just want to ask you a few simple questions. How well did you know Cora?" Martin looked genuinely surprised.

"She came in with Mistress Dolly from time to time, to help serve the meals and clean up and such. She was always friendly, but she never spoke to me direct-like, if that's what ye're asking."

"Had you ever seen her with anyone? Was she friendly with any of the men?" Valerie was watching Martin carefully, but she couldn't see any tension or annoyance.

"I cannot say as I've seen 'er with anyone, ma'am. I think I saw 'er walking out of the spring house with Master Charles once, but I cannot be sure. I was too far away."

"Thank you, Martin. Can you send in Richard now?" Valerie felt like a detective, asking all these questions. It was actually kind of fun.

"Richard. I will only keep you for a moment. I was wondering how well you knew Cora." Richard cocked his head to the side and stared at Valerie, his eyes narrowed in thought.

"I saw 'er when she came with Cook."

"Did you ever speak to her?"

"I did. We spoke a few times. She liked little trinkets, so I carved her a wooden box to keep them in." Richard looked sad at the thought of Cora, leaving Valerie to wonder if he had been in love with her.

"Were you courting her?"

Richard looked at Valerie with a smirk. "I 'ave five years left on my contract, Mistress Whitfield. I 'ave no house, no money, and at this moment, no future. How could I court anyone? What would I 'ave to offer a girl who lives in a big house and sleeps in a warm bed? I liked 'er, yes, but we weren't courting. I never touched 'er, if that's what ye're getting at. May I go now?"

Valerie nodded and watched him leave. She had no idea if Richard was telling the truth. He seemed to feel angry about his lot in life, but would that drive him to murder? And why kill Cora? Valerie wondered if Cora might have rejected him, driving him into a rage. She walked back out into the summer sunshine. She was suddenly tired, and very sad. She would go find Louisa and read her a story before her nap. That always made her feel better.

FORTY-SEVEN

Louisa stood on deck, inhaling deeply. She had been smelling it for a few days now—the smell of the tropics. The turquoise water sparkled in the blazing sun, and seagulls dived for fish into the tranquil blue of the sea. Louisa turned up her face, allowing the golden rays to warm her before retreating back beneath the brim of her hat. She hadn't had one of her own, so Agnes pilfered a hat from the belongings of Anne Collins, which were still onboard. Louisa didn't like to take the girl's things, but for a woman to have a tanned face simply did not do in the seventeenth century.

Anne and her mother were always in Louisa's thoughts, and she prayed for them daily, hoping against hope that they were all right somehow. She was beginning to understand why people throughout history had been so devout. Their faith was probably the only thing that stood between them and the abyss. They had to believe that their God was loving and just, and if only they prayed hard enough, would hear them and answer their pleas. She had certainly been praying more since her arrival in the seventeenth century. She didn't expect God to help her, but it did bring her comfort.

Louisa squinted at the speck in the distance. Kit said they would be able to see land by midafternoon, and it was nearly eleven. They would be putting into port at Kingston for supplies and repairs. She looked up at the bridge. Kit was at the wheel, his face shaded from the sun by his cavalier hat. He had let the word slip that he was now betrothed to Mistress Jamison, so the crew and Reverend Blakeley were forced to turn a blind eye to some unseemly behavior, such as Louisa coming up on the bridge without an invitation and standing next to their captain.

The reverend usually tried to hide his scowl when he saw her with Kit, but he had no say in the matter. She was the captain's betrothed, after all. They still had to be extremely discreet. For a woman to be seen coming out of a man's cabin in the morning, even if he was her intended, would mean immediate ruin. Louisa usually left in the dead of night, making sure the coast was clear before dashing to her own cabin, her face covered with the hood of her cloak. Since there were only two women on board, it could only be her or Agnes, but she still didn't want anyone to see her face.

Once she accepted Kit's proposal, she felt a certain peace settle over her. She hadn't realized how scared she'd been until Kit said that he'd take care of her and help her find Valerie. She'd tried not to think of what she would do if she couldn't find her sister, which would be catastrophic. She would be alone in a struggling colony with only the Reverend Blakeley as an acquaintance. Unless someone was able to tell her the whereabouts of the Whitfields, her search would be at an end. Knowing that Kit would be there with her allowed her to breathe again, and she blew him an affectionate kiss. He blessed her with an affectionate smile in return. She would share a midday meal with him in his cabin and talk to him then.

* * *

"You can't be serious. Please tell me you are joking." Louisa jumped out of her seat, her pottage forgotten. It was disgusting anyway, but now she'd completely lost her appetite.

"Why are you so upset?" Kit looked at her in puzzlement. "You must understand my position."

"Position? You're going to go to the slave market and buy human beings." She was horrified that he saw nothing wrong with that, but Kit simply shrugged and continued to eat.

"Louisa, someone is going to buy those people anyway, one way or another. At least if I buy them, they won't be ill-treated. Sweetheart, we are barely keeping afloat. We have no master gunner, no surgeon, no rigger, and the carpenter is falling off his feet. We have a cracked mast, seeping hull, and yards of sails that need to be replaced. We also need a cooper to check the state of the cargo, and tighten any lose barrels before there is permanent damage, as well as a couple of able-bodied men to make up the ranks of the sailors. We might actually make it to Virginia if we don't encounter another storm, but I don't want to take any chances."

"And you expect to find all this skilled labor at the slave market?" Louisa sat back down and faced him, ready for an argument.

"The pirates take all kinds of men captive when they seize a ship. Most of them are shipped off to North Africa, but you never know. Some turn up on the islands. I might be able to find a few skilled slaves. I promise you, I will give them their freedom once they've worked off their purchase price."

"You are despicable!" she spat out, furious.

"Am I really? I realize you've led a sheltered life, but this is the way things are, my sweet. Human life is cheap, especially in less civilized parts of the world. Now, I take it you won't be joining me at the market?" He gave her an infuriating smile, hoping he'd won the argument.

"I don't think so. I will stay right here fuming, while you're bidding on human cargo."

"All right then. By the by, are you going to eat that? It's awful, but I'm famished. We desperately need supplies. We just might have some mutton for supper tonight. Something to look forward to." He reached over and took her bowl of the revolting pottage. Louisa didn't even know what that was, until the steward informed her that it had something like a combination of oats with something unidentifiable mixed in, and boiled beyond all recognition.

"Enjoy your expedition. I'm going back up. It has suddenly become too stuffy in here." Louisa swept from the cabin, not bothering to look back. *Impossible man*, she thought, as she went up on deck.

All thoughts of the slave market fled as soon as she saw land. She felt as if she hadn't seen land in years, when in fact, it had only been about six weeks. Louisa could see the shaggy heads of palm trees nodding in the tropical breeze and pristine beaches of white sand in the distance. The water had begun to change color a few days ago, going from the blue-gray of the Atlantic Ocean, to the turquoise of the Caribbean. They were so close to land, she could see people moving about in the distance, but they were the size of ants.

"That's not Jamaica," Reverend Blakeley stated at her elbow. "That's actually Hispaniola. We have to pass it in order to reach Kingston. I have been studying the map. I hope you're not planning to go ashore, Mistress Jamison. No woman is safe in these heathen lands." The reverend's lips were pressed so tight they virtually disappeared from his face.

"No, I plan to stay aboard. I have my own reasons for not going ashore. It does look lovely though, doesn't it?"

Reverend Blakeley gave her an odd look. "Not the word I would use, but I suppose the water is a pretty color. What are those strange trees?"

"Palm trees. They grow coconuts." Louisa answered, her eyes never leaving the shore.

"I am sure I don't know what a coconut is, but you seem very well informed. I presume Captain Sheridan has been familiarizing you with the local flora and fauna when you visit him in his cabin," he said, sarcasm practically dripping from his tongue.

"Yes, Reverend. We spend all our time discussing geography and astronomy. As a matter of fact, Captain Sheridan was able to help me see stars I hadn't had the pleasure of seeing before. He is quite knowledgeable." Louisa tried to stifle a smile as she saw Reverend Blakeley absorb what she'd said. She could see his baser side grasp her meaning and then push it away, assuming that a well-bred young woman would never intentionally say such things.

"Good day to you, Mistress Jamison. I think I'm correct in assuming that you won't be joining me at prayer."

"Not today, Reverend."

FORTY-EIGHT

AUGUST 1620

Louisa paced the deck, feeling like a caged animal. They had been in Jamaica for nearly two weeks now, and she was anxious to get on their way. She had gone ashore several times with Kit, but was forced to spend most of her time aboard while he went about business. Louisa had been curious to see the Jamaica of the seventeenth century. She and Doug had been there on vacation once, but she never actually saw Kingston. They stayed at a resort in Montego Bay.

She tried to imagine Kit at a resort. What would he look like with his hair cut short and his face clean-shaven, lounging by the pool with a tropical drink in his hand? She simply couldn't see it. Kit was so at home in his surroundings she couldn't picture him anywhere else. The thought of him with his hair cut, wearing a pair of jeans and a shirt, seemed just ridiculous, and she gave up on it. She liked him just as he was.

Louisa had enjoyed their trips to Port Royal. The city was a kaleidoscope of sound and color, with people from various countries seen on the streets and in the markets. The strict moral codes of European nations didn't apply here, and people were drinking, gambling, and whoring quite openly. Kit led her past the solid stone walls of the fortress, fortified by cannon, and into the heart of the city where she actually saw several white women walking along with their male protectors.

She couldn't remember the last time she had enjoyed a meal as much as she had at Morgan's Tavern. After weeks of eating salt pork, hard biscuit, and the nasty pottage, she was drooling at the smell of roasting meat and fried plantains, but the best part had been sliced pineapple and mango for dessert. Louisa hadn't had a fruit since she left the twenty-first century, and she savored every bite, asking Kit to buy some bananas and pineapples to take back to the ship. He was a little suspicious of bananas, but he liked the pineapple, which he'd tasted on an earlier voyage.

"Are any of these men pirates?" Louisa asked as she looked around the crowded street.

"More than a few, I should say, but most of them congregate closer to the docks. This part of town is favored by British subjects and sailors."

"Where is the slave market?" She couldn't help wondering where all those wretched people were held.

"It's not far from the quay. Makes it easier for the owners to bring them to market, and for the buyers to drag them off to their ships and plantations. Convenience is everything," he said sarcastically. "Now, why don't we go to a regular market and see if we can find you something pretty?"

Kit led her to a bustling street market where numerous stalls fought for space under the broiling sun, their colorful awnings providing welcome shade for merchants and shoppers. Louisa was drawn to the mountains of tropical fruit, but Kit steered her further down toward the silks and jewels. Luisa thought giddily that it would be nice to buy a bikini and go swimming, but of course, a swimming costume wouldn't be invented for centuries, and Kit would never allow her to go swimming anyway. Going to the beach wasn't a seventeenth-century pastime. She sighed and allowed Kit to lead her through the crowded market.

He didn't let her out of his sight, and held on to her arm at all times. At first, his overprotectiveness annoyed her, but she quickly came to realize just how easily someone could snatch her and deprive her of her freedom. This was a different world, where life was very scary without the protection of a man. Kit wore his sword whenever he left the vessel, and tucked a pistol into his belt. There was also a dagger in his boot. After her first foray into the city, Louisa understood the necessity, and hoped Kit would never need to use his weapons.

Kit stopped in front of a stall selling jewelry. His eyes lit on a necklace of silver and larimar. He held it up for her inspection. "What do you think, my sweet? Will you try it on for me?"

It was beautiful, and she agreed to try it on. The cloudy blue stone looked just right against her creamy skin, the chain heavy and warm from the sun. Kit threw the owner a few coins and told her to keep it on.

"Perfect," he said as he led her to a stall selling silk. Louisa loved the colorful selection of fabrics and ribbons. She ran her hand over the cloth, enjoying its smooth texture. The colors were varied and vibrant, shimmering in the morning sun. *So, this is shopping seventeenth century style*, she thought. She reached for an embroidered shawl the color of twilight. The silk was so fine, it slid through her fingers.

"It matches your eyes, Louisa. Shall I get it for you?" He didn't even wait for her to reply before paying for the shawl. Louisa threw it over her shoulders, despite the heat. The silk felt wonderful against her skin. "Why don't you go and choose a pineapple and some of those yellow things you are so fond of, and I'll be right back. Don't worry. I'll keep my eye on you," he promised when he saw her panicked expression. "You have my word." He handed Louisa some silver coins and led her to the stall.

Louisa selected two pineapples, three mangos, and a bunch of bananas by the time Kit reappeared at her side, looking satisfied. "Ready to go back? It's getting awfully hot, and you look like you would be much more comfortable wearing nothing but that necklace."

"Is that why you bought it? To buy sexual favors?" She slid her arm through his, kissing his cheek. He was really good to her, and made her feel protected and desired. Doug had begun to take her for granted toward the end of their relationship. Would Kit grow tired of her after several years and do the same? Would she ever get to find out? Louisa wondered. It was difficult to make any long-term plans, given the unpredictability of life in this dangerous time.

Louisa was glad to get out of her heavy clothes once they returned to the ship. It was hot as hell in the cabin, so she opened the windows, letting in the fresh breeze. The steward had cleaned the cabin, but he had a morbid fear of open windows, believing the air outside to be full of unseen dangers. She supposed that could be true in the city, but out here, the air was fresh and fragrant, bringing with it the smell of sun, sea, and exotic spices.

Kit had unbuckled his sword, put away the pistol, and was carefully pulling off his shirt. He winced as he lifted his left arm. His wound was still hurting him. Louisa wished she had some painkillers to give him, but had none left. She'd used up the pills she brought with her immediately after the pirate attack. She'd ground the pills and added them to his ale to ease his pain, and took a few for the terrible headaches she had after hitting her head.

She stretched out on the bed, enjoying the cool embrace of the sheets, and closed her eyes while she waited for Kit to come to her. They flew open in surprise as something silky touched her wrists. Kit bound her wrists with her new shawl and tied them to the headboard. His eyes were like pieces of burning coal as he looked at her, no longer smiling.

"What are you doing?"

"Something I've dreamed of for a while," he said softly, pushing her legs apart. Louisa was torn between anxiety and overwhelming desire. No one had tied her up before. She knew Kit wouldn't do anything to hurt her, and her wrists were tied loosely enough for her to yank her hands out, but she was still tense. The idea of being bound did not appeal to her at all.

"Untie me, Kit. I don't like this. Please."

"Not just yet, my sweet. Keep quiet, or I will have to gag you." He pulled out a kerchief and blindfolded her, making her heart race. She wanted to kick him, but he held her, pinning her to the bed. For a few moments, he did absolutely nothing, allowing the tension to mount until she felt like a coiled spring, vibrating at the lightest touch. What was he planning to do to her?

Louisa nearly jumped out of her skin when she felt Kit's lips on her inner thigh. They were like butterfly wings, light and soft. He kissed her a few times and stopped, waiting, making her squirm. She thought he would kiss the other thigh, but he didn't. His lips trailed across her belly and then downward. She sucked in her breath, expecting him to go lower, but he stopped again, running a finger between her breasts and then squeezing her nipple, first gently, then harder. Louisa was trembling with desire, wanting him to go on.

"Don't stop," she moaned.

"Want to be gagged, do you?" Kit whispered, as he took her other nipple in his mouth.

She felt his arousal against her thigh, but he seemed in no rush to make love to her. Instead, he slid down again, leaving a trail of kisses down her belly. He was driving her crazy. She gasped when his tongue slid inside her, probing and exploring her, slowly and deliberately. He was teasing her mercilessly, making her vibrate with unbearable tension. His tongue was replaced by the tip of his shaft. Louisa arched her hips, but he pulled back again, chuckling softly.

"I'll get you for this," she whispered.

"I told you not to talk, or I'll gag you," he replied, his voice low and silky.

She expected him to gag her with his handkerchief, but he went with a more creative option. Louisa wrapped her lips around him and flicked her tongue over the tip, making him gasp. It was her turn to tease him, and she took her time, enjoying her brief moment of power over him. He seemed to be enjoying it too.

He shifted his weight again and she wondered what he would do to torture her next. She cried out when he finally slid into her and moved with torturous slowness.

"Kit, please," she moaned. "I can't take it."

"You asked for it," he replied, and thrust into her with all the force of his body. She wrapped her legs tightly around him, taking everything he had to give her. After a few seconds, she went off like a 4th of July firecracker. It didn't take Kit long to join her. He'd been as inflamed as she was. She was still quivering when he pushed up the blindfold, his gaze intense. "I think you liked that," he mused. "In fact, I am almost sure."

"You are an absolute beast," she breathed.

"I'll take that as a compliment. Now, I must leave you." He began to get dressed.

"Aren't you going to untie me?" she asked, alarmed.

"If you insist. I was going to leave you like that until I came back from the slave market. I am sure I'll be ready for more by then."

"Kit!" He untied her and kissed the tip of her nose. "Thank you," he said, suddenly serious.

"For what?"

"For making a fantasy come true. That doesn't happen often in this world."

"Glad I could help," she replied with a wide smile.

"I have to go. We'll be sailing with the tide tomorrow, and I want to try my luck one more time. Pickings have been slim the past few days. Oh, I got you a little something at the market."

He pulled a ring out of his pocket as he sat next to her on the bed. The ring felt heavy on her finger. It was gold, with a large sapphire in a diamond setting. This was no delicate modern ring. It was large and solid, weighing her hand down. She had never owned anything so extravagant. Louisa knew from her experience as an art restorer that a piece like this would cost a small fortune in modern times.

"A betrothal ring. Do you like it?"

"I love it. Thank you, Kit. I didn't get you anything."

"Oh, I think you did," he answered, running a finger down her inner thigh.

Louisa stretched out on the bed. She'd take a nap while Kit went to the slave market. He had managed to acquire a few people over the past ten days, but no one was particularly skilled. He did get a rigger, but no master gunner or cooper. The men were overjoyed to be aboard a British ship again, and were recovering from their ordeal as they prepared to set sail. Louisa had to admit that Kit had been right. The fate he offered them was preferable to anything else that might have befallen them had they been purchased by a planter and forced to remain in Jamaica.

Louisa tried to sleep, but sated as she was, her mind wouldn't settle. What Kit had done to her wasn't what she would expect of a seventeenth-century man. She'd assumed that relations between men and women were unexciting and brief— a few minutes in the missionary position, with the nightshirts still on, but perhaps she'd been wrong, or maybe it was only Kit who was so hot-blooded. He'd spent several years in France, but he'd intimated that he'd been faithful to his wife and didn't partake of what Paris had to offer. What had his life with Helena been like? Louisa wondered. He didn't speak of her, and Louisa didn't ask, but once Kit overcame his sensibilities and took her to bed, he was just like any other man she'd known. He didn't want to just copulate, he wanted to play and experiment. He wanted to bring her pleasure, and take pleasure for himself. She couldn't have imagined desiring a seventeenth-century man so much, but at the moment, she was greatly looking forward to sharing her life with him.

Louisa smiled as she drifted off to sleep. Perhaps he'd made her fantasy come true as well.

FORTY-NINE

By the time Louisa woke up it was late afternoon. The heat was beginning to subside, replaced by a cool breeze blowing through the open windows. She was hungry. She poured some water into a basin and freshened up before going up on deck. What she wouldn't give for some deodorant and a razor. Kit didn't seem to be put off by her hairy armpits and legs, but she felt self-conscious. Ah, a bikini wax. How nice that would be. At least there would be something decent to eat today. They had been eating much better since putting into port, and Louisa had even convinced Cook to make some fish. He presented her with something that might have been fried grouper, making Louisa clap her hands in delight. It tasted wonderful.

There were few people on deck when she came up. Since the ship had been in port, the sailors had been getting a well-deserved rest, taking naps and going ashore to drink, dice, and search for willing wenches eager to take their coin. The sails were furled, the vessel bobbing gently on the calm waters of the Caribbean. The necessary repairs were completed at last, and the hold was full of supplies that would see them to Virginia. There wasn't much to be done at the moment.

Louisa sat on a barrel, leaning against the mast. It was nice just to sit and enjoy the lovely weather. She would wait until supper. It was only an hour away. She wished Agnes would spend more time on deck. The girl was pale and drawn, spending most of her time in the small cabin, sewing and rearranging their few possessions.

Louisa rose from her perch to gaze over the rail. Was that Kit? He was walking toward the ship slowly, carrying something large and heavy. Louisa couldn't believe the stubbornness of the man. Didn't he realize his wound would start to bleed again? It would never heal properly at this rate. He went about his business as if his arm hadn't been practically lopped off. Kit stopped for a moment to catch his breath and continued walking, his sword slapping against his thigh. Was that a carpet? Why would he buy a carpet?

"Master Willis," Louisa called out to the cabin boy. "Would you please help the captain? He seems to have acquired a very heavy carpet."

"Right away, ma'am," the boy replied, already heading to the ramp leading to the quay. He skipped down the ramp toward Kit, who looked up in gratitude. Louisa leaned against the railing watching their progress. Kit held one side of the rug while the boy held the other, enabling them to walk faster. Louisa sucked in her breath in shock when she saw an arm come out of the wrapping. That was not a carpet. That was a person wrapped in something colorful. She ran down the ramp toward Kit, her heart hammering.

Louisa saw her face before she even reached Kit and Daniel Willis. Her eyes were closed, her skin sunburned and blistered, but it was definitely her. "Anne!" She called out. "Oh, Anne." The girl didn't seem conscious. Her arm swung limply as the men carried her onto the deck. Anne's hair was dirty and matted, her gown torn to shreds, exposing her breasts.

"Take her to her cabin," Louisa told Kit. "I will be right there."

Louisa stopped by the galley for fresh water and broth, and got some clean rags from Agnes. By the time she got to Anne's cabin, Kit had laid her out on her berth, having unwrapped the colorful blanket. Louisa stifled a scream as she pushed aside the strips of torn fabric. Anne's chest was covered with livid blue welts. "Her back is worse," Kit said. "She has been beaten, more than once."

"How do you know that?" Louisa put her hand to the girl's face. It was hot and sweaty.

"Some of the bruises are turning yellow, while others are still purple," Kit answered matter-of-factly as he held up her wrists. "She'd been fettered too."

Louisa took Anne's wrist, searching for a pulse. She could feel it under her fingers—faint, but definitely there. She would be all right. She just needed care. "Kit, where did you find her?"

"I was just about to leave the market when they brought her up on the platform. I had to engage in a bidding war to get her. I have very little money left."

"How did she come to be here?" Louisa thought Anne had been taken to Africa and here she was in Jamaica. "Did you see her mother?"

"No, I didn't see Mistress Collins anywhere. The man who sold Anne to me was Flemish. He must have either bought her from the pirates or traded her for someone else. I can't really say. He had a few others for sale. She didn't even recognize me, poor thing. She collapsed halfway through the auction, which was actually fortunate, since it kept the others from bidding. They want healthy slaves, although she would have fetched a considerably higher price had she been with child."

"Why don't you leave us? I need to get these rags off and try to get some food into her. Hopefully, she'll come around soon."

Kit nodded and left the cabin, closing the door behind him.

Louisa turned her attention to Anne. Her breathing was shallow, her eyes still closed. Louisa dipped a rag into the water and began sponging Anne's face. She kept a cup of water aside for drinking and put it to Anne's dry lips. Anne's eyes fluttered open in panic. She stared at Louisa, unseeing, and full of fear.

"Anne, it's me, Louisa Jamison. You are aboard the *Gloriana*. Do you remember me?" The girl just stared, her lips moving silently. Louisa gave her more water and continued to apply a wet rag to her face.

"Anne, you'll be all right now. Captain Sheridan will keep you safe." The girl closed her eyes again. Louisa gently wiped her cheeks and smoothed the filthy hair away from Anne's face. Anne turned away, silent tears sliding down face. She looked emaciated and broken. Where was her mother? Louisa thought it best not to ask.

Anne tried to push Louisa's hands away as she began to peel off what was left of her gown. Anne's body was covered with bruises, but the skin hadn't been broken, which was fortunate. Less chance of infection. Louisa pulled off the torn and soiled petticoat and looked at Anne's thighs. They were bruised on the inside, and smeared with dried blood. So, she must have been raped, poor girl, and brutally. Anne whimpered as Louisa began to wash the blood away, trying to be as gentle as possible.

"Anne, are you badly hurt?" The girl didn't answer. She seemed to be in shock. Louisa finished washing her and took a clean shift out of her trunk. She pulled it carefully over Anne's head, helping her to lie back down.

"Here, try to drink a little broth. You need nourishment." Anne took a few sips then turned her head away.

"Go to sleep, Anne. I'll get Agnes to come and sit with you for a while."

"Father," Anne whispered through cracked lips. "Father."

"He's not here right now. Just try to sleep. I'll come back later."

Louisa let herself out of the cabin, her eyes swimming with tears. The poor girl had been through absolute hell, and now she would have to tell her that her father had committed suicide. Anne would be left alone in the world with no one to take care of her or protect her. Louisa went to get Agnes. She didn't want to leave Anne alone for any length of time. God only knew what she might do.

FIFTY

Valerie put on a wide-brimmed hat to shield her face from the sun and picked up a basket. She'd go pick some wild strawberries at the edge of the forest and make jam for Finn. She had discovered the strawberry patch shortly after coming to Rosewood Manor, and picked the fruit every year, making pots of jam. She didn't have real sugar for sweetening, but a little honey or molasses usually did the trick, and eventually everyone overcame their suspicion of the little red berries.

It had been several weeks since Finn's ordeal, but he was still sulking, hardly eating anything, and refusing to leave his room. His leg was on the mend, but he was bed-bound for at least another two months. Every day, Alec offered to take him outside, but Finn refused. He stubbornly remained in his room, sullen and alone, reading and rereading his favorite book on astronomy. Valerie knew exactly what was troubling him, but had no idea how to get through to her son. She would keep trying. Maybe a little jam would sweeten his temper.

"Going strawberry picking, Mistress?" Bridget asked as she came out of the parlor, her sewing basket slung over her arm.

"I've just finished all my mending. Would ye care for some company?"

"Of course, Bridget. I'd love it."

The two women strolled companionably toward the strawberry patch, their baskets swinging as they walked. After so many years, Bridget was more friend than servant, but Valerie never asked her about her daughters in Ireland, since it was a sore subject for the woman. She missed her girls terribly, but at this stage saw no reason to return home. Both girls had married within the past few years, and now had lives of their own. Bridget got the occasional letter delivered from England by Captain Smith. The girls would send the letters to an inn at Plymouth where the captain would collect them when in port.

"Is Master Finn still fretting?"

"I'm afraid he is. He feels guilty about the baby, and blames himself for bringing on the early labor," Valerie answered with a sigh. "I keep telling him that it wasn't his fault, but he doesn't believe me."

"I told 'im much the same thing," Bridget replied. "He will come around in time. He just needs to be up and about again. It will take 'is mind off 'is troubles."

"Speaking of troubles, Bridget, I can't get Cora's death off my mind. I keep trying to figure out who killed her."

"Why do ye think someone killed 'er?" Bridget set her basket down and began to pick the fruit with both hands.

"It's the way she was positioned. If she was in the spring house alone and simply slipped and hit her head, she wouldn't have been behind all those cans. It's as if someone was trying to hide her, but didn't do a very good job. I can't imagine that it was a planned attack, but maybe she argued with someone, and the argument got out of hand. She also had a little piece of fabric clutched in her hand, as if she tore it while fighting off her attacker, or trying to grab the other person to retain her balance. Alec didn't think anything of it, but I think it might be significant." Valerie popped a strawberry into her mouth, enjoying the sweetness of the little berry.

"Hmm. I reckon it could 'ave happened that way, but who would do that?"

"I have three suspects so far: Master Whitfield, Master Charles, and Richard Squires." Valerie turned to look at Bridget to see her reaction.

"Ye suspect yer own husband?" Bridget exclaimed.

"No, but Charles accused him of dallying with Cora and of killing her, and although I don't believe he did it I have to keep him on the list. I suspect Charles only did that to divert suspicion from himself. It seems they were lovers."

Bridget nodded thoughtfully. "I can believe that. Cora was not the kind of girl to remain a maid for long. It wasn't in 'er nature. Now, Amelia, she is a different sort altogether. They fought more often than not, those two." Bridget continued to pick the berries, her basket filling much faster than Valerie's who kept putting the berries in her mouth.

"Did they? I thought they were fond of each other."

"Oh, they were, but they fought something fierce. I heard them through the wall of my room. Couldn't hear what they were fighting about."

"Hmm, I didn't know that," Valerie said. "Was Amelia carrying on with anyone?"

"Not that I know of. Ye should consider the women too, aye? Maybe someone was jealous." Bridget straightened out and rubbed her back for a moment before bending down for more fruit.

"Who would be jealous of Cora? We only have me, you, Amelia, and Barbara Dolly in the house, and I don't believe any one of us bashed her head in."

"What about the field workers? There are four women. Master Charles could have been dallying with more than one lass, did ye think of that?"

"No, I haven't. I can't see Charles being even remotely interested in any of those women, but I supposed they can't be ruled out completely. Bridget I never knew you had such powers of deduction," Valerie laughed. "You can be my sidekick."

"Yer what?"

"My assistant. I will share everything I find out with you from now on," Valerie promised.

"Sounds fine to me, Mistress, so long as ye don't think I killed 'er." Bridget sat down on a patch of grass and took a handful of strawberries, popping them into her mouth one by one, smiling sheepishly at her mistress.

FIFTY-ONE

Valerie buttered two pieces of bread and impaled them on a stick, holding them out over the hearth. The jam was ready and cooled, filling the kitchen with a sweet, fruity aroma. She would bring Finn jam on toast. Even he couldn't resist that. Finn had a sweet tooth just like his father. He wouldn't say no to jam. Valerie slid the toasted bread off, spread it with more butter and jam, and put it on a tray with a glass of cold milk. She hoped this would work.

Finn was studying a map when she came in, his face pale and sad. Valerie noted that he was wearing a clean shirt, and his hair was brushed and pulled back into a neat ponytail. Definite improvement from a few days ago when he was sitting around in a soiled nightshirt, hair messy, and face unwashed.

"What are you looking at, Finn?"

"All the places I'd like to visit once I get older. I want to be an explorer, like Columbus." He put down the map and glanced at the laden tray, his eyes brightening. "Is that strawberry jam? Did you just make it?"

"I made it especially for you. Bridget and I picked the strawberries only this morning. Would you like some?"

"Yes, please. Thank you, Mama. That was good of you, considering..." Valerie set the tray down in his lap and sat on the side of the bed.

"Finn, I know you blame yourself for what happened, but I keep telling you, it wasn't your fault. It takes more than worrying for a woman to go into labor."

Finn took a bite of toast, his gaze sliding guiltily away from his mother. "You don't have to say that to make me feel better. I know what I've done."

"Finn, listen to me. While I was carrying you, terrible things happened. First, I was very ill. I didn't even know you existed then, and later on, your father was arrested and taken to the Tower. You know what happened. I saw him in in his cell before he died. He'd been tortured, and he was barely recognizable. I could have lost you then, but I didn't. You hung on and lived, and were born healthy and strong when the time was right. Baby Alex wasn't strong. Babies born at seven months often survive, but he didn't. He just wasn't strong enough. You can't blame yourself for that. No one can."

Finn stopped chewing and gave her a pleading look. "Really? Is that really true? I didn't kill him?"

"No, my darling, you didn't kill him."

Finn looked relieved, as if a heavy burden had been lifted from his shoulders. "Thank you, Mama. Do you think Father can help me go outside later? I'd like to sit in the garden."

"Of course, but before that, you can help me with something. Have you ever seen Cora with anyone?" If anyone saw anything, it would be Finn. He was always coming and going, and his powers of observation were keen.

Finn looked thoughtful for a moment. "I saw her kissing Charles in the woods. She told me it was a secret and not to tell anyone. I didn't tell."

"Of course, you didn't. Have you ever seen her with anyone else?"

"No, but I saw Amelia with Charles too. They weren't kissing though." Finn drained his cup of milk and put it back down on the tray, not bothering to wipe his milk moustache.

"What were they doing?"

"They were quarrelling, but they stopped as soon as they saw me and pretended to be civil."

"Are you sure it was Amelia and not Cora?" Valerie was perplexed.

"Of course, I'm sure. They don't even look alike, do they?"

"No, I suppose they don't." Valerie removed the tray and made for the door. "Father will come and help you soon." Finn was already looking at his map again, a small smile on his face.

FIFTY-TWO

Louisa gently pulled a brush through Anne's hair. The girl seemed to like having her hair brushed, and Louisa was only too happy to do something, anything, to help her feel better. She still hadn't spoken, but managed to take some food and stroll around the deck on the arm of the reverend. Louisa plaited the hair and twisted it onto a chignon at the nape of Anne's neck, securing it with several pins.

"Would you like to take a walk with me, Anne?" The girl didn't answer, but got up slowly and went to the door. Her bruises were beginning to heal and fade, but the emotional damage would not be so easily dealt with. Reverend Blakeley spent hours reading to Anne from the Bible in an effort to comfort her, but she remained silent and detached. Louisa was relieved to hear from Agnes that Anne had begun to bleed. Thank God she wasn't pregnant.

Louisa led Anne toward the prow of the ship. She seemed to like that spot, and stood looking out over the horizon, her eyes wistful and moist. North America was already visible in the distance, as they drew closer to the shores of Florida. They would be sailing up the coast until they docked in Virginia in a week's time.

"They slit her throat," Anne whispered suddenly. She sounded detached and matter-of-fact, but Louisa knew this was a breakthrough. She didn't ask any questions, just took Anne's hand in her own and squeezed it reassuringly.

"She kept screaming, demanding to be released. I begged her to be quiet, but she wouldn't stop. She just screamed and screamed."

"Are you speaking of your mother, Anne?" She nodded sadly. "Yes. My mother. My poor mother." She continued to stare out over the water for such a long time that Louisa thought she wouldn't say any more, but Anne suddenly spoke again.

"They beat her, and then they gave her to the sailors. Many of them were Mussulmen and wouldn't touch her, but some did. They took turns with her and made me watch. They cut her throat and threw her overboard once they were done. I begged them to kill me too, but they said I would fetch a much higher price than my old, fat mother, and shackled me down below."

"What happened after that?" Louisa thought she shouldn't ask, but she needed to know. It would help her help Anne if she knew what happened.

"One of the other captives told me they were sailing to Algiers, but they met another ship on the way. It was Flemish. The captains seemed to know each other from before. The Flemish captain came aboard to look over the slaves. He chose me and a few men, and we were dragged aboard his ship. The men were taken down below, but I was taken to his cabin. I went willingly, thinking he might be a civilized man and help me, but I was so wrong." A sob escaped Anne as she continued to stare straight ahead, shaking slightly.

"He wanted me to do things, horrible things, but I refused. He beat me, then raped me again and again. I would have thrown myself into the sea if I was able to get free long enough to reach the deck, but he kept me fettered in his cabin. He took me to the slave market once we reached Jamaica. He said I gave him no pleasure, and he could still get good money for me." Anne was crying hard now, her face contorted with grief. "Captain Sheridan saved my life, but he shouldn't have bothered. My life is worthless now. I wish I were dead, like my parents. There is nothing left for me in this world."

"Oh, Anne. Don't say that. We will take care of you. We won't let anyone harm you again." Louisa put her arms around the girl, but nothing she did could comfort her. Anne no longer cared what happened to her. She would have to watch her carefully to make sure she didn't do anything foolish.

Louisa slid off Kit's lap as she heard the persistent knock on the door.

"Enter," he called out. The reverend entered the cabin, not bothering to hide his disapproval when he saw Louisa seated demurely by Kit's side.

"Captain Sheridan, a word if you please." The reverend took a seat offered by Kit, his hands folded in his lap. "I understand that you intend to look after Mistress Collins once we dock, and I think I might be able to help."

"I am listening," Kit replied, leaning forward. He felt it his duty to look after Anne Collins, but at this time, he had no idea what form that care would take. Kit would be sailing back to England in due time, but taking Anne along was out of the question. He hoped to find a suitable home for her in Virginia.

"I wish to marry her. Would you be so kind as to perform the ceremony? I am afraid I can't marry myself." The reverend looked anxious and Louisa felt some sympathy for the man.

"Reverend, do you think Mistress Collins is in any condition to marry at the moment?" Kit asked. "Have you even discussed this with her?" He seemed genuinely shocked at the suggestion, especially since Louisa had just told him of her conversation with Anne. Kit poured a cup of wine for himself and offered one to the reverend.

"No thank you, Captain. I have, indeed, discussed this with Mistress Collins, and she has agreed to become my wife. I feel that it's my Christian duty to offer her any help I can, and as her husband I will be able to protect and guide her. If you are concerned with her physical state, I can assure you that I won't trouble her with any demands. That side of things is not important to me. I am simply concerned with her spiritual and emotional well-being."

Kit looked over at Louisa, silently asking for her opinion. She gave him an imperceptible nod. Marrying the reverend would give Anne a home, a position, and security, which would all help her recover in time. If they chose to consummate their union, it would be a decision they would make together. Louisa had no doubt that the reverend would honor his promise, and not force Anne to do anything she wasn't ready or willing to do.

"If Mistress Collins is of like mind, Reverend, it will be my pleasure to marry you. When would you like the ceremony to be performed?"

"Tomorrow morning would suit. We've no time to call the banns, since we'll be arriving in Virginia shortly, and I think it best for everyone if we're married by the time we dock."

Reverend Blakeley stood and turned toward the door. "If you wish, I could return the favor, and marry you and Mistress Jamison as well."

He didn't wait for an answer and walked out, back erect, head held high. Louisa knew he disapproved heartily of her spending time alone with Kit without the benefit of a chaperone. Kit snuck a peek at Louisa and looked away. He didn't want to press her and she was grateful to him for that, but suddenly she felt strangely unsettled. Would it be so terrible if she married Kit tomorrow? The thought of marrying Kit filled Louisa with happiness. It wasn't just fear that made her want to marry him—it was love. Whether she found Valerie or not, she wanted Kit by her side.

Louisa glanced at Kit. He was making an entry in the log, completely oblivious to her inner turmoil, and suddenly she knew. Louisa walked over and put her palms on his desk, prompting him to look at her. His gaze was full of affection as he reached out and took her hands in his. "What is it, my sweet? Do you have doubts about letting Anne Collins marry the reverend?"

"No, I think he will be good for her. I was just thinking that a double wedding might not be such a bad idea. What do you say, Captain?" Kit's look of surprise turned to one of pleasure.

"What prompted you to change your mind?" he asked, rising from his seat and taking her into his arms. "I thought you wanted to wait until you found your sister."

"I've come to understand that my life wouldn't be complete without you, Captain Sheridan. It seems that I love you." Kit came around the desk and gave her a tender kiss.

"A double wedding it is, then. I promise to love you all the days of my life, Louisa."

FIFTY-THREE

"Anne, are you sure this is what you want?" Louisa stood next to her at the prow of the ship, looking out over the horizon. This had become Anne's favorite spot, and she could usually be found here, just staring off into the distance. Anne turned to face Louisa, her smile wistful.

"Louisa, my parents are dead. I realize that people lose their parents all the time, but it's so much easier to accept death from an illness, rather than a murder and a suicide. I am damaged beyond repair, and will only bring disgrace to any man who might possibly want me. The reverend makes me feel safe and protected. He is a man of God, and if he is willing to take me on, then I must accept. I told him that I cannot be a full-fledged wife to him, but he seems willing to accept that." Anne gave Louisa something resembling a smile.

"He wants me to help him with his work, and in time, maybe even accompany him on missions to convert the heathens and teach them the ways of Our Lord. After what happened, I couldn't ask for a more fulfilling or productive life. I don't care what happens to me, but if I can be of help to someone else it would make me content. I know you don't care for the reverend, but he is a kind and patient man, and his visits have been a balm to my soul." Anne's brown eyes had lost the glazed look they had immediately after her rescue, the light of hope beginning to peek through the grief.

"Then I wish you all the best, Anne. You sound as if you've thought this through. I only wish there was something I could do to help."

"Oh, but you have helped. You have been so kind to me, both you and Captain Sheridan. I cannot begin to imagine what would have happened if he hadn't seen me at that market. I know you're not planning on staying in Jamestown, but I very much hope that we will see each other again. Where will you be settling once you are wed?" Anne seemed a little more animated now, and Louisa was only too happy to talk to her.

"I really don't know. I came here to find my sister. I believe she lives in Virginia with her family. Captain Sheridan promised to help me. Everything depends on that. If I find Valerie, then I would like to stay where she is. The captain is not averse to settling in Virginia. If I can't find Valerie, then I will return to England with my husband. There would be nothing for me there." A chill ran down her spine at the thought of not finding Valerie, but she stubbornly pushed it away. She wouldn't even entertain such thoughts.

"Then I will pray for you. I hope you find your sister soon, then you and the captain can settle in the New World. It would be lovely to have a friend there, and I would very much like to meet your sister."

"Thank you, Anne. At this point, I would very much like to meet my sister as well."

FIFTY-FOUR

Valerie raised her dress a little off the ground to prevent the hem from getting soaked by the dew. The day dawned misty and gray, sounds of distant thunder rumbling somewhere in the distance. The rain would come soon, but she had a little time. In truth, Valerie didn't care if she got soaked to the bone. The heat and humidity made her feel sticky and irritable, and she would enjoy nothing more than walking in the cooling rain, drops of water bathing her flushed face.

It was only an hour since the sky began to lighten, but she wasn't sleeping well these days. Her breasts stopped aching and leaking milk, and her body was healing, but her heart was still sore. The baby was always in her thoughts, as was Finn's self-loathing, Cora's suspicious death, and the feud between Alec and Charles. Alec hadn't spoken to Charles since their fight, leaving Valerie to doubt that the brothers would ever be able to mend their fractured bond.

Alec didn't want to talk about Charles, but she could see the hurt in his eyes every time Charles walked into the room or joined them at the dinner table. Alec was heartbroken and confused, shaken to the core by Charles' betrayal. He couldn't ask his brother to leave, but he couldn't bear for him to stay, and Valerie had no idea how to help him.

She would have thought that Charles would apologize once he had a chance to cool down and think things through, but he was defiant and angry, not seeking reconciliation with his brother. What could have prompted such resentment and anger? Finn was oblivious to the strain between Alec and Charles, but Louisa was starting to ask questions. She was sensitive to any undercurrents, and the obvious discord affected her deeply. She'd always been partial to Charles, following him around like a puppy and seeking his approval, but in her heart, her first loyalty was always to her father, and she felt torn between the two men, unsure how to act. Valerie tried to reassure her that both Alec and Charles still loved her despite their differences, but the girl was upset and moody.

Valerie picked some flowers and began her ascent up the hill to the cemetery. She was surprised to see that she wasn't alone in her desire to pay her respects and thought Alec had beaten her to it, but on closer inspection, she realized the tall man standing with his back to her was Charles. They looked so alike sometimes, especially from a distance. Charles was an inch or two shorter than Alec, but he shared his dark hair and lithe physique.

"Good morning, Charlie. You're up early." Valerie noted the flowers on Cora's grave as she came closer. "You miss her, don't you?"

"Yes. I suppose you know about us." Charles looked down at his hands, unable to meet Valerie's gaze.

"Yes, I do. Did you love her?"

"I was very fond of her. I know what you are thinking, Valerie, but it wasn't me. I didn't kill her." Charles looked up, a picture of defiance.

"Do you really believe it was Alec?"

"No."

"Then why did you accuse him? You broke his heart." Valerie was angry with Charles, but she needed to understand. Charles turned to her, his green gaze blazing with anger.

"I wanted to hurt him. He took Finlay away from me. I know what he did, Valerie. I overheard you talking. Alec killed Finlay to get you. Is Finn even his, or were you playing the whore to both brothers?"

Valerie had an overwhelming desire to slap Charles' smug face, but she held back, mentally counting to ten, before answering him. He obviously harbored a lot of resentment toward Alec, but he needed to get his facts straight. Whatever he believed had nothing to do with what really happened.

"You have it all wrong, Charlie. No one forced Finlay to do what he did. He chose his own path, and it led to his death. Do you know what it means to be hanged, drawn and quartered? You grew up far away from England, so you wouldn't understand. Your brother would have been hanged until almost dead, disemboweled, and emasculated, then cut up into four parts. His remains would be displayed as a deterrent to future traitors. Is that the death you would have chosen for him? Alec gave him a quick death because he loved him. It had nothing to do with me."

Valerie watched the emotions playing over Charles' handsome face. He might not have seen an execution of a traitor, but he'd heard enough to know that she was telling him the truth. The idea of Finlay suffering such a horrible, prolonged death, left Charles shaken, his belief in Alec's guilt undermined.

"But Alec married you soon after," Charles retorted.

"Finlay's last wish was that Alec marry me and raise our child as his own. Alec and I were bound in grief, but he never laid a finger on me until we were married. Never. He loved Finlay, and he loves him still." Charles nodded, a look of abject misery on his pale face. Valerie could see him relenting and decided to change the subject. He needed time to process what she told him about Finlay's death.

"Now, tell me, Charlie. What did you and Cora argue about? Louisa saw you."

"We argued about Annabel. Cora overheard me talking about courting her and was angry. Cora knew I could never marry her, but she was still hurt. I told her that it had nothing to do with my feelings for her, but she didn't really believe me." Charles gave Valerie a sheepish look. "No girl wants to share."

"What about Amelia? Seems you argued with her as well."

"My, you have been busy, haven't you? Yes, I argued with Amelia. She wanted me to stop dallying with her sister. She thought I would ruin any chance Cora had of getting married. It seems one of the workers was trying to court her, and Amelia thought he would be a much better choice. I told her to mind her own business. Now, if you've finished interrogating me, I will go have some breakfast." With that Charles, turned on his heel and walked down the hill toward the house.

Valerie laid her flowers on the baby's grave and sighed. "Your father, uncle, and brother could all benefit from some psychotherapy, Alex. Probably wouldn't hurt for me to join them. Too bad it won't be invented for another couple hundred years," Valerie said to the tiny grave. "Rest in peace, my darling."

The rain began just as Valerie left the tiny graveyard. Rivulets of water poured down her face and between her breasts, making her feel instantly cooler. She turned her face up to the sky, enjoying the downpour, and twirled around. Her skirts were plastered to her legs, but she didn't care. It felt heavenly. The roar of thunder reminded her that it was time to go home. Valerie ran through the rain, sliding on the wet grass.

Valerie stripped off her wet clothes and crawled into bed, cuddling next to Alec for warmth.

"You're all wet! Where have you been so early in the morning?" Alec pushed her wet hair out of his face and pulled her closer.

"I went to visit baby Alex."

"Oh," was all he said.

Valerie pressed herself closer to him and moved her hand downward. Her breasts were still sore, and her body was telling her it wasn't ready, but she didn't care. She'd missed Alec terribly and wanted him to touch her.

"Make love to me, Alec," she whispered.

"Are you sure? It hasn't even been a month yet."

"I'm sure. I need you."

The pain was excruciating, but she bit her lip and wrapped her arms around him, holding on tight. She wanted to feel pain. She wanted to feel something other than sorrow, and eventually it began to hurt less. She wasn't enjoying it, but she wanted him to find comfort in her body. Alec was hurting too, and now they could share their pain, both physical and emotional. Alec rolled off her, and propped himself on his elbow.

"You didn't enjoy that, did you? Did I hurt you?" He looked upset at the thought, angry with himself for letting his instincts overrule his brain.

"Yes, you did, but I wanted you to." Alec gave her a strange look, knowing better than to ask for an explanation.

"Alec, I want to get away from here for a while. Sometimes I feel like I can't breathe."

"I was thinking of going to the West Indies to see if I could find some new suppliers. Would you like to come with me? The *Misty Dawn* should be coming into port in a few days, and leaving once the cargo is loaded. We'd be gone for a few weeks, but I think Bridget and Mistress Dolly can hold down the fort. Besides, Charles will be here." That was the first time Alec had mentioned Charles in weeks. Maybe he was beginning to thaw.

"Yes, I'd like that very much. I'll start making arrangements today."

FIFTY-FIVE

Agnes curled into a ball and turned toward the wall of the cabin. She didn't want her mistress to see the tears sliding down her face. She had prayed for months for a miscarriage, but that was before she felt the child move. At first, the movement was so slight that she barely registered it, but the last few days it began getting stronger, and she couldn't deny any longer that there was an actual human being growing inside her. A terrible guilt stole over her as she held her hands to her stomach, feeling the rippling movement in her womb. Was it a boy or a girl? Would it look like her?

Agnes wiped the tears away with the back of her hand and sighed. Mistress Jamison had just informed her that she would be marrying Captain Sheridan tomorrow. That certainly complicated things, not that they were easy to begin with. As of tomorrow, Captain Sheridan would become her master, and God only knew how he would react to having an unwed mother under his roof. Would he turn her out? Fresh tears began to flow as she pulled the blanket over her head to stifle her sobs. With no money, no friends, and no husband, how would she be able to survive in the New World? Who would give her a job once her belly could no longer be hidden beneath an apron?

"Agnes, are you all right?" Mistress Jamison sat down on her berth, her cool hand on Agnes' forehead. "Are you ill?"

"No, Mistress, just very scared." It was time to tell the truth. Agnes swallowed hard, knowing that the next couple of minutes would alter the course of her whole life.

"Why are you scared?" Her mistress took her by the chin and forced her to look at her. "You can tell me."

"I am nearly five months gone with child," Agnes covered her face in case Mistress Jamison was going to slap her, but she simply smoothed back her hair and smiled.

"Yes, I was beginning to suspect as much. No one has seasickness for two months, and only in the mornings. Did you think I would throw you out?"

"Yes, Mistress. Once ye marry Captain Sheridan 'e might dismiss me." Agnes continued to sniffle, but she was beginning to feel slightly more hopeful.

"Captain Sheridan will not dismiss you, Agnes. I'll see to that. I will still need a maid, pregnant or not. Was it some boy you knew in Plymouth?" This was the hard part. It would have been much easier to tell Mistress Jamison that she had been in love with some young lad, who'd deceived her, but her mistress had been kind to her, and she didn't want to lie any more than she already had.

"No, Mistress. It were me uncle."

"Do you want to tell me about it?" Mistress Jamison looked horrified.

"Mam died of the flux three years ago, leaving me alone. Me da died afore I were born. I walked from our village all the way to Plymouth to find me mam's sister. Mam always spoke lovingly of 'er, so I hoped she'd take me in. Aunt Susan welcomed me with open arms and gave me a home and a job. I was to help 'er and Uncle Gerald at the inn, cleaning rooms and doing the washing. I didn't mind the work as long as I 'ad a roof over me head and people who cared about me. Uncle Gerald was always nice to me, bringing me sweets and giving me an afternoon off, here and there. I was 'appy."

Louisa nodded. She could see exactly where this was going, but she let Agnes continue. "I saw Uncle Gerald watching me sometimes, and it made me feel ever so queer. He'd just smile and wink at me. It wasn't until about a year ago that 'e finally made 'is move. I was cleaning one of the back rooms, and 'e came in and locked the door. Aunt Susan was in the taproom serving customers, so there was no one to stop 'im. He said that I was beautiful and drove him mad with desire, and could 'e just touch my tit. I didn't want 'im to, but I was afraid that 'e'd throw me out, so I pulled down my bodice and let 'im touch me. He was gentle and just kissed me on the tip of my nose after 'e'd had 'is fill."

Agnes sighed loudly. "I knew 'e wouldn't stop at that. The next time 'e asked me to lift my skirts and let 'im touch me down there. I was so scared, but 'e didn't 'urt me. He just stroked me for a bit and let me go. He gave me a ribbon and told me not to tell my aunt."

"Did you?" Louisa asked.

Agnes shook her head. "I was afraid to. I thought that if that's all 'e wants, I can live with that. He didn't ask for anything more for a few weeks. Just wanted to fondle me a bit. I let 'im. Eventually, 'e asked me to give 'im my hand. He wrapped it around 'is cock and put 'is hand over mine, moving it back and forth. It was such an odd thing to do, but 'e seemed to like it. By the time I turned fourteen, 'e was having me regular-like. I prayed that 'e would get tired of me and stop, but 'e didn't. He never hurt me, but 'e made me understand that if I refused 'im, there would be a price to pay."

Agnes wiped away angry tears. "And then my aunt found out. She walked in on us one day, and she beat me black and blue. I could not sit for a week. She said she would put me out, and it wasn't long after that Master Dobbs showed up, looking for a servant for ye. I already knew I was about three months gone with child, and thought my aunt would kill me if she found out, so I offered to go with ye and prayed that I would lose the baby." Agnes was crying hard now, her eyes averted from her mistress.

"Agnes, you shouldn't blame yourself for what happened. You were just a child. You still are."

"I was so scared of being thrown out on the street, Mistress. I know what 'appens to girls who cannot find a position. They end up whoring until they either die of disease, or some drunken sod does 'em in."

Louisa drew Agnes to her and held her tight. "You'll be all right, Agnes. I promise. I will keep you with me, no matter what, and your baby will be safe with us. Captain Sheridan is a kind man, and he won't let any harm come to you. Now, help me prepare for my wedding." Agnes nodded and slid off the berth, happy to have something other than her own problems to think of.

FIFTY-SIX

Valerie waited until midmorning to go speak to the cook. Mistress Dolly was usually done with breakfast by then, and took a break before starting on lunch. The house was quiet, with only the sound of rain drumming on the windows. The morning was so gloomy that candles had to be lit, and they threw flickering shadows onto the walls of the corridor as Valerie walked to the kitchen, which smelled of the freshly baked bread and wild garlic that Cook used to season the meat for lunch. Mistress Dolly was eating a buttered bun spread with some leftover jam and enjoying a cup of ale. She always liked to eat after everyone was fed and the kitchen was quiet and cozy.

"Mistress Dolly, the master and I will be going away for a few weeks," Valerie began as she reached for a bun and began to spread it with butter. She forgot to have breakfast this morning and was suddenly hungry.

"Don't ye worry, Mistress Whitfield. Everything will be right as rain while ye're gone. It will do ye good to get away from this place for a while. There's been too much sadness here of late."

"Yes, there has. How has Amelia been?" Valerie took a bite of her bun, licking a drop of jam off her lips.

"Better, I think. She misses her sister, but seems more at peace than she has been for the past few months." Mistress Dolly poured Valerie a glass of milk and pushed it toward her. She knew Valerie didn't care for ale.

"Had she been troubled before Cora's death?"

"She had been sullen the last few months, always picking fights with Cora, but ye know how sisters can be. One minute they are inseparable and the next they are fighting over nothing." Cook got up and began to peel turnips and carrots.

"I never really fought with my sister," Valerie said.

"Well, ye're a rare case then. Most sisters fight. I even sent the two of them to different places, so they would get a little break from each other."

"Mistress Dolly, where was Amelia when Cora went to the spring house?" Valerie forgot all about her bun and stared at the cook's back.

"She went to the barn to milk the cow, but I cannot be sure that's where she actually was." The cook threw a peeled carrot into a basin and moved on to another one.

"Did she come back with the milk?"

"She said she took it directly to the spring house before coming back to help me wash the crockery. Why?"

"No reason. Just curious."

Valerie finished her breakfast and went out onto the porch. The rain was coming down hard, making it almost impossible to see anything. Huge puddles formed in the natural depressions in the earth, worms suddenly crawling all over the wet ground. The thunderstorm had passed, but Valerie could still hear rumblings and see flashes of lightning in the distance. She liked the smell of ozone in the air after a storm.

If what Cook said was correct, then Cora had gone to the spring house while Amelia went to the barn to milk the cow.

Cora never left the spring house, so Amelia must have seen her when she got to the spring house with the fresh milk. It was impossible not to notice Cora lying there.

Had Amelia run into Cora at the spring house, or was Cora already dead by the time she got there? If she was, why didn't Amelia tell anyone? None of this made any sense. Why would Amelia want to hurt her sister? They came over from England together, and did everything in their power not to be separated. What drove a wedge between them? Was it Charles? Was Amelia jealous of Cora's relationship with Charles enough to kill her? The idea seemed preposterous, but Valerie needed to speak to Amelia again.

FIFTY-SEVEN

Kit waited until the crowd of sailors quieted down before opening the Bible to the place Reverend Blakeley had marked for him. He'd never performed a wedding ceremony before and was a little nervous. The bridal couple stood before him, looking grimmer than any couple getting married had a right to. The reverend was pale and tense, while Anne Collins just seemed vacant. She wasn't unhappy, just indifferent. Kit looked away from them and began to speak. He had no desire to do this, and secretly thought that Reverend Blakeley and Anne Collins had no business getting married.

Plenty of marriages were based on things other than love, but this just seemed all wrong to him. The reverend was marrying Anne out of pity and giving up his husbandly rights, and Anne was simply looking for someone to protect her. She was like a wounded bird that needed tending, but even wounded birds eventually healed and wanted to take flight.

Kit wondered how he'd feel if he had to agree to a loveless marriage. He could see Louisa standing behind Anne, a picture of feminine grace and good health. She'd worn a fine blue gown, and she looked beautiful enough to be presented at court. He was proud to have her for his own, and couldn't wait to be her husband, in name as well as in deed.

Helena had loved him since he was a boy and tried to please him in all areas of their marriage, but his relationship with Louisa was different. Helena deferred to him in everything, accepting his word as law. She never questioned him, or volunteered her opinion, unless he asked for it. She was the same way in their marriage bed. She gave herself to him, but never asked for anything in return, and certainly never dared to try anything that might be considered improper for a decent woman. Kit fantasized about doing certain things, but never broached the subject, afraid to offend his wife. Helena would see those things as depraved and humiliating.

Louisa was completely different. Her appetite matched his own, and she seemed open to anything he wanted to try. He had never tied anyone up before, and had been apprehensive about Louisa's reaction, but she had been so aroused he had to think of mundane log entries and lists of repairs to be undertaken to hold himself back. Louisa didn't just lie there, allowing him to take her; she wanted to give him pleasure as well, and felt no embarrassment about touching him and exploring his body in ways no woman ever had.

Kit felt sorry for the miserable pair in front of him, knowing that some of the greatest pleasures of being human would be completely out of their reach. He concluded the ceremony and asked the reverend to kiss his bride. The kiss was tight-lipped and chaste, with the bride nearly pulling away at the last second. Once the ceremony was over, the reverend seemed to relax a little and reached out for the book. He switched places with Kit and flipped it open, ready to begin. Kit held out his hand to Louisa, who took it without reservation, and stepped in front of the reverend. She gave Kit a radiant smile, and his heart fluttered with happiness.

FIFTY-EIGHT

Valerie had several chances to speak to Amelia, but every time she saw the girl alone, something stopped her. If she were truly honest with herself, she didn't want to know if Amelia was responsible. She liked the girl, and feared finding out the truth, but if Cora was truly murdered she couldn't just let it go. She owed it to the poor girl to find out the truth, especially since they would be leaving Virginia next week. How could she leave her children alone when there was a murderer on the loose?

Valerie saw Amelia heading for the spring house and decided not to waste the opportunity. She gave her a head start and then followed discreetly, waiting for Amelia to disappear inside the dim confines of the little structure. Amelia was just lifting a can of butter out of the spring when Valerie quietly slipped inside. The girl looked ashen as Valerie faced her across the spring.

"So, is this where it happened, Amelia?" She wasn't sure what happened, but hoped the girl didn't know that and would blurt out the truth. Amelia's eyes slid away from Valerie's, but she didn't say anything. "Why did you do it?"

Amelia looked up, her expression one of terrible pain. "I

didn't mean to, Mistress. As God is my witness, I didn't mean to." The can of butter fell to the stone floor as Amelia sank down in a heap, her legs no longer holding her up. "I was just so angry. She laughed at me."

"Why did your sister laugh at you?" Valerie remained in her position, not daring to get too close to Amelia. If she killed once....

"She wasn't my sister," whispered Amelia.

"Who was she then?" Valerie sat down on the floor across from Amelia, waiting for the girl to answer. She didn't want to tower over her, making her feel intimidated.

"Cora and I grew up in a brothel in Plymouth. Our mothers were employed by Madame Tilly, who was only too happy to 'ave free help around the establishment. Cora and I cleaned, washed, took out the chamber pots, and swept out the hearth. The women were always nice to us during the day, but we had to become invisible at night once the customers came. By the time I was seven, I'd seen and 'eard more than any grown woman. I was scared of men. They were like wild beasts that panted and grunted and sometimes lost control and hit the girls. I didn't want that life for myself."

Valerie could only imagine the life these poor little girls had in the brothel, but she asked Amelia to go on.

"As Cora and I got older, it was understood that we would start working for Madame Tilly once we began to bleed. She was already planning to sell our maidenheads to the highest bidder. There is quite a market for such things, believe it or not. So, Cora and I decided to run away. We would go to the docks and sell ourselves as indentured servants, telling everyone we were sisters, to stay together. It worked. A captain bound for Virginia took us on board, then sold us on to Master Whitfield." Amelia wiped her eyes and hung her head even lower than it already was.

"You see, I've always loved Cora, and I wanted her to love

me. I wanted to give her comfort and affection." Valerie thought she understood what the girl was trying to say.

"Were you lovers?" The girl nodded miserably. "It wasn't sordid like it was with the men. It was wonderful and pure. We simply gave each other pleasure and love. Then Cora took up with Master Charles."

"Were you jealous?" Valerie asked.

"Not at first. If that was what she wanted to do I couldn't stop her, but after a while she started pushing me away. She said that she liked his prick, and it gave her more pleasure than I ever could. We started fighting and avoiding each other."

"What happened that day, Amelia?"

"I went to milk the cow, and found Cora here when I brought the milk. She was fetching something for Mistress Dolly. I tried to reason with her, but she was so angry. Master Charles wished to marry some uptight virgin, and Cora was in a state. She started yelling at me, telling me that I was unnatural, an abomination. She called me names and told me to leave 'er alone. She said I disgusted 'er and made 'er feel soiled."

Amelia sniffled loudly. "Then, she began to laugh and said that what I needed was stiff prick to show me what loving was really about, and that since I was still a maid I couldn't possibly understand the needs of a woman. I was so hurt, I thought I would die. She slapped me across the face, so I pushed 'er."

Amelia was crying into her apron and whimpering like a kitten. "I didn't mean to kill 'er. I really didn't, but I was in such a rage. I went over to 'er and slammed 'er head against the floor again and again, then dragged 'er behind the cans and ran. I knew she'd be found, but I didn't know what to do. I was so scared and sorry. I prayed and prayed for forgiveness, but I knew I would 'ave to tell the truth if Master Charles was accused of killing 'er. 'E was good to 'er. I couldn't stand by and watch 'im pay the price for my crime." Amelia stood up slowly, leaving the can of butter on the floor.

"What will ye do with me, Mistress Whitfield? Will I 'ang?"

"I don't know what to do, Amelia. I am horrified by what you've done, but I feel pity for you. I will need to speak to the master. In the meantime, let's go back to the house, shall we?" Valerie took the girl by the arm and led her back to the main house, her mind still trying to comprehend what she'd heard.

Valerie locked Amelia in her room and went in search of Alec. Murder was punishable by death, but Valerie hoped she could somehow persuade Alec not to turn her over to the law. A new governor had recently arrived from England and might wish to send a message to the colonists that murder would not go unpunished. It's not that she didn't think Amelia should pay for what she'd done, but having come from the future, her stance on capital punishment was a little different than most of the people around her. She wondered what Alec would say.

"She bashed her head in?" Alec gaped at Valerie. "She admitted that to you?" He was in the stable, mucking out a stall when Valerie found him. Alec returned the pitchfork to its rightful place and sat down on a bale of hay, stunned. "I can't believe it."

Valerie sat down next to him, leaning her head against his shoulder. "What should we do with her? Will you turn her over to the marshal? Can you imagine what they'll do to her if they find out about the fornication? They might whip her, or put her in the pillory before hanging her. Oh, it's too much, Alec."

"No one knows the whole story, so no one has to find out about that side of things. I cannot imagine that they even have a specific punishment for relations between two women. It's usually the buggery they are concerned with. But they will hang her for murder. I suppose she could use the "Benefit of clergy" to get out of hanging.

"What is that?" Valerie had never heard of that term before.

"It's a type of loophole found in the Bible. It's the first few lines of Psalm 51.

"Have mercy upon me, O God, according to thy loving kindness: according unto the multitude of thy tender mercies blot out my transgressions." Alec recited the lines by heart, no doubt thinking of Finlay.

"Does that actually work?" Valerie was shocked. Was that all a person had to say to avoid hanging?

"In most cases, if the accused knows about it. I suppose I'd better go speak to the girl." Alec rose from the bale of hay and turned to Valerie. "I wish it had been an accident."

"Me too."

FIFTY-NINE

Alec slowly walked back to the house, reluctant to face Amelia. He strongly doubted that the girl would escape the noose. He knew Valerie felt sympathy for her, but he wasn't sure that he did. Murder was murder. Would he have been justified in killing Charles for accusing him of the crime? Of course not. A human being had the power to control their actions, and Amelia had killed Cora, no matter what her reasons were. Alec sighed as he approached the house. He truly wished that Amelia had just run away while he was in the stables with Valerie. He wouldn't search for her, just let her disappear. She wouldn't be able to go to Jamestown or any settlement close by. The harsh conditions of the wilderness would be punishment enough. If she found a new life for herself someplace else, then so be it.

Alec climbed the stairs to the attic and approached the door. He stood on the landing and listened for a moment before inserting the key into the lock. It was too quiet. Amelia wasn't crying, so she probably didn't feel much remorse. The sight that greeted Alec was one that nearly made him sick. Amelia was hanging from the beam, her body slowly turning. She had used a sheet to make a rope, and must have stood on the bed to tie it to the only sturdy piece of wood in the attic bedroom. Amelia's eyes were bugging out of her head, her tongue protruding from her mouth, already swollen and nearly black.

Alec felt for a pulse, knowing full well there wouldn't be any. She was gone. He pulled a dagger out of his boot, and sawed through the twisted fabric until he cut the body down. He laid Amelia on her bed and sat down next to the body, covering his face with his hands. Another death in such a short time. He couldn't help but feel sorry for the foolish girl. She had been so young. He would have to tell Valerie and the children, and he dreaded the task.

SIXTY

Valerie kissed the children goodbye for the tenth time and allowed Alec to assist her into the trap. Their luggage was already stowed in the back, and it was time to go. The first rays of the sun were just visible in the morning sky, the rosy light painting the house in a warm glow. Mist was still gathered in the valleys and between the trees, but the sun would soon burn it away and envelope everything in the muggy heat of August. The *Misty Dawn*, appropriately named for mornings just like this one, would be leaving on the morning tide. Valerie waved to Louisa and blew a kiss to Finn, who was sitting on the porch, his leg propped on a stool. She was secretly glad that he was still wearing the cast, since being housebound would keep him out of trouble until they returned in four to six weeks.

Valerie had to admit that she was excited at the prospect of getting away for a while. She'd probably be bored aboard the ship, but the idea of being on the open sea on the way to a tropical place was enticing. Valerie suspected that Alec was also eager to get away. Charles had approached him and apologized profusely, but the peace between the brothers was fragile, both of them still tense and awkward with each other. Charles was planning to take a trip of his own after they returned, possibly to England. He wanted to see his ancestral home and visit London, which he'd heard so much about. He talked of going to France as well, but time would tell.

Valerie felt a twinge of excitement as the masts of the ships in the harbor finally came into view. There weren't that many vessels, but they were imposing with their furled sails, and thick chains, stretching into the murky water and anchoring them in place. Several sailors came down from the *Misty Dawn* to take their trunk, but there was still time before the tide. It was fully light now, the sun already warm on their faces. Alec suggested going into a tavern for a tankard of ale, and Valerie agreed. She wasn't thirsty, but she didn't want to be in the way as the crew prepared to set sail in an hour. She might get a cup of cider.

There was no one in the tavern at such an early hour. Most sailors breakfasted aboard their vessels, or were still dead to the world somewhere, sleeping off the drink consumed the night before. Alec finished his ale and glanced out of the window to check the position of the sun. It was about eight o'clock. Time to go aboard. Alec threw a few coins on the scarred, wooden table as rose to leave.

The dock was getting busy, the fishy smell growing stronger as the sun warmed the refuse floating in the water. It was already warm and humid, leaving Valerie to wonder how Alec didn't boil alive in his leather doublet, but his mind was already on the voyage as he absentmindedly took Valerie's arm and guided her toward the waiting ship. They walked along the quay toward the *Misty Dawn*, passing the *Gloriana* which had come into port the night before. The barkeep had mentioned that it had been attacked by pirates, but Valerie hadn't been paying attention. She looked up at the hull of the ship, rising above her head. The creaking of sails and the scream of seagulls filled the air, making her suddenly happy.

Valerie took one last look around before walking up the

ramp to the ship. She noticed a tall man and a woman descending the ramp from the *Gloriana* and her heart gave a painful squeeze. Something about the woman reminded her of Louisa, but of course that was ridiculous. She took Alec's arm and headed up the ramp, eager to get going. Valerie wasn't sure what made her stop and look again. It was some gut instinct that understood something before her brain did. She looked at the woman one more time, taking in the dark blond hair, just visible underneath her cap, and the trim figure in the brown dress. There was something apprehensive in the woman's walk as the man steered her toward the tavern.

The woman suddenly looked up, as if she felt Valerie's gaze on her. Their eyes met across space and time and held each other's gaze for a moment, before Valerie's brain finally accepted what her heart was screaming so loudly. A great sob tore from her, and then she was running, screaming, and crying, desperate to get to Louisa, who was running toward her, her skirts raised above her ankles to avoid tripping.

They flew into each other's arms with cries of pure joy. They clung to each other, afraid to let go and discover it had all been an illusion. Valerie was dimly aware of Alec behind her, but she had no time to explain, couldn't break away. Louisa was squeezing the life out of her, soaking her face with tears. Neither one said a word, but it was all right there in their eyes. Valerie held Louisa away from herself, still unable to believe that her sister was there.

"Lou," she whispered. "Oh, Lou. I thought I'd never see you again."

"I'm here, Val. I am really here. I've found you and I will never let you go again. Never." Louisa suddenly looked at Valerie in shock. "Were you leaving?"

"Not anymore." She turned to Alec, but he just smiled at her.

"I take it you are my sister-in-law. Alexander Whitfield, at your service. It's my pleasure to make your acquaintance at last. You must have traveled an awfully long way to get here."

Louisa saw something in his eyes, but wasn't sure how much he knew, and just nodded happily. She could see why Valerie looked so happy in the portrait. The man was, in a word, hot. She suddenly remembered Kit, who stood off to the side, patiently waiting.

"Val, this is my husband, Captain Christopher Sheridan." Louisa saw Alec look up in surprise.

"Any relation to Lord Robert Sheridan?"

"He was my father," Kit replied shyly. Valerie gave Louisa an amused look.

"Five minutes in the seventeenth century, and not only does she snag a husband, but a lord to boot. Well done, big sister. Well done," she whispered into Louisa's ear. Louisa looked at Valerie. She had vanished when she was twenty-six and had been here for fifteen years, so she was now forty-one to Louisa's twenty-nine.

"Who is the big sister now?" she asked bemused. They burst into hysterical laughter that left the men watching them in mutual confusion.

"Alec, you go on without me. I have to stay here with Louisa. I hope you're not angry." Valerie threw him a winsome smile. Louisa had a feeling that Alec was rarely angry with her sister.

"I can go another time. I will just have them take the luggage off the ship. I wouldn't miss this for the world." He turned away, leaving the sisters to stare at each other, still unable to grasp that they were truly together at last.

SIXTY-ONE

"That was by far the absolute stupidest thing you've ever done in your life, but I am so happy you did it," said Valerie, slightly slurring her words with too much brandy. The sisters sat curled together on a settee in the parlor, their faces illuminated by the glow of the candles. "Here is to the memory of Mom and Dad," proclaimed Valerie, raising her glass of brandy.

"Technically, they haven't been born yet," mused Louisa as she took a sip of her own drink, "but here is to them. I only wish they knew that we'd been reunited. Think of how happy they would have been."

"Especially if they knew it was in seventeenth-century Virginia," Valerie snorted, hiccupping. "So, tell me about Kit. How long have you been married?"

"Two and a half days," Louisa muttered. She was getting a little drunk herself.

"Seriously, Lou, do you love him?" Louisa stared off into space for a long moment before replying.

"Yes. Yes, I love him. I wasn't sure at first. I always thought that you had to know someone for ages to truly love them, but it's not like that, is it? I'd been with Doug for nearly a decade and I loved him, I really did, but this is different. These men are different. He made me feel as if I was the only woman in the world for him. You know how guys are in the future. They're always thinking that something better will come along, and want to keep their options open. I never felt that way with Kit. It was as if no other woman would do, and suddenly I felt as if no other man would do for me."

Valerie nodded. "It's funny, but that's just how I felt. When Finlay asked me to marry him, I thought that he couldn't possibly be serious. We barely knew each other, but he was dead sure. Once he made up his mind that was it. It was the same with Alec. There was never any question that we would be together after Finlay died. It was just a matter of time."

"It's strange the way you talk about them," Louisa said, getting more comfortable. "It's as if you loved them both all along."

"I did. I knew they were two separate people, but in my heart, they were like extensions of each other, just two separate halves. I never really felt guilty about loving Alec after Finn. It's what Finn would have wanted, and there was no one else to whom he would have entrusted his wife and child. Alec wasn't just fulfilling his promise by marrying me; he'd loved me all along. I knew it the whole time, and I sometimes wonder what would have happened had Finlay lived?" Valerie put down her glass and stared into the flames of the candle.

"What do you mean, Val?"

"I mean that we couldn't have gone on all living together without incident. It was like sitting on a powder keg. Someone would have had to leave in order to avoid an explosion. But what about you? Will you be going back to England when we've only just been reunited?" Valerie looked devastated at the thought, and Louisa reached for her hand.

"We hadn't really talked about it much since we didn't know if we'd find you or not, but Kit's home is in England. I won't leave you though, not yet. I want to stay with you until I can't stand looking at you any longer," she said with a smile. "And that will take forever."

"In that case, I hope that Christopher Sheridan is a very patient man."

"Val, how did you feel when you found yourself in the past?" Louisa asked.

"Bewildered, terrified, but most of all alone. I went up to the castle, not knowing what else to do, and met Alec. He offered me protection and a home. At first, I still thought I might be able to get back somehow, but I quickly realized that there was no way back. I had to adjust. Life goes on."

"Oh, God. Remember that *Beatles* song? Mom and Dad kept singing it on the way to the Grand Canyon, and we kept asking them to stop because we wanted to listen to *our* music. What I wouldn't give to hear them sing it one more time." Louisa began to sing "Ob-La-Di, Ob-La-Da" softly.

Valerie joined in, their voices rising in unison. They must have gotten pretty loud, because Kit materialized in the doorway, looking slightly alarmed.

"What kind of song is that?" he asked, advancing into the room.

"The kind happy sisters sing when drunk," quipped Alec as he put his hand on Kit's shoulder and led him out, giving Valerie a meaningful look, which made them dissolve in hysterical laughter.

"He doesn't know, does he?" Valerie asked.

"No. Do you think I should tell him?" Louisa had pondered this question for some time, but decided to hold off.

"Probably not at the same time as telling him you want to stay here and not go back to England with him. It might be just a bit much for him all at once."

"How did Alec react when you told him?" Valerie had told Louisa that Alec knew all about her past.

"Surprisingly well. His grandmother had come from the future, and filled his head with visions of cars and airplanes."

"Oh my God!" exclaimed Louisa. "Was his grandmother Erzsebet? I read about her online."

Valerie nodded. "One and the same. Shall we go to bed? I'm quite drunk. You know, this is the first time I've been truly happy since losing the baby. I still can't believe you are really here."

"Get used to it. Now point me in the direction of my bed. I'm exhausted." Louisa yawned and followed Valerie upstairs.

"The 'Honeymoon Suite' is through there. I can't offer you a hot shower, but you can have a bath if you like. Breakfast is at eight. Starbucks coffee, served with freshly baked bagels with cream cheese and smoked salmon, followed by freshly squeezed orange juice. NOT!!!" Valerie was still giggling as she went into her own room.

SIXTY-TWO

Louisa woke up with a huge grin on her face. She could hear the sounds of breakfast being prepared in the kitchen, little Louisa's voice asking Valerie if she could go say good morning to her aunt and uncle. That almost brought tears to Louisa's eyes, but they were tears of joy. A lot of decisions would need to be made, but they could all wait for a few days. There was no rush. Today she just wanted to be happy, and now that she'd found Valerie, there was something else she wanted to start working on.

Louisa snuggled closer to Kit, kissing his chest and stroking him gently. She wanted a baby, and she wanted one soon. Meeting her niece and nephew had been very emotional, making her longing for a child stronger than ever. Kit wanted a child as well, so there was no time like the present.

By the time they came down to breakfast the whole family was already downstairs, waiting for them. Finn was reserved, but Louisa gave them both a hug and a kiss, and asked if she could sit next to her aunt.

"Christopher, I was wondering what your plans are," Alec said as he reached for a hot bun. "Will you be returning to England with the *Gloriana*?"

"That all depends on my wife. I can't imagine that she would want to return to England having just found her sister, so I am entirely at Louisa's disposal. I will need to go back to the docks to see to the ship and crew. I left the first mate in charge, but it's my duty as captain to be there." Kit seemed reluctant to go back to the ship, but he had no choice in the matter. He had things to do.

"The reason I'm asking is that one of my captains is ready to retire. The *Morning Star* sails to England and back, but I'm sure you wouldn't want to be away from your wife for so long. It would be possible to transfer the captain of the *Misty Dawn* to the *Morning Star* and have you take over the West Indies route. Louisa can remain with us while you're gone. Does that sound like something you might want to take on?"

Louisa watched Kit with interest. Alec was proposing the perfect solution, and she hoped that Kit would be willing to accept it. He wouldn't be content to sit around and do nothing, but sailing to the West Indies would only take him away from her for a month or two at a time, versus the trans-Atlantic voyage which would take anywhere from four to six months to get to England, unload, load the goods, and return.

"That sounds ideal, Alec. I would very much like to take you up on your offer. I would also feel relieved to know that Louisa is not alone, and safe in the bosom of her family. Thank you." Kit smiled happily and took a sip of ale.

"Actually, Alec, I would like to sail to England on the *Gloriana*," Charles piped in. "I've been thinking of returning to England for some time, and this would be a good opportunity. I've asked Master Gaines for permission to wed his daughter, and he'd given his consent, on the condition that we wait until she is sixteen to marry. I will be back in time for her birthday in the spring."

"That sounds like a fine idea, Charles," Alec answered. "It's time you saw something of the world. I am sure Mistress Gaines will gladly wait for you."

Valerie squeezed Louisa's hand under the table. Louisa couldn't fully understand the tension she sensed between Alec and his younger brother, but she didn't need to understand. That was between them, and right now she was just happy to have her domestic situation almost worked out. The thought of living with Valerie made her very happy, and Kit didn't seem to mind. In time, they would probably want a home of their own, but for now, she would be thrilled to be close to Valerie and her family.

With breakfast finished, everyone began to file out of the dining room. Alec and Kit retired to the study to discuss Alec's plan further, and the children left with Charles.

"Val, have you seen Agnes this morning?" Louisa asked.

"I told her she can sleep in this morning. I hope you don't mind. The poor girl looked so worn out last night. Cook will see to her. I put her in the attic bedroom. Unfortunately, it became vacant recently, but I'm sure Agnes will like having her own room. I think she will need the space," added Valerie meaningfully.

"Thank you, Valerie. The girl was more terrified than tired. She's pregnant and thinks we'll throw her out. I keep telling her we won't, but she is still fearful. The child is her uncle's."

"Poor kid. I wonder if she wants the baby."

"She doesn't, but what is there to do? I think she might change her mind once she sees it," Louisa said. "It's not like she can put it up for adoption."

"I'm sure it will all work itself out. It usually does. Now, how would you like to take a walk with me? I still have so many questions for you, and they are best answered away from the house."

"Lead the way, sis. After being cooped up on that ship for over two months I'm only too happy to go for a walk. Can we stop by the cemetery? I'd like to put some flowers on my nephew's grave." Despite the joy of their reunion, there was still a shadow of pain in Valerie's eyes when she spoke of baby Alex, and Louisa wished she could do something to alleviate her pain.

"Of course. Let's go."

SIXTY-THREE

CHRISTMAS EVE 1620

Louisa threw on her cloak and stepped out the door into the frosty December afternoon. Thick snowflakes were silently falling from the colorless sky, twirling in the chilly air, before settling on the ground and blanketing it with a pristine, fluffy quilt. The frozen grass crunched satisfyingly beneath her boots as she made her way to the spring house, swinging the empty can as she went. Cook needed some more butter, and Louisa was only too happy to take a walk.

Normally, Agnes helped Mistress Dolly with the kitchen chores, but she was near her time and could barely waddle up the stairs, much less trudge all the way to the spring house over the slippery layer of new snow. She was due any day now, her eyes full of anticipation and fear. Despite everyone's assurances, she still believed that God would strike her down for her sins and she would die in childbirth together with her ill-begotten child.

Louisa stopped and looked up at the leaden sky before sticking out her tongue to catch a few snowflakes. They tasted fresh and cold, making her feel like a kid again. This was her first Christmas in the seventeenth century, and it was vastly different from anything she was used to. Finn and little Louisa decorated the front room with boughs of pine, but there was no Christmas tree or any other ornaments.

Christmas was a solemn occasion marked only by a church service and a meal. Anything considered frivolous was strongly discouraged by the Church. Louisa had remembered reading somewhere that the Christmas tree tradition didn't actually come to North America until the nineteenth century, when a picture of Queen Victoria, Prince Albert, and their children appeared in a newspaper depicting the royal family standing around a decorated tree. Prince Albert had brought the tradition to England from his native Germany, where the practice had begun as early as the sixteenth century. It was said that Martin Luther had been the first person to bring a fir tree into his house, and decorate it with candles to mimic the beauty of the forest and stars. Louisa sorely missed decorating the tree and singing Christmas carols, but she had to get used to the way things were done in the here and now, and foregoing the tree was the least of her concerns.

She hoped Alec would come down for Christmas Eve dinner. He'd been ill since his last trip into Jamestown a week before. There was an epidemic of influenza going around, no doubt worsened by the lack of hygiene and close living conditions. Alec frequently stopped into the tavern for a tankard of ale, and Louisa couldn't help wondering if the barkeeper ever bothered to wash the tankards between customers. Valerie had quarantined Alec as soon as he began running a fever to protect the rest of the household, and went about trying to heal him.

Louisa had been fascinated with Valerie's arsenal of medicines. She looked up some holistic remedies while planning her trip to the past, but this was an education. Valerie kept a special wooden casket on the highest shelf of the scullery containing her 'pharmacy,' which she was proud to show her sister. There were linen strips for binding wounds, emetics for inducing vomiting in case of ingesting something poisonous, purgatives for moving bowels, and poultices for irritations and burns. There was even a small bottle of laudanum. Louisa looked away from the jar of leeches, suddenly feeling queasy at the sight of the slimy creatures. Luckily for Alec, he had been spared that particular remedy. Valerie made an infusion of willow bark several times a day to bring down the fever and applied mustard plaster to Alec's chest and back.

"Where did you learn that?" Louisa asked her sister, intrigued.

"I learned a lot of things from Bridget. Her mother and grandmother were real country women, familiar with the medicinal properties of herbs and plants. She taught me about cupping." Valerie showed Louisa a dozen small jars neatly arranged in the corner of the chest. "Cupping is good for bronchitis and pneumonia. It stimulates the flow of blood and draws out the infection. It's surprisingly effective."

"How does it work?" Louisa picked up a small jar and held it up for closer inspection. She couldn't imagine how an empty jar could stimulate or draw out anything.

"You have to use fire. A lit taper will do. You insert the lit taper into the jar, heat it up, and then immediately place it on the patient's back. The heat creates suction, which in turn, stimulates the blood."

"God Val, that sounds positively barbaric. Alec lets you do this?" Louisa put the jar back, eyeing it with distaste.

"Oh, it doesn't hurt at all. It's kind of nice actually. It just makes you feel warm. Alec doesn't mind. He hates being sick."

"I think he probably just enjoys you fussing over him," Louisa giggled. "You haven't been paying much attention to the poor man since Kit and I showed up."

"Oh, he gets his share of attention."

Valerie took out a piece of willow bark and a jar of mustard paste and closed the lid of the casket. "I make sure of that. In either case, these are the only types of medicine available to me, and I leave nothing to chance. You know what the mortality rate is these days. Any slight fever or scratch can turn into something deadly. Poor Alec nearly had a heart attack the first time I used some of his French brandy to disinfect a cut. He's used to my eccentricity by now. He hides the brandy though, and leaves me the cheap stuff."

Louisa followed Valerie into the kitchen to make the willow bark infusion. "What about Agnes? Will she be all right, do you think?" Agnes was frequently on Louisa's mind as her time drew near.

Valerie shrugged. "She is young and healthy, and the baby seems to have turned and moved into position for birth, according to Bridget. She is as knowledgeable as any midwife in the twenty-first century. She'll do everything in her power to assist Agnes, but there is only so much even a doctor can do." Louisa knew she was thinking of baby Alex and dropped the subject. Valerie still went to the little cemetery nearly every day, leaving a bunch of wildflowers or a sprig of holly on the tiny grave.

Louisa filled the can with fresh butter and closed the door of the spring house behind her. She'd heard about Cora's death and was always a little wary of entering the place. She turned her steps back toward the house. The snow was falling faster now, the flakes illuminated by the feeble rays of the setting sun. It would be dark within the hour. Nearly all the windows of the house were aglow with candlelight, shadows visible from time to time as the family prepared for their holiday meal. Everyone would be there except for Charles, who'd sailed to England on the *Gloriana*.

Louisa saw Kit emerge from the stables and gave him a wave. He was doing all of Alec's chores while Valerie kept him in bed. Kit waved back and came toward her. "Let me," he said, as he took the can from Louisa's cold hand.

"It's not heavy," she slipped her hand inside his to warm it.

"I know, but your hands are cold." Kit pulled up Louisa's hood, kissing the tip of her nose. "You'll catch your death out here."

"Oh, how you fuss," she answered happily, smiling up at him. "Alec might be joining us for dinner. Valerie says he hasn't had a fever since yesterday."

"That's good news. I almost wish I'd gotten a touch of the catarrh to get that kind of attention from my own wife." Kit gave her a wicked grin and drew her to him as they trudged through the newly fallen snow.

Louisa found many things difficult to adjust to in this primitive, rugged life. She often dreamed of working on a painting at the museum, or driving a car while singing along to the radio. Just last night, she'd dreamed of walking down Fifth Avenue at dusk, admiring the exquisite Christmas windows, colored lights making ordinary things appear magical. She tried to hold on to the dream for a few moments after waking up, reluctant to let the image go.

Things that she had taken for granted now seemed like unimaginable luxuries, real only in her and Valerie's memory. When alone, they often talked of their old life, reminiscing about things and people they missed. Louisa still hadn't worked up the courage to tell Kit the truth about her past, but she would eventually. With Valerie and Alec to back up her story, he was less likely to think that his wife had lost her mind.

Louisa gazed at the golden light spilling from the windows of the house and smiled. The warmth she'd found at Rosewood Manor more than made up for the harsh reality. Some days, she still couldn't believe that only a year ago she was bereaved and alone, contemplating the mad idea of going in search of Valerie, and here she was, reunited with her sister, and married to a wonderful man. Valerie routinely referred to her as 'Lady Sheridan' as a joke, but Louisa secretly liked the title. *Lady Sheridan indeed*, she thought to herself, grinning.

"Come, Lord Sheridan," she said laughing. "I think you need a bath before supper. You reek of horses and worse."

"Makes it more authentic. After all, Our Lord was born in a manger."

"You are not Our Lord. Now off with you." Louisa gave Kit a push toward the stairs and went to bring the butter to Mistress Dolly. Something called 'Christmas Pudding' smelled heavenly, making her mouth water. Christmas tree or no Christmas tree, this was going to be the best Christmas ever.

EPILOGUE
VIRGINIA 1622

Louisa spread a blanket beneath the shady canopy of a maple tree in front of the house and sat down, gently setting baby Dottie next to her. Dottie was too intent on chewing the tail of Finn's wooden horse to pay much attention to her surroundings. She gripped the toy with both hands, trying to get a bigger bite. She was at the stage where she pulled everything into her mouth. Louisa wiped the drool from her face and adjusted her bonnet. She usually took Dottie on Agnes' afternoons off to allow Agnes to spend time with Richard Squires. The couple was to be married after harvest, since both Alec and Kit agreed to terminate their indenture contracts to allow the newlyweds to start a new life. Richard had been a carpenter in Cornwall, and intended to open up his own workshop in Jamestown after the wedding. Louisa was happy for Agnes, but she would miss Dottie. She had grown attached to the little girl and would miss spending time with her.

Louisa hoped that Kit would be back from Tobago in time for the wedding. She had asked Reverend Blakeley to officiate, since both the bride and groom were Protestant. Louisa visited Anne Blakeley at least once a month, but the Blakeleys were leaving also. The reverend intended to go to a settlement further west, where a clergyman was needed. Anne supported her husband's decision and looked forward to the new place. All in all, she was doing remarkably well. Anne would never fully recover from her ordeal, but she seemed happy with the reverend and had actually grown fond of him. Louisa had no idea if they ever consummated their marriage, but it didn't matter. They both seemed content with the arrangement, and that was a good thing all around.

Louisa thought of contentment and smiled. She couldn't wait for Kit to get back. They had been married for just over two years, but she still missed him like a new bride every time he went away. Absence did indeed make the heart grow fonder. She thought of how happy Kit would be when she told him her news.

They'd been trying to conceive since they came to Rosewood Manor, but month after month went by without results. Louisa suspected that Kit blamed himself for her failure to get pregnant. Helena never had a child, so Kit just assumed that the fault lay with him. Louisa knew he was tormented with guilt at not being able to give her the baby she wanted, and that made her news all the sweeter. She suspected she was pregnant before he left a few weeks ago, but wanted to be sure. According to Bridget, she was almost three months gone, and would be in the second trimester by the time Kit returned. Louisa smiled, imagining his joy when he heard the news.

Her reverie was interrupted by the arrival of Valerie, who plopped down on the blanket and pulled Dottie onto her lap, wiping her face with the hem of her gown and giving her a kiss. "I'm going to miss her," Valerie said wistfully. "She is such an angel. I miss having a baby around the house. Guess I'll have to wait to spoil yours. I bet you can't wait to tell Kit."

"I wish he was coming home today," answered Louisa, reclining on the blanket. "I miss him madly."

"Lou, if you had to do it over again, would you still follow me back in time?" Valerie asked, snatching her finger away from Dottie's teeth.

"Yes, only if I knew how well it would all work out, I wouldn't have been so scared. What about you, Val? If you knew then what you know now, would you still turn the hands on that clock?" Louisa peered at her sister, knowing her answer already.

"I would. It's funny, but I've been able to find here that which always eluded me in my own time. Seems you've found it too. Now all you have to do is tell your husband that you came from 2012," giggled Valerie. "Tell him right after you tell him that you're expecting. He might attribute it to pregnancy hormones and not think you're insane."

"Thanks for the advice, sis. I think I'll hold off. He never asks about the past, so why bring it up? Why burden him with things he can't understand? It's not like we are going back to the future."

"No, it's not. But what if we could?"

Valerie and Louisa looked at each other in silence, contemplating the possibility.

A LETTER FROM THE AUTHOR

Huge thanks for reading *A Leap of Faith,* I hope you were hooked on Valerie and Alec's epic journey. It continues in book three, *A World Apart.* If you want to join other readers in hearing all about my new releases and bonus content, you can sign up for my newsletter.

www.stormpublishing.co/irina-shapiro

If you enjoyed this book and could spare a few moments to leave a review that would be hugely appreciated. Even a short review can make all the difference in encouraging a reader to discover my books for the first time. Thank you so much.

Although I write several different genres, time travel was my first love. As a student of history, I often wonder if I have what it takes to survive in the past in the dangerous, life-altering situations my characters have to deal with.

Thanks again for being part of this amazing journey with me and I hope you'll stay in touch – I have so many more stories and ideas to entertain you with!

Irina

facebook.com/IrinaShapiro2

x.com/IrinaShapiro2

instagram.com/irina_shapiro_author

Printed in Great Britain
by Amazon